Until You

CATHARINA MAURA

This is for those of you that believe your past defines your future.

It doesn't.

Contents

Chapter One

GRAYSON

My eyes shift from my watch to the familiar city landmarks that pass us by. I tap my foot impatiently. We're getting closer, the surroundings getting more and more familiar, but it still feels like we aren't moving fast enough.

Damn flight delay. I spent all month ensuring that I'd have a full week off and that I'd get here in time. It shouldn't have taken me more than six hours to get from California to Miami, but it ended up taking almost all day.

My patience is wearing thin by the time we pull up in front of Noah's house. Noah is a lot like me. Neither one of us has a lot of friends. Hell, we're probably each other's only friend. I hate the thought of him expecting me, and me keeping him waiting — on his birthday, no less.

I place my suitcase by the front door and press the doorbell, reaching into my pocket to retrieve the two season tickets I bought him. I'm not really into football, but Noah is obsessed. A few years ago, tickets like these were nothing but a dream, but now? Now there isn't much that's out of reach for me.

1

Noah opens the door, a wide grin on his face. He looks thrilled, and to this day, it still surprises me that someone could be so genuinely happy to see me.

"Happy birthday, buddy," I say, holding up my gift for him. "I'm sorry I'm late."

Noah's eyes widen and he snatches the tickets out of my hand. He looked happy to see me, but he looks even happier to see these tickets. I shake my head and smile.

"No way," he says, holding up his gift. "Are they real?"

"Of course they are." I chuckle. "You can keep both so you can take someone with you. Your schedule is insane, so I figured season tickets were my best bet. You're busier than I am, man."

He smiles at his tickets and nods at me as he puts them away. "I can't wait to drag you to the next game," he says, leading me into the house. "You'll learn to enjoy it at some point."

I look around, unable to wipe the smile off my face. Stepping foot in this place still feels like coming home, even though I've never lived here.

This house is filled with warmth. It always has been. It isn't just a house, it's a home in every sense of the word. Noah and his little sister made sure of it.

It's nothing like my penthouse apartment. No matter how much money I spend on it or how I decorate it, it'll never feel like this place does.

I frown when I realize that it's uncharacteristically quiet. "Where is Aria?" I ask involuntarily.

I place my suitcase at the bottom of the stairs, my eyes falling to the family photos on the wall. Just like me, Noah and his sister grew up parentless. You'd never be able to tell by looking at them, though. They're never engulfed in sadness and sorrow. They work hard — not just at their education and jobs, but at being happy and building lives they can be proud of.

I've always wondered if it's because they got to spend a few years with their parents before they were brutally taken from them. The way they are... was that instilled in them by their parents?

I'm not sure what's worse, never knowing your parents at all and never knowing why they left you, or having them taken from you the way Aria and Noah did.

"She moved out," Noah says, grimacing. "She's living with her boyfriend now. He seems like a nice guy, and I'm happy that she's finally building a life of her own, but I miss her, you know?" Noah is rambling, so he's lying about something. I bet it's about liking Aria's boyfriend.

He runs a hand through his hair and smiles, his expression sorrowful. "Ever since our parents were murdered," he says, grimacing. He inhales shakily, his eyes falling closed. "I can barely say it even now. It's been fifteen years, and it still kills me. Ever since they were... taken from us... I've been scared to let Aria out of my sight. This is good for her. Brad is good for her."

Brad, huh? In all the years I've known her, she's never dated anyone. I wonder who this guy is. Somehow, I doubt he's good enough for Aria.

Throughout everything they've been through, Aria has remained the light in Noah's life. He's never told me the full story, but from the bits and pieces I've been able to put together over the years, they've been through hell. I don't understand how they both smile the way they do. To this day, I count myself lucky that Aria has always gone out of her way to ensure that I feel like I belong with them too, like I'm part of their family.

"How long has she been dating him? I saw you guys just a year ago, and I don't think she was dating anyone then. Isn't it too soon for her to move in with some guy?"

Noah smiles, but his smile doesn't reach his eyes. "I can't be an overbearing brother anymore, and you can't act like one either. Aria is twenty-six, and I have to let her live her own life. I can't keep her trapped in the past. I can't protect her from life itself."

I smile wryly. "Those sound like Aria's words, not yours."

I can just imagine her expression as she tells Noah exactly

what he just told me. Her dark chocolate eyes flashing with fury, her cheeks flushed.

Noah smirks and shakes his head. "You know us too well, man. Fucking hell, she lost it when I forbade her from moving out."

I cringe. No one tells Aria to do *anything*. Forbidding her something is straight-up dumb, and even attempting to would have pushed her straight into her boyfriend's arms.

"They'll be here soon," Noah says, walking into the kitchen. "I think you'll like Brad. Go easy on the guy, or Aria will have your fucking head too."

I have a feeling I'm not going to like *Brad*, but I'll manage to keep my mouth shut. I always do.

Noah hands me a beer and turns on the TV. "Wait a minute," I say, stopping him from changing the channel.

I sit down next to him and grin when the reporter announces that a well-known politician has been sentenced to fifteen years in prison, courtesy of countless sexual harassment cases. My smile widens when the cameras settle on his face, his disbelief apparent. He knows he was set to get away with what he did, and he would have. Until a few hours ago.

My phone buzzes, and I sit up when I see the logo of the Nemesis Platform on the screen, a thrill running down my spine.

Nyx: *Was it you?*

I glance back at the TV, satisfaction washing over me. Fucking scumbag, using his money and power against those weaker than him. He had this coming.

Ash: *Yes.*

Nyx: *Check the forum. The victim is so grateful, she's offering you a reward.*

I smile as I type my reply. Nyx and I have never met. I don't even know if she's actually a woman, since she won't confirm or deny that. I'm just assuming she is, based on the Greek goddess she named herself after. All I know is that she's the founder of the Nemesis Platform — a platform where victims let down by

4

the justice system have a chance to tell their stories and ask for help.

Members can take on cases and attempt to balance the scales, the way I just did, and every once in a while, a few of us collaborate to crack a tough case.

Most of us, like Nyx and I, prefer to remain anonymous, since many of the methods we employ aren't quite legal. But there are many lawyers and social workers on the platform too, offering pro bono legal and emotional support. Nyx allows reward money after cases have been resolved, but never payments upfront. I think that's a key part of why this platform is so successful. She doesn't allow any opportunity to scam or hurt those that are already vulnerable.

Ash: *I don't need a reward from her, but I'll take one from you. Tell me something about you.*

I tap my foot as I wait for her reply. I'm hailed as one of the best software engineers alive right now, but no matter what I do, I can't find out anything about Nyx. Her platform is coded so brilliantly that I can't even find a single vulnerability. There's no way to hack into the Nemesis Platform — no way to find out who she is. I might be good, but Nyx is better. Far better.

Nyx: *I'm trying to grow out my beard so I can braid it. Like Rapunzel, you know? Brapunzel? No, that doesn't sound right. Beardarunzel. I intend to become Beardarunzel.*

I bite back a smile and shake my head. She won't give me anything.

Ash: *Okay, now you have me worried I've been dreaming about meeting some hairy noob. Put me out of my misery, Nyx. At least tell me you're a woman, albeit a bearded one.*

I clutch my phone tightly as I await her reply. It wouldn't surprise me if she ignores me altogether, but I hope she won't.

Nyx and I have been friends for months, and it's only recently that I've started to throw slightly flirtatious lines at her. She's never responded to it, and I can't tell if she's not interested or just clueless.

Nyx: *Yes, I'm a woman, Ash. There. That's your reward.*

I grin as I stare at my screen. She has this way of making me feel giddy like I never have before, and I don't even know her. Hell, she didn't even give me a reward — I already know she's a woman. Despite that, she has me smiling like an idiot.

"Huh, I'll be damned," Noah says, his eyes on me. "You're texting a woman."

I freeze and look up at him. I'd totally forgotten where I was. I'd forgotten Noah was sitting right next to me. Lately Nyx has started to have that effect on me. I don't even know what she looks like, but she's got me enthralled.

"Who is she?"

I shake my head. "I don't know, man. I have no idea who she is. It's complicated."

Noah grins and leans back in his seat. I sigh as I prepare myself to tell him all about Nyx. As much as I know, anyway.

Chapter Two

ARIA

I hold my breath as I finish the last bit of icing, my trembling hand threatening to ruin Noah's birthday cake. I need this cake to be perfect, and I swear the icing gods conspire against me every year.

I exhale and take a cautious step back when it's done, the edges of my lips turning up into a smile. It looks almost exactly like the inspiration image I used.

This year I went with a medical themed cake, since we're also celebrating Noah finally finishing his residency after years of hard work. He always told me he'd be a doctor by age thirty, and he did it. It shouldn't even surprise me, since my brother is the hardest-working man I know.

I bite down on my lip as I resist the urge to readjust the fondant stethoscope I made. If I touch it now, I'm bound to ruin it.

"Wow, looks great!" Brad says, and I jump, almost knocking the cake over. I turn around, my brows scrunched up in annoyance. Brad holds his hands up in surrender and smiles. "Sorry, doll," he says. "I didn't mean to scare you."

I place a hand on my chest and shake my head, my heart beating a mile an hour. Brad walks up to me and wraps his arms around my waist, pulling me in for a kiss, and I relax against him, a smile finding its way onto my lips as he pulls away.

"How was your day?" he whispers. "That cake looks like it took you hours to make."

I glance back at it and smile in satisfaction. It *did* take me hours. I took half a day off work to make it, but it was worth it. I can just imagine how happy Noah will be when he sees this. I've made him a cake every year for the last twelve years, and I know it's something he looks forward to.

"It was good," I tell him, dragging my eyes away from the cake. "How was your day? How did the presentation go?"

Brad grins and nods, his hands tightening around my waist. "It went so well. God, doll, if you hadn't helped me out with those last few bugs, I'd have made a fool of myself today. The client asked for a few final changes, but overall it went really well. I'll show you the client's requested amendments later. I can't wait to see what your brilliant mind comes up with." He sighs happily and presses a kiss to my forehead. "You're amazing, you know? I don't understand why you stay in the sales department. Selling software isn't the same as creating it."

The smile melts off my face, and I pull away. He knows as well as I do that my applications to move departments keep getting rejected. "Someday soon," I tell him, holding onto those words with all the hope I've got left.

I turn away from Brad, allowing sadness to overwhelm me for one single second, my heart clenching painfully. Brad's job is all I've ever wanted. Creating software that changes the world... that's what I want to do.

I'm lost in thought as I pack the cake. I can feel Brad's eyes on me, but thankfully he doesn't say anything. I don't have the energy to respond to his words of encouragement, no matter how well he means.

I have a software engineering degree, just like he does, yet no matter how hard I try, I keep being told that I'm more of an asset in the sales department, that it's rare to find an 'approachable' woman that actually understands the tech behind our products. The worst thing is that it isn't even a lie. I'm one of few women in the company — and the only woman in the software engineering department is so introverted that I've barely managed to say two words to her.

I'd move companies if I could, but it's too late now. I've worked in sales too long. I have no actual work experience as an engineer, and whether I like it or not, being a woman doesn't work in my favor. If I could go back in time, I'd never have accepted this job right out of college. I was foolish to think that working for any tech company would be good enough, that getting my foot in the door was all I needed to do. It isn't that simple.

I'm still lost in thought by the time we reach my brother's house and struggle to snap out of it. It's silly, and I know it, but I can't help it. The more time passes, the more it feels like my dreams are getting further and further out of reach.

"You okay?" Brad asks, as we walk up to the front door. "I didn't mean to upset you."

I turn to look at him, taking in his bright green eyes and his concerned expression. I shake my head and force a smile. "I'm totally fine," I tell him, just as the front door opens.

"Aria!" Noah yells, smiling from ear to ear, his voice radiating excitement. And just like that, every bit of worry, every regret, every hint of sadness disappears. "Show me the cake!"

I laugh when he takes the box from me, his eyes wide. His excitement is palpable, and it warms my heart. This. This is why I spent hours baking a cake that'll be devoured in minutes.

"Well, good to see you too," I say, feigning dismay. "Happy birthday, by the way."

Noah hums in acknowledgement, but doesn't take his eyes off the cake box. He carries it toward the kitchen reverently, and I can barely stop smiling. His response is exactly what I was hoping for.

When we were kids, Mom baked us a themed birthday cake every single year. She'd surprise us with something astonishing every time, depending on what we were into at that age, and it was always the highlight of our day.

When we lost our parents, birthdays became more of a memorial than the celebration they'd have wanted for us. It was hard on me, but it was even harder on Noah. It killed me to see him heartbroken on his own birthday, so when I was fourteen, I set out to make him a cake. It was barely edible, but from the moment Noah laid his eyes on it, he was filled with the same excitement and happiness I was used to seeing. I've made him a cake every year since, and it's become one of my favorite family traditions.

Noah hugs the cake box to his chest and moves so carefully that I can't help but chuckle as he disappears around the corner, taking his prized possession to the kitchen. I glance at Brad, expecting him to share my amusement, but instead he looks angry. I raise my brows, and he grits his teeth.

"He always does this," Brad says, his eyes flashing with anger. "He always ignores me. I was standing right there, but he only greeted you. It's so obvious that he hates me. I don't know what I've done to deserve that type of rude treatment. I shouldn't even have bothered coming. I doubt Noah wants me here."

I pause in the hallway and lift my hand to Brad's shoulders. "He didn't mean it that way," I say, my voice soft. "He's just excited about the cake I made him. The cake... it's our thing, it's a tradition, and this particular tradition is sacred to us."

Brad looks away and exhales loudly, his annoyance on display. "You can't even tell me he doesn't hate me, can you?"

I sigh, wishing we didn't have to go through this right now. Brad has been convinced that Noah hates him from the start, but Noah has never done anything to make him feel that way. Even when I question Brad about his feelings, he can't give me concrete examples, and I have no idea what to do.

"I've told you he *doesn't* hate you so many times now," I say, my voice soft. "He wouldn't have invited you over today if he did."

I get where Brad is coming from, though. Noah hasn't been the friendliest, but then he's always taken a while to warm to strangers, and that's what Brad is to him. I've never brought anyone home before. And with how busy Noah is, he hasn't had a chance to get to know Brad, to figure out how our family dynamics work with him added to the equation. Noah doesn't like change, and Brad has been the biggest change we've been through in the last couple of years... since we lost our parents.

I sigh and rise to my tiptoes to kiss Brad in an attempt to ease his worries. Much to my surprise, he takes a step away, his eyes wide.

I blink in confusion and turn to follow his gaze, coming face to face with stormy, dark brown eyes that I know all too well.

"Grayson," I whisper.

Chapter Three

GRAYSON

I lean back against the doorframe, my eyes on Aria and the man standing next to her. She's wearing some ridiculously high heels tonight, and she's almost as tall as her boyfriend with them on. Her long hair flows down her back in dark waves, and her stunning chocolate eyes are flashing.

I watch as her smile melts away because of something he said and cross my arms, forcing myself to stay put. Aria is always smiling. I've always known her as the girl that'll smile through her tears, the girl that won't let the world see the pain that lives inside her. She's one of the strongest women I know, so who the fuck is this asshole that's putting that frown on her face?

I watch as she places her hands on his shoulder, her eyes on his. She speaks to him so softly that I can't make out her words, but her expression tells me she's placating him somehow. She's appeasing him, so they must have been arguing. I don't like the anger in his eyes, the way Aria seems to reason with him. Something about this whole exchange doesn't feel right to me.

Aria rises to her tiptoes, as though she's about to kiss him, and

I tense. Right before her lips meet his, he notices me standing in the hallway and takes a step back, his eyes widening with recognition.

Aria follows his line of sight, her lips tipping up in a familiar smile when they settle on me.

"Grayson," she whispers.

Aria walks up to me, her heels clicking against the wooden floor. She pauses in front of me, the top of her head barely reaching my shoulder.

"Aria," I say, my voice soft. Her name has always felt like a sin on my lips.

She tips her head to the side and smiles at me, her eyes twinkling. I breathe a sigh of relief — this is the Aria I know, ever surrounded by a hint of mischief.

"I didn't know you'd be here," she says, her voice as sweet as it's always been.

I nod, and her smile widens.

"Still so incredibly eloquent," she adds, her eyes filled with amusement. "It's nice to see you. I'm not sure Noah will ever get used to not having you around anymore."

It's been five years since I moved back to California, and I'm not sure I've gotten used to it myself. During the time I was studying, Miami became home to me, and in some ways, it still is. After all, it's where Noah and Aria are.

I tense when Brad wraps his arm around Aria's waist and glance at him, assessing the man that seems to have stolen Aria's heart. What does she see in him? Must be his character, because surely she isn't into this type of guy? He's wearing more hair product than she is, and his teeth are weirdly white. It's unnatural, and it creeps me the fuck out.

"Darling, won't you introduce me?" he says, not a trace of his previous annoyance present.

Aria's eyes light up, and it irritates me. It annoys me she lights up for him like that.

"Grayson, meet my boyfriend, Brad."

Brad holds his hand out for me and I glance at it, part of me wanting to leave him hanging. I grab his hand and shake it with far more force than I need to. He pulls his hand away and slides it into his pocket, struggling to hide a grimace. "It's so great to meet you, Grayson," he says. His tone gets on my nerves. I see the eagerness in his eyes, the irritating smile. I know his type, and I can't stand people like him. Sleaze ball. What does Aria see in this guy?

My eyes roam over him, taking in his far too tight shirt and his douchebag haircut. How much hair gel does this guy use? I can't help but wonder if his hair would budge if I place a tennis ball on top of his head. I doubt it would. If anything, it might permanently fuse to his hair.

Brad turns to Aria and holds her tighter. "Darling, you never told me you knew Grayson Callahan."

He sounds far too excited, and his tone grates on me. Aria smiles tightly, her eyes shifting away, as though her connection to me makes her uncomfortable. "He's my brother's best friend," she says, her voice soft.

Her brother's best friend, huh? I guess that *is* what I am, but she's always treated me like I'm one of her friends too, like I'm family.

Brad turns to her, his brows raised. "The CEO of one of the world's largest software engineering firms is your brother's best friend, and you work for a boutique firm?"

Aria shrugs him off and walks toward the dining room, where Noah has already put his birthday cake on display.

I watch her as she forces her signature bright smile onto her face, but she isn't fooling Noah or me. He glances at me with raised brows, and I shake my head slightly.

Brad follows and stares at her. It annoys me that he so obviously demands an answer. "Not everyone can get into Aequitas," she says eventually, her voice soft. "Besides, I'm not working as an engineer. I have no relevant work experience. You know that."

Aria sits down at the dining table and starts fussing with the plates and cutlery, her expression stormy. Brad sits down beside her, his arm on the back of her chair, and I drag my eyes away. He's fucking clueless. He doesn't even seem to realize that Aria is angry.

Noah clears his throat awkwardly and smiles at me. "Aria and Brad work together," he tells me, breaking the silence. "They work for a small firm that mostly dabbles in communication software. It's nothing like yours, of course, but it's the same field, I think."

I stare at Aria, my heart tightening at her haunted expression. I don't know what's going on, but her sadness is clearly tied to her job, and it looks as though Brad is rubbing salt in an open wound.

"You can," I say, and Aria looks up at me, her gaze questioning. "You can get into Aequitas."

She blinks, her cheeks reddening just a little. I've caught her off-guard. I can tell by the way her eyes widen, the way her lips open, as though she wants to say something, but doesn't know what.

"You have an engineering degree, no?"

She nods slowly. "I specialized in software engineering." Her gaze lingers, yet I can't read that look in her eyes. Is it admiration? For a split-second I wonder if I inspired her to follow my path, but then I shake my head and smile. Of course not.

"You will always be welcome at my firm, Aria."

She looks down at her plate, her cheeks turning crimson. She looks like she doesn't know what to say, and I love that expression she's wearing. Aria is rarely at a loss for words, but I've got her speechless. Over something so simple too. She should've known there's always space for her by my side.

Noah sits up excitedly and grins. "That's a great idea," he tells her. "You should consider it. There isn't a better company to work for, especially in your field."

Brad nods. "I agree," he says, his eyes on me. "I'd absolutely love to work for you," he tells me. "Do you have a business card? Maybe we can chat sometime next week."

I lift my wine glass to my lips and take a sip before placing it back down on the table, trying my best to suppress my irritation. "Not you."

Brad blinks in confusion, while Noah bites back a smile. "I apologize for his abrasiveness," Noah says, not sounding apologetic at all. "He means that his invitation only extends to Aria."

I shake my head. Noah has always done this, translating my handful of words into full sentences. I never understood why — it's not like I'm ever unclear. I just don't see the point in wasting my words where they'll remain unheard.

Aria glances at me, and the way she looks at me makes my heart feel strange. Her eyes are filled with so much hope, as though working for me actually means something to her. I wonder if she's ever applied... *fuck*. What if she did and her application got rejected? I should've created an alert for her name.

Noah clears his throat and straightens in his seat. "Let's cut the cake," he says, smiling. "I've been looking forward to this all day."

His eyes drift to the photos on top of the fireplace, and I expected him to rise and choose a photo of his parents to place on the table with us. Aria and Noah have made it a tradition to include their parents on special occasions. They've done it for years, so I'm surprised when Noah tears his gaze away from the photos. He glances at Brad and then picks up the cake knife.

"Wait a minute," I say, rising to my feet. I walk over to the fireplace and grab one of the photo frames, carrying it back to the table carefully. Noah looks up at me with gratitude in his eyes, and I can't help but wonder if he'd have ignored their standing tradition because of Brad. Surely not?

Aria's eyes meet mine, and I can't quite decipher her expression. It looks a lot like helplessness blended together with gratitude. She rises to her feet to sing happy birthday to Noah, and I sit back to look at her. Her voice still renders me speechless. It's as sweet and beautiful as she is.

I drag my eyes away and stare at the cake she made for Noah. It's obvious she put a lot of thought into this year's design, and I fight the tinge of jealousy I feel. To have someone care about you that much... to have someone hand make you a birthday cake, what would that be like?

My eyes fall to Brad, and I tense involuntarily. He'd better appreciate Aria, he'd better treat her like the queen she is. I've taken men far more powerful than him down, and I won't hesitate to ruin him if he ever hurts her. For his sake, I hope he never does.

Chapter Four

ARIA

"He's even more intense than I expected him to be. I've read so many articles about him, and you *know* I idolize the guy, yet you never thought to mention that you know him personally?" Brad says, his words tumbling out in rapid succession. "He's quiet but domineering, and he's even taller and broader than he looks in photos. Where does he even find the time to work out? Don't you find that all successful people are like that? They prioritize their health in ways we don't."

He hasn't stopped talking about Grayson since last night, and I should probably find it cute, but it just makes me uncomfortable. I'm not entirely certain why, but it does.

In part, it might be because I'm a little protective of Gray, and I know Brad wants to make use of my connection to him. I've always treated Gray the same way I treat Noah, and neither one of them seems to realize just how amazing they are. Noah continuously gets approached for free medical advice and treatments, when he barely has time to sleep as it is. Gray, on the other hand, is always hounded for his money and his connections. I don't want to become another person who does that to him when I should be on his side.

Noah and Gray both look domineering, but they have hearts of gold. They don't know how to turn down requests for help, because they both know what it's like to be in a vulnerable position, to have nothing.

My phone buzzes, and I smile when I see a notification from the Nemesis app. I glance over at Brad, but he's so busy obsessing over Grayson he doesn't even realize I'm barely listening.

Ash: *Did you manage to braid that beard of yours? Send pics.*

I suppress a smile, amused with Ash's continuous efforts to find out who I am. We've never met, but lately I've come to consider him a friend.

Nyx: *I French braided it. It was beautiful.*

Ash: *Ok Beardarella. Did you see the new case that popped up? One week tops. You wanna bet we can get this case resolved in a week?*

I click on the case icon and find a new request. It's a death row appeal. My heart drops at the mere thought of someone dying for a crime they didn't commit. Looks like this person was convicted for murder based on nothing more than a witness testimony.

Nyx: *It won't be easy, but let's do this. I'm betting five days. We'll need to work quickly.*

Ash: *What are we betting?*

Nyx: *Favors.*

Ash: *A favor from the illustrious Nyx? Count me in.*

"Aria?" Brad says, snapping me out of my thoughts. He looks annoyed, and I smile at him sheepishly as I put my phone down. "Do you think you could score me an interview?" he asks, wrapping his arm around my waist.

He pulls me closer until our bodies are pressed against each other. "Please, honey," he murmurs, his lips lowering to mine. I sigh in delight when he kisses me, my heart fluttering in a way it never has before. When he kisses me this way, I can barely think straight. The way Brad makes me feel... I've never felt anything like it. I never thought I'd ever have any of this — a normal life, a boyfriend, a well-paid job.

Brad pulls away and looks at me pleadingly. "Wouldn't it be amazing if we could both work for Aequitas? I know you aren't happy with your current job. This could be the perfect solution. It could be a new start."

I tense, my heart fluttering as I cautiously allow hope to fill me. "We could move to California together," I whisper, my thoughts filling with everything that's currently out of reach. A job I actually *love*, being surrounded by people that motivate me and that'll teach me more than I can learn by myself... and most of all, I'd have Brad by my side.

Brad nods. "Exactly. It's time we start thinking about our future. We can't stay here forever. If we want to make it, we need to be in Silicon Valley."

Our future... I like the sound of that. We've only been together for a year, but I'm happy that we seem to be on the same page about our life together. Brad knows I've been applying for jobs for two years now, and I'm unable to find anything due to my lack of relevant work experience. I've been thinking about the next steps for my career, and honestly, working for Grayson would be a dream come true.

"Okay," I whisper. "Whenever Gray visits, he always makes sure to spend a week with my brother, to catch up and hang out. He should be here for a few more days."

Brad grins. "Do you think he'd want to have dinner with us?"

I nod. Gray has never said no to dinner before. Just like Noah, he's always been there for me, in both big ways and small.

Brad hands me my phone in a rush and I shake my head as I scroll through my contacts, amused by his excitement.

I'm oddly nervous as I raise my phone to my ear. Gray has never said no to anything I've asked of him, yet now I feel... bad. I feel bad asking him to dinner, knowing my intentions aren't pure. I don't want to be another person who uses him. I bite down on my lip, second guessing myself. Just as I've convinced myself that I can't do this, he picks up.

"Aria," he says, his voice deep and his tone as unhurried as ever. The way he says my name has always been unique, almost intimate.

"Gray," I whisper, before clearing my throat. "Hi."

He chuckles, and I feel heat spread across my cheeks. Brad stares at me, a hint of impatience in his expression.

"Hi," Grayson says.

I laugh nervously and shake my head. This is Gray. My Gray. The same Gray I've known for years, Gray who treats me like his little sister. Noah has always told me that the three of us are a family, and that he and Gray will always be there for me. I shouldn't be so scared to ask for a simple favor.

"I... um," I mutter. "I... is Noah going to be late today? He always is these days, you know? They work him to the bone. You're probably alone at the house, right? It can't be nice. Or is it? Maybe you're enjoying the solitude? I don't know. But what will you eat? Do you have food?"

My eyes flutter closed in mortification. So much for asking for a favor. I'm messing this up. Grayson bursts into laughter, while Brad stares at me with raised brows and a confused expression.

"What is it you want, Aria?" Gray says, his tone teasing.

I sigh and shake my head. "You saw straight through me, huh?"

"You always ramble when you're nervous, Ari. Either you've done something, or you want something. Which is it?"

The use of my childhood nickname warms my heart, and I relax instantly. "Fine, you're right," I admit. "Food. You don't have any, do you?"

Gray pauses before he replies. "I do not. Why?"

"Would you like to have dinner with me?"

"Dinner... me and you?"

I glance at Brad and purse my lips, a hint of uneasiness making me hesitate. "And Brad," I say, my voice soft.

Gray is silent, and I swallow hard as I wait for his reply. My heart is beating in my throat, and for a second I'm certain he'll say no. Part of me hopes he does. That way my conscience won't weigh so heavily on me.

"Was this your idea or his?"

How... how does he know? "Gray, you and I always hang out when you visit. You don't want to?"

He sighs, and guilt settles in the pit of my stomach, weighing on me. "You're evading my question, Aria. Was it your idea?"

"I... no, Gray."

"And this, me having dinner with you both, it matters to you?"

I hesitate. Part of me wants to say no. I don't want Gray doing anything he doesn't want to do, and I know he'll do this for me if I ask him to. He'll do it, but I doubt he'll enjoy it. I glance at Brad, and the hope in his eyes fills me with resignation. Having dinner with Gray could change everything for us. I could get my dream job and Brad could move with me. Working for Gray would definitely be a good career move for Brad, too.

"It does, Gray," I say, my voice barely above a whisper.

He sighs, falling silent for a moment. "You'll cook for me?"

"I'll make your favorite.".

"You still remember what that is?"

I smile. Like I could ever forget. "Always, Gray."

"Hmm... at least you'll feed me a homemade meal while your boyfriend feeds me bullshit. Done. I'll see you at seven?"

I bite back a smile. "See you at seven, Gray."

Brad fist pumps and mouths 'Yes!' as I end the call. I should be happy that Gray agreed, but somehow, I'm left wishing he hadn't.

Chapter Five

GRAYSON

I pause in front of Aria's apartment, dreading the dinner I'm about to be forced to sit through. Even after all these years, I can't deny her anything. She's no longer the teenager she was when I first met her, but I still want her to have everything her heart desires. Even if that means sitting through an evening of Sleazy sucking up to me.

I inhale deeply and raise my hand to knock. The door swings open a second later, and I can't tell whether I'm amused or annoyed to find Brad standing in front of me. I glance at his hair, suppressing my frown. How? How does it stay like that? Seriously, what does he put in it?

"Grayson, my man," he says, taking a step closer to me. I take a step back. The fuck does he want to do? Hug me? I barely even know the guy.

His expression falls, and he straightens awkwardly as he opens the door wider. "Please, come in."

I nod and follow him in, my eyes taking in every detail. The place is small, and it's old, but it's got character. Aria's signature touch is all over the place. There's color everywhere, but somehow, she makes it work. Where I'm all black and white, Aria is everything in between. She always has been.

"Ah, this shabby little place probably isn't what you're used to," Brad says. "I told Aria it'd be better to eat out, but she was being stubborn tonight. I'm sorry. I'm afraid you'll have to suffer through one of Aria's meals."

I clench my jaw. What the fuck is that supposed to mean? Does this guy not realize how lucky he is that she makes him food at all? That she spends time and effort, putting endless love and care in every dish he has the honor to eat? Fucking asshole.

"I insisted."

He blinks, confused, and I sigh. Of course he's a fucking dumbass, unable to comprehend a simple response.

Relief washes over me when I hear Aria's laughter. I turn to find her standing in the kitchen doorway, an apron tied around her waist, her hair in a bun and her feet bare. She looks cute, and those eyes of hers are twinkling with that expression that's uniquely hers: mischief and provocation.

"Gray," she admonishes. "Full sentences, please."

She walks up to me, and I hold my arm out for her. She walks into my embrace and I lift her off the floor with one arm, side hugging her. She's so fucking small, and I've always loved that about her. Aria giggles when I put her down, and the sound of it puts me at ease. It melts away the annoyance I felt at seeing Sleazy's face.

"Gray meant he insisted on me cooking for him," she explains, and I shake my head. She acts like I don't speak, but I do. Just not to people that aren't worth my time. I speak just fine to Noah and her.

Brad nods, his expression guarded. There's just something about him I don't like, and it's more than his dumb hair. I should've done what my instincts told me to do, and hacked into his phone. The operating system is likely one my company created, after all. I didn't, because Aria would never forgive me if she found out, and I don't want to intrude on her privacy like that.

She pulls on the edge of my sleeve and leads me to the dining table, where a stunning meal has been laid out already. "Ta-da," she says, grinning and gesturing at the food. Her eyes are filled with warmth, an intimate smile on her lips.

Brad looks horrified and he clenches his jaw as he turns toward her. "Darling," he says through gritted teeth. "You made *scrambled eggs*? As the main dish?"

I pat the top of her head and slide my hand down to her neck until my hand is resting on her shoulder. "Thank you, Ari," I say, unable to wipe the grin off my face.

Her eyes aren't on me, though. They're on Brad, and her expression is filled with shame and sorrow. I pull her closer to me, the top of her head hitting my bicep. She looks up at me. I hate seeing this sadness in her eyes.

"Thank you for making my favorite food," I tell her. She stares into my eyes, and slowly but surely, the tension in her shoulders eases. She smiles, and I breathe a sigh of relief.

"Of course, Gray," she says, grinning.

Back when Noah and I first met, in our first year of college, eggs were the most nutritious and filling food we could afford. He and I both attended a college we couldn't really pay for, and the fees were too high for us to bear. Noah had the additional responsibility of taking care of Aria, and from what I understand, they spent most of their parents' life insurance paying for the mortgage of their house and legal fees related to their parents' case.

Similarly, I worked my ass off just to be able to pay the school fees and my rent in a tiny shared flat. There often wasn't much left for food, so Noah and I would split grocery bills and eat together. Aria's creativeness saved us. She learned to whip up eggs in ten different ways, making us feel like we were having something else every day. It wasn't just that, though. I doubt she knows it, but Aria is the first person who's ever *wanted* to cook for me. Her scrambled egg dish was the first meal I ever had that was made with care and affection. It's been my favorite food ever since, and I still can't have eggs without thinking of her.

"Come on," she says, her voice soft. She pulls out my seat for me, and I chuckle, shaking my head.

"No way, Ari," I tell her, placing my hand on her shoulder. "You sit."

She sighs in mock exasperation as she sits down, but I see the appreciation in her eyes, and I hate that. For her to look at me that way can only mean one thing: she's not being treated chivalrous enough, she's not used to this.

Brad clears his throat awkwardly as I sit down next to Aria. "I didn't know eggs were your favorite," he says.

I stare him down as Aria fills up my plate. "Why would you?" I ask him.

Brad blinks, clearly uncomfortable, and Aria taps my thigh underneath the table, sending me a pleading look before pulling her hand away.

I sigh and remind myself to be *nice* to Brad, when all I can think about is what would happen if I cracked an egg on his head. Would it stick in his hair gel, or would it run down his head like it's supposed to? I don't know, but I'd like to find out.

"So, Aria told me she's seriously considering accepting your job offer."

I see Aria stiffen from my peripheral vision and instantly gather she told him no such thing. I lean back in my seat and stare at Brad, wondering what other crap will come out of his mouth.

"We'd love to move to Cali together, and honestly, we'd both love to work for Aequitas. If there's anything you can do, we'd really appreciate it."

He's smart. He's capitalizing on my affection for Aria. I glance at her and find her staring at her plate, her entire body tense. She seems uncomfortable, and I don't know what to make of the situation. He's using her, and she seems to realize it, yet she's letting it happen.

"*She's* already in," I tell Brad, tipping my head toward Aria. "But you... you'll have to prove yourself."

He sits up, his eyes filled with determination. "Test me any way you want. I'm a great developer. Anything you need, I can probably do it."

I smile at him. Moron. "Have you ever heard of the Nemesis Platform?"

He frowns at me, and I've got my answer. Fucking noob. He works in tech and hasn't heard of the Nemesis Platform? He stands no chance in my company. Probably wouldn't even make it through the first round of interviews.

"It's a vigilante platform, for a lack of a better explanation. It's all the rage with my developers and engineers right now. Find a weakness in their systems. If you do, I'll hire you on the spot."

Brad looks excited, but Aria looks disappointed. She probably knows as well as I do that I've just given Brad an impossible task, and the fact he doesn't even know it doesn't bode well for him.

She wears that same sad expression throughout the rest of dinner, and I feel fucking awful. I did this. I did this to her. Would it really kill me to hire Sleazy? Truthfully, he likely wouldn't last long, anyway. He'd be fired after his first performance review. Yet I still can't budge on this. I can't sit here and let him capitalize on my affection for Aria. I won't let him use her this way. If he wants to apply the regular way, he's welcome to do so, but I'm not handing him a job.

The atmosphere between Aria and me is tense as she walks me to the door, but Brad barely notices. He's already got his laptop out, ready to meet the challenge I set.

"Why?" Aria asks as we reach the door, hurt flashing through her eyes.

I turn to look at her and gently brush her long hair out of her face. "Because he doesn't deserve you, and you should never let a man hold you back from chasing your dreams. Not Noah, not me, and certainly not *Brad*. Follow your dreams, Aria, and if he's the one, he'll follow *you*."

She stares at me and then nods, crestfallen.

The look in her eyes haunts me the entire way home, and I can't help but second-guess myself. Did I just make the wrong decision?

Chapter Six

ARIA

I stare at my screen, lost in thought. I told Brad I'd help him find the last few bugs in his software during my lunch break today, and all I can think about is wanting to do this full-time. I want projects of my own.

I'm glad I get to gain some practical experience through Brad's projects, but none of the stuff I've worked on will have my name on it. And that shouldn't matter, because how many people really care who developed the software they use? But still... I want to be known in the industry as someone worth working with. Someone worth hiring.

My mind involuntarily drifts to Grayson. He said I'd be welcome at Aequitas, and he seemed to mean it, but then he made it impossible for Brad to join alongside me. I don't understand why he'd do that. Is it a way of offering me something yet making sure I won't take him up on it? Was it an empty offer?

Aequitas is my dream company. It has been since Gray founded it. I've applied every single year, and not once did I even make it to the interview rounds. I've never had the guts to ask

Gray for a job directly — not because I'm opposed to using connections, not at all — but because I'm scared he'll tell me that I'm not good enough, that the rejections from his HR department mean I'm not cut out for Aequitas.

Working at Aequitas could change everything for me. But is a dream job worth risking my relationship?

I grab my phone and stare at the photo of Brad and me that I've set as my background. For years I was convinced that I'd never have a normal life, that I'd never recover from the loss of my parents. I've always believed no one would ever be able to see through the smiles I force onto my face every day. And no one did, until Brad. I can't leave now. I can't move all the way to California. I'm not sure our relationship would survive, and I'm not willing to take the risk. Not even for my dream job. All I've ever wanted is to have a normal life. I want to live the life my parents would have wanted for me. I can't risk the happiness I've finally found.

I'm startled out of my thoughts when my phone rings. My heart drops when I recognize the number, and my stomach twists violently. If our lawyer is calling, it can't be good news. I grab the edge of my desk as I lift the phone to my ear.

"Hello?" I say, my voice barely above a whisper.

"Aria," Jack says, his voice tinged with regret, as though he doesn't want to be making this call. My eyes flutter closed, and I bite down on my lip, bracing myself.

"They released Peter Simmons on good behavior. I only just found out, and I wanted you to hear it from me."

His words reverberate through my mind, taking a while to click. This can't be happening. He can't get away with what he did. Not after everything we went through to finally put him in jail.

"Good behavior? Jack, he *murdered* my parents. You told me he'd serve twenty-five years. How could he possibly be out ten years early? How is that possible?"

Jack sighs, as though he doesn't know what to tell me. "I'm

sorry, Aria. If his behavior was exemplary, it's possible for part of his sentence to have gotten commuted."

I swallow hard. "He was supposed to be in for another ten years. This shouldn't be possible," I repeat, panic gripping me.

"I'm looking into it as we speak," Jack says, but the tone of his voice tells me all I need to know. It's too late to do anything about this. "I'd better call your brother."

I shake my head. "I think it might be better if I tell him myself," I say, my voice breaking. It's been hard on Noah, celebrating his birthday without our parents, becoming a doctor after years of hard work and being unable to see the pride in their eyes. He won't deal well with this news.

I don't even realize I ended the call, not until my manager calls out my name. I don't remember rising from my seat, yet here I am, with my bag in hand, my feet moving me toward the door.

"Aria," he says. "Where are you going? I need you to give that presentation to the board for me later today. I have plans tonight. Make sure you make a good slideshow as well."

I look up at him, my eyes lingering on his face. He looks unkind, and he is. He's always fobbing his work off on me, and I've always taken it. I've done it, because I always thought it'd increase my chances of moving departments.

"No," I say, my voice soft but clear. I'm barely thinking straight, but it still feels right. I walk past him, ignoring the way his face reddens.

"If you walk out now, you'd better not dream of returning tomorrow morning."

I pause and turn back to look at him. All eyes in the office are on us, and most people look amused. There's not a single glance of sympathy, there's no outrage on my behalf, and not a single person here will stand up for me. No one seems to care I might lose my job. All this seems to be is a moment of entertainment for them. Every single person in this department has at some point reached out to me for help, and I've never asked for anything in return. I've given this company everything for years. What for?

"Understood," I tell my manager, and then I walk out, slamming the door behind me. The regret sinks in the second I walk into the lift and I place a steadying hand against the cold metal. I'm tempted to go to Brad's floor to find him, but I'm scared I won't make it there without bursting into tears. The last thing I want to do is embarrass myself even further.

I'm shaking by the time I get home. My thoughts are whirling, and I feel sick. The news I received combined with the loss of my job has me sinking to my knees as soon as the front door closes behind me.

I inhale deeply, trying my best not to panic, forcing myself to breathe. I glance around, my eyes settling on a flash of red.

I start to tremble, a chill running down my spine when I realize what I'm looking at.

That flash of red... they're red heels.

And they aren't mine.

Chapter Seven

ARIA

I reach out hesitantly, a small part of me hoping that I'm wrong. A thousand different excuses run through my mind. Maybe they're a gift for me. Maybe they're a pair of old shoes I've just forgotten about. I know I'm lying to myself, and I hate myself for it.

I grab the shoes, my grip tightening around the heel. They look familiar, and my heart sinks when I realize why.

I tense when I hear a sound... a giggle. I'm in a strange state of denial as I stand up and force my feet forward, toward our bedroom. It's like my brain knows exactly what's happening, but my heart refuses to believe it.

My stomach twists painfully when I notice the trail of clothes leading to the room. Part of me wants to walk away, to pretend this isn't happening, but a larger part of me refuses to do that to myself.

I take the last few steps toward the bedroom, my entire body trembling. They didn't even close the door. The sounds coming from the room break my heart. A strange helplessness fills my body. It's like I'm on a collision course, yet I can't get myself to walk away.

I swallow down my tears as I make it to the doorway. I knew what I'd find, yet somehow, I struggle to make sense of what I'm seeing. Brad, the man thought I'd spend my life with, is in bed with another woman. Not just any woman — Britney from HR. The same girl that keeps encouraging me to apply, that promised me she'd do whatever she could to get me the job I want. She's been so friendly to me, and she got even friendlier when I started dating Brad. I should have known her intentions weren't pure.

I lean back against the wall, out of sight. My eyes fall closed, yet the image of the two of them haunts me. Brad has her in his arms, his lips pressed to her forehead. He's never once held me that way. Every single time we've had sex, he's gotten up to shower straight after. He always told me that it wasn't personal, that he hated laying in his own sweat. Yet he doesn't seem to have an issue with it right now, with Britney. The two of them are tangled in the sheets I spent *weeks* choosing.

"There's always another excuse," Britney says, her voice whiny. "You told me you'd ditch her the second she finished that software for you. I'm tired of only being able to see you during our lunch hour."

I wrap my arms around myself but that won't stop the tremors, it won't ease the pain.

"I know, honey. But I told you, she knows Grayson Callahan. This is my chance to get a better job. Working for him would mean I'm set for life. You and I would be set for life. The pay is good, the benefits are even better, and the opportunity for growth is limitless."

I hear the mattress squeak, and I can just imagine him leaning over to console her. I don't have it in me to look.

"It sounds like you just want to keep dating her. When you first approached her, you told me you'd only be friends with her so she'd help you with your work. Then you suddenly started dating her, and now you won't break up with her? I'm not a fool, Brad."

I hear him sigh, and I can tell he's frustrated. "Honey, I told you... I only started dating her because she thought I was flirting with her, and at the time she was doing half my work for me. I couldn't risk her walking away from that project, and it's a good thing I didn't. Her work got me a promotion, it paid for our holidays and those expensive clothes you love."

I bite down on my lip to keep my sobs in. All the projects I've helped him with, all the software I've helped him develop... he was just using me. We initially became closer because of the coding I'd help him with. He used to take me out for drinks or dinner to thank me for my help, and I misunderstood. I thought he liked me, that he was falling as hard as I was, but to him I was just a tool. My throat closes up and angry tears run down my cheek, my lungs burning from trying to keep it in.

"That doesn't explain why you stay with her every time you tell me you're ending things with her, and it sure as hell doesn't explain why you *live* with her."

"Honey," Brad says, sounding annoyed. "Why do we have to do this every time? I told you it's so she could cover half my rent, so we'd have more money for the house we're buying. The deposit and renovations aren't cheap, darling. That's why you're staying with your parents for now, isn't it? So we can save up. Besides, I needed easy access to her for some of the projects I had going on. The few hours I saw her weren't enough to convince her to do as much work as she's doing for me."

A tear rolls down my cheek and I will myself to walk away, but I can't. I can't get myself to move.

"Tell me the truth. You want her, don't you? Did you really fall in love with her after all that play pretend? Just tell me, Brad. Tell me the truth. I'm tired of waiting for you. I'm tired of waiting for our life together to begin."

Brad laughs, the sound vicious. "Want her? Don't mess around, Brit. Have you seen her? Those short fat legs, the disgusting stretch marks all over her body. I put up with her, but I do not *want* her. Fuck. She disgusts me. Every time she touches me my skin crawls, and you know it. I put up with it for you, for us. She's a fucking psycho. Every other night she wakes up screaming about her dead parents or some shit, disturbing my sleep. If I'd known she was this crazy, I'd never have bothered with her, but it's too late now. I'm already in it, so I might as well milk her for all she's worth."

I've heard enough. More than enough. I wouldn't have forgiven him for cheating, but this? This kills me. None of what we had was real. While I was ready to put my dreams on hold for him, he was using me to make Britney's dreams come true.

I just about manage to swallow down a sob as I walk away. Part of me wants to confront them, but I can't do it. I can't stand any more of this. I need to get out before I fall apart. I don't want them to see. I don't want them to know that they broke what was left of me.

Chapter Eight

GRAYSON

I love moments like these. I love the tranquility. Nothing but me and the tapping of my keyboard. The rain outside just adds to my sense of peace.

This is one of the reasons I love staying with Noah. Being in this house always takes me back to a time when things were simpler. To a time when Noah and I were just students doing all we could to ensure a better future for ourselves. Back then, the company I now run was nothing but a dream, a simple concept that I didn't think would ever come to fruition.

So many years have passed since Noah and I met, and so much has changed, but our friendship has always stayed the same.

As has this. The search for my parents. I still don't know who they are, or why they left me in front of a church as a baby. I've considered dozens of scenarios, and the ones I keep clinging to are the situations in which they had no choice. Maybe they were too poor. Maybe my mother had me too young and wasn't allowed to keep me. I don't know, but I have to find out.

My eyes scan the medical records in front of me, and I'm

unsure what I'm hoping to find. I've exhausted all leads I had, and at this point I'm looking for a needle in a haystack.

I'm startled when the doorbell rings and check my watch. Noah isn't meant to come home from work for another hour or so. I rise from my seat and walk to the front door, finding Aria standing in front of me, completely drenched with mascara running down her face, her hair sticking to her cheeks, despair filling her eyes. She looks up at me, and the sob that tears through her throat guts me. She steps forward and throws herself into my arms.

"Grayson," she says, her voice breaking.

I wrap my arms around her and hold her tightly. The sound of her despair goes straight to my heart. "What happened, Ari?"

She's crying so hard she's almost choking on her sobs. I lift her into my arms and carry her into the house, kicking the door closed. Her entire body feels ice cold and she's shivering. I've never seen her in this state before, and I don't know what to do. I'm worried sick, and my heart hurts just seeing that look in her eyes.

I lead her to the sofa and sit down, placing her on my lap. Aria tightens her grip on me, her arms wrapped around my neck and her face pressed against my throat.

I grab the blanket from the sofa and throw it around us, trying my best to warm her up. I can't tell if she's shaking because she's cold or due to the force of her tears. I bury my hand into her hair and hold her tightly, unsure how to console her.

"Aria, what happened? You're scaring me," I whisper, one hand in her hair, the other rubbing her back soothingly. Every muscle in my body is on high alert, ready to do some serious damage to whoever made her cry like this.

"Gray..."

She sounds heartbroken, and she's crying so hard that she's unable to get her words out. I hold her tightly, her body pressed against mine. She's clinging onto me like I'm her lifeline, and it kills me. I've never seen her cry like this, not once.

"Ari," I whisper. "Please, tell me what happened. Tell me why you're crying. I can't make it better if you won't tell me what's wrong."

She shifts in my lap, and I loosen my grip on her as she draws herself up in my arms, tucking her knees underneath her chin, her cheek resting against my chest.

"Was it Brad?"

She nods hesitantly.

"Did he hurt you?"

She nods again, and I start to see white. I force myself to stay calm, but I can't keep my body from tensing.

"Where? Where did he touch you?"

Aria shakes her head and turns to face me. Her eyes are red and swollen, and dark mascara lines run down her face in a way I've only ever seen happen in movies. Seeing her like this makes me want to put Brad six feet under.

She places her hands on my shoulders and shakes her head. "I'm not physically hurt, Gray," she says, her voice barely above a whisper. "He... Brad, he... he cheated on me."

She bursts into tears at that last word and hides her face in my neck, her arms wrapped around me. I hold her and stroke her back gently, my thoughts whirling. What the fuck? Who in their right mind would ever cheat on Aria? I knew Brad was a dimwit, but fucking hell, I didn't think he was this stupid.

I hug Aria as her tears continue to drench my shoulder. She hasn't lived an easy life, not in the least, yet I've always known her as the girl with the perpetual smile on her face. To see her like this, with tears in her eyes? It both shocks and angers me. Brad will pay for this. These tears of hers will cost him everything.

I hear the door slam closed and tighten my grip on Aria. Noah freezes when he walks in and finds her in my arms, the sounds of her sobs breaking the silence in the house.

His eyes widen, and he rushes up to us, alarmed. His eyes meet mine, and the rage in them startles me. "What did you do? Why is she crying?" he asks, his voice raised.

His tone makes me tighten my grip on Aria involuntarily, protectiveness washing over me. She trembles in my arms and shakes her head, unable to get the words out.

I cradle her head gently and glare at Noah. "It wasn't me. It was Brad."

Noah freezes. I see the guilt he struggles to hide, and it hits me right in the chest. I'd never do anything to hurt Aria. Rather than assuming something must have happened, he assumed *I hurt her.* Me. I can't even blame him for his assumption. No one knows me better than Noah. He knows about my criminal record. He knows I've beat someone up to the point that he'll never be the same again, and he knows I still don't regret it. He knows what I'm capable of.

I stroke Aria's back, her breathing slowly calming. Noah sits down next to us, and Aria turns to face her brother. I recognize the helplessness in Noah's expression. He can barely stand to see her like this either.

"Brad," she says, her voice breaking. "He's been seeing someone else all along."

Noah's hands shake as she finally tells us both exactly what she walked in on earlier today, the things she heard and saw. Noah clenches his jaw and listens patiently, but I know he's already plotting Brad's demise. I know, because I am too.

Noah raises his hand to her face and pushes her hair out of the way carefully. "You've got me, Aria," he says. "*This* is your home. Gray and I, we're your family. You don't need Brad. Fuck him, okay? Fuck that asshole. I never liked him anyway."

Aria smiles at his words, but another tear drops down her cheek. Noah looks at me, and I nod. Brad's going to pay. He'll regret hurting Aria the way he has.

I'm going to hit him in ways he won't ever see coming. He'll never recover. I won't stop until his life is in pieces, and even then, it won't be enough.

Chapter Nine

GRAYSON

Noah closes Aria's bedroom door and leans against it. He looks devastated and it's obvious he's feeling Aria's pain as though it's his own. He straightens and clenches his jaw, his expression shifting from pain to angry determination. He turns resolutely and heads toward the stairs, and I fall into step with him.

"You're a doctor," I remind him. "Your hands are precious. Do you really want to damage them? Those hands should be used to save lives."

He glances at me and clenches his jaw. "She's my sister. I haven't seen her cry like that in over a decade. I don't give a fuck about my hands, Gray. I'm burying that douchebag."

He reaches the door and bends down to put on his shoes. I sigh. I get it. I want to beat Brad up just as much as he does, but will it help?

"All right. I guess I'll have to bail you out for aggravated assault, then. How much do you think it'll cost me? Do you think they'll still let you work in a hospital if you have a criminal record? I'm not sure, you know."

Noah freezes and looks down at his shoes. He looks defeated and helpless, feelings I understand all too well. "What do you want me to do, Gray? I can't just let this slide. He broke her heart. He made her *cry*."

I nod and lean against the front door, blocking his exit. "What I want you to do is leave this to me. I'm here, aren't I? Beating him up might put him in the hospital, but he'll recover. He'll get over it, and in a month, it'll be like it never happened. We can't have that. Aria is my family too, Noah. I won't let him get away with what he did. I'll ruin his fucking life. Trust me, okay?"

Noah looks into my eyes, as though he's wondering whether to put his faith in me. He nods hesitantly, and I breathe a sigh of relief.

"I want him to pay for using her, Gray. I want him to regret hurting her the way he has."

I smile at him smugly and cross my arms. "Noah, I'll make him regret ever approaching her."

Noah nods and I tip my head toward the living room. "Come on," I tell him. "Let's make this son of a bitch pay."

I lead him to the dining table where I've been working this week and start up my laptop as we both sit down. Noah is restless as he watches me type line after line of code, and I sigh, forcing myself to talk him through what I'm doing, even if it's just to ease his worries.

"Aria said she helped him with software, didn't she? If not for her, he'd never have a working project. I've just gained access to both his work computer and his laptop, and I'm corrupting all his files and back-ups. Not in an obvious way, though. That'd be too easy. I'm altering the code," I say, pointing out specific lines of code that likely mean nothing to Noah, but he nods nonetheless. "This makes it so that every piece of software he's worked on starts to act more and more buggy over the next few days, and every day, the issues will get worse. He won't realize until the software has already been delivered to his clients, and by then, it'll be too late for him to fix it."

Noah grins and looks at me with wide eyes. "You can do that?"

I nod as my fingers fly over the keyboard. "This will ruin his reputation in the industry. He'll lose his job, but more importantly, he'll never be able to work as a software engineer again. Not after the mess he'll be left with. Issues this big will result in a big investigation, and they'll trace it all back to him."

Noah crosses his arms and frowns. "He won't know?"

I shake my head. "It's quite obvious which parts of his software were coded by him, and which were crafted by someone else. Aria, I assume. His coding is a fucking mess, using ten lines where he could use one. He's never going to figure it out, and I've made sure all issues point back to him."

The short, tight lines of code look familiar to me. There are patterns I recognize, but I can't quite place where I've seen them before.

Noah sits with me and stares at my screen intently as I finish writing the amendments that will ruin Brad's life before removing every trace of my presence.

I sit back and sigh in relief when it's done, but I don't feel much better. It's not enough. The damage I've done is extensive, but it doesn't ease my anger.

"All done," I tell Noah.

"Thank you, Gray. If you hadn't been here, I might actually have ruined my career in a fit of rage. Aria would blame herself if that happened, and that's the last thing I want to do to her. I don't know, man. Just... thank you."

I nod awkwardly. I've known Noah for over a decade, but I still don't know what to say to stuff like this. He smiles knowingly and rises from his seat.

He claps me on the back and walks toward the stairs as I turn my laptop off. I watch him walk away, looking far more relaxed than he did an hour ago. I'm glad I was able to stop him from potentially ruining his career. He's right. Aria wouldn't have forgiven herself, and they'd both end up heartbroken. Noah's career means the world to him. It's all he's ever dreamed about, and he's only just finally finished his residency. I can't let him risk it all now.

I'm restless as I walk to the guest room. Even though I know I did some irreversible damage to Brad, it doesn't feel like enough. I can't shake the image of Aria standing in front of me, tears streaming down her face. She felt so cold in my arms, and the way she was shaking... she didn't even have her home keys — she had nothing but her phone on her. Aria must have rushed out of her apartment in a state of despair.

I sit down on my bed and run a hand through my hair. It's not enough. Ruining his career isn't enough.

I rise to my feet without a second thought and slip out of my room. Noah has too much to lose, but I don't.

I grab Noah's car keys on the way out, and twenty minutes later, I'm standing in front of Aria's apartment. I raise my hand to the doorbell, barely able to restrain my anger.

Brad opens up almost immediately. "Aria?" he says, his voice tinged with mock concern.

His expression drops when he sees me standing in front of him, and I smile as I pull my arm back and punch him square in the jaw. He stumbles back and loses his footing, falling to the floor. A rush of satisfaction overcomes me, and the feeling is almost... thrilling. I've felt this way only once before when I put my former foster father in the hospital. This feeling... it's addictive. It's dangerous.

"That's the last time you'll ever say her name," I tell Brad.

I lean in and pull him back up by his collar before punching him again, enjoying the loud crack upon impact. Brad falls back to the floor, blood trickling from his lip. The expression on his face tells me he knows exactly what he's done — and that Aria knows. I'm tempted to do to him what I did to my foster father, breaking as many bones as I can, leaving him paralyzed. I struggle to push down my need for vengeance, my need to make him pay the ultimate price for his betrayal.

"Don't try to contact her. Don't appear in front of her. If I catch you anywhere near her, I'll do far worse than I did today."

Brad laughs mockingly, but I hear the desperation underneath it. "You won't get away with this," he tells me. "I'll sue you. This is assault, and you can more than afford to settle, can't you?"

I smile and look down at my fist. I hit him so hard that my knuckles are red. I sigh and look back at him. "Do you really think I'll appear on any of your building's security cameras? Noah's home cameras will show me walking in a few hours ago, and they won't capture me leaving again until tomorrow morning."

I take a step back and shake my head. "Spread any rumors, and *I'll* sue *you* for defamation. But that's not all I'll do. Watch your back."

I want to say more, but I can't have him suspect that I messed with his software. I doubt he'll be able to find my little alterations to his code, but just in case, I don't want to hint at it. I'm tense as I walk out of the building, my hands shaking with suppressed violence. This anger, this inability to accept injustice... it runs through my veins like a compulsion. I can't give in to it again. I wanted to do so much worse to Brad, and I barely restrained myself. I should have put him in the hospital for what he did to Aria — but this will do.

It'll do, for now.

Chapter Ten

ARIA

I stare at myself in the full-length mirror in my bedroom, dropping my towel to the floor. I'm nowhere near as tall as Britney, and my body type isn't anything like hers either. My stomach isn't flat and I have no thigh gap to speak of. My legs are big, they always have been. I don't have her long, beautiful legs. Looking at myself, I now see what Brad must have seen. The stretch marks, the fat around my stomach and thighs. Even my breasts aren't what they used to be. My weight fluctuations made them look far more saggy than they once were.

Is that what it was? Was it my body? Or was it a combination of things?

Brad and I didn't even sleep together until we'd decided to move in together, and now that makes sense. He didn't want me. Sleeping with me was another way to keep me under his thumb, to keep me happy.

Whenever we did have sex, it was usually over quickly. Brad never held me the way he was holding Britney. He always, *always* showered straight after sex. I didn't use to think much of it and just assumed it was a personal preference. That maybe he just didn't like the idea of being even remotely sweaty. Now I know that's not what it was.

It was me.

I turn away, disgusted by the image in the mirror. I dress hurriedly, wanting to cover myself up. I've never felt so uncomfortable in my own skin, and I can't help but overthink everything.

Why wasn't I good enough? What does Britney have that I don't? Was any of it ever real? Thinking back on it, Brad and I first started talking because I offered to help him with an app he was asked to develop. He kept coming back for more help, and I thought he was flirting with me. Why didn't he just clarify that he wasn't? Why didn't he steer us toward friendship instead? I would've been happy to be friends. He didn't have to manipulate me the way he did. I've never denied anyone help, and had he asked for it, I probably *would have* helped him out.

Britney's words keep replaying in my mind. Those two have obviously been together for months, if not years. I was thinking of my future with Brad, but Brad... he was building a future with Britney.

I grab my phone and scroll through old photos of us, looking for signs. In the few photos of Brad, Britney and me, he's always in the middle, his eyes on her and his grip on her tighter than it is on me. How did I never notice this? I grit my teeth and delete the photos one by one, wishing I could delete these memories from my mind, too.

I inhale shakily and place my palm against the wall, trying my hardest to pull myself together. I won't cry again. I won't. I swallow down a sob and straighten my back. Brad doesn't deserve my tears.

I look up when my phone buzzes on my desk, and my first thought is that it must be Brad. That he must be wondering why I haven't come home. But it isn't him — It's Ash.

Ash: *I found something promising. It might be nothing, but it* *might be something. Old records of keycard logging. If this is accurate, this guy was at work at the time of the murder. It can't be right though... surely his lawyer never would have missed this?*

Nyx: *I'll look into it. It might be something. If there's just one crumb, we can follow it.*

Ash: *I'll send everything I've got over.*

I sit down on my bed, feeling numb. My heart feels broken, and I know it can't be fixed. But this man... this man's entire life might get taken from him. My life might be falling apart, and there's nothing I can do about that... but I can try to save a life.

Ash: *Hey, are you okay? You're usually quite talkative when we're on a case together. You seem a bit off.*

I stare at the screen in surprise. How did he know? I tighten my grip on my phone and swallow hard. Ash, he's probably the only friend I've got left now, and I don't even really know him. I guess that's the only reason he and I *are* friends — because he doesn't know how messed up I am, because he only sees the best parts of me.

Nyx: *I'm okay, Ash. Thank you for checking.*

I lock my phone and place it back on my desk, mentally bracing myself to finally leave my room. I can't stay cooped up in here. It'll worry both Noah and Gray too much.

I'm nervous as I walk down the stairs. The way I cried last night... I made a fool of myself. I must've looked like a mess, and I bet Noah and Gray feel sorry for me. I hate that. I don't want to be pitied, no matter how pitiful the situation.

The kitchen is uncharacteristically quiet as I walk in. I expected Noah to be waiting for me with hundreds of questions. I'm relieved to find that he isn't here — it's just Gray. I'm not ready to face my brother yet. He told me I was rushing into things, and I knew he never liked Brad, yet I dismissed his concerns.

Gray is staring at his laptop and looks up when he sees me, a smile on his face. "Morning," he says, grinning as though everything is normal, and I breathe a sigh of relief. He's not looking at me the way I thought he would. He's not acting out of the ordinary at all.

"Morning, Gray," I murmur, walking past him to make myself a cup of tea. I glance over at Gray's cup and find it empty, so I refill it for him without thinking. I don't realize I didn't ask him if he wanted any until I notice him staring at me in that way he does sometimes, as though he's in disbelief somehow.

"Thank you," he says, his voice soft. I nod as I take a seat next to him. His eyes roam over my face and I see the concern in them, but I'm grateful he doesn't ask me any questions. Instead, he just raises his mug to his lips.

I frown when I notice his bruised knuckles and lift my hand to his, tracing over his bruises with the tip of my finger, careful not to hurt him. Gray tenses, a flash of guilt in his eyes, and the edges of my lips turn up in a reluctant smile. I should have known that my brother and Gray wouldn't let Brad get away with what he did, and I'm glad. I'm glad to have both of them in my corner.

"Thank you," I tell him. "Thank you for always being there for me."

Gray puts his mug down and lifts his hand to my face, gently brushing the hair out of my face. "I always will be, Ari."

I nod, my smile widening. "I know," I murmur, looking into his dark brown eyes. There are specks of green in them, and I've always found them mesmerizing. "You know I'll always be there for you too, right?"

Gray nods, but I see the way he draws himself up defensively. It's subtle. It's in the way he tenses his shoulder and locks his jaw, the way the warmth seeps out of his gaze. He's always been this way. It's like he still doesn't trust that I mean what I say. Even after all these years, he struggles to believe that Noah and I consider him family.

I lean back in my seat and inhale deeply. "Yesterday... I left work early because I got a call. I've been so selfish, so lost in my own issues..."

Gray stares at me, his gaze intense. "You weren't selfish, Aria.

You were hurt. Big difference."

He wouldn't think that if he knew what I've been keeping from Noah. I look away and I gather my courage. "Where's Noah? I need to speak to him."

Gray stares at me as though he's trying to read me and shakes his head. "He was called in for an emergency this morning. Not sure when he'll be back. He ran out of the house yelling random medical terms. Sounded serious."

I nod and stare down at the table.

"Hey, what's wrong?"

I glance at Gray, my heart breaking — for different reasons this time. "Our lawyer called yesterday. That's why I went home early. He... he told me that our parents' killer was released on good behavior, and I... instead of telling Noah, I..."

"Fuck."

Gray reaches for my hand and places his over mine. His hands are so big that mine feel tiny in his, and his touch brings me unexpected comfort.

"You okay, Ari? I can't imagine how you must've felt last night."

He squeezes my hand, and I bite down on my lip in an effort to stay in control of my emotions. I have no tears left to cry, yet my heart still weeps.

"I have to tell Noah. Last night all I thought about was myself and Brad, like that even matters compared to the news I should've shared with Noah."

Grayson shakes his head. "Ari, you didn't do anything wrong. Telling him a day later won't change the facts."

I nod, but I feel guilty nonetheless. I feel like I've been a burden over the last twenty-four hours, and I hate that. "I need to tell him as soon as possible."

Gray nods. "I'll be there if you want me to be. For both of you."

I look into his eyes and nod. He always has been, and Noah and I are beyond lucky to have him in our lives.

Chapter Eleven

GRAYSON

"How was she today? I should've turned my phone off and ignored the emergencies they called me in for. It's not like I'm the only doctor they've got. Someone would've handled it. I should've known better."

I shake my head. "Let's be honest," I say. "She wouldn't have wanted you around today, and you know it. If you truly believed Aria needed you today, you would've stayed. You knew she needed space as well as I did."

Noah falls silent and turns to look at Aria. We both watch as she busies herself setting the table, having refused our help. "She's made a whole chicken roast, so she's not okay," he says. "She only does a roast when she feels guilty. I don't want her to feel guilty. None of what happened was her fault, and I don't know how to tell her that without reopening her wounds. I don't want to make her cry, man."

Her eyes are still red and swollen, and her smile is missing. Noah is right. She probably does feel guilty, but not for the reasons he's thinking. My mind drifts back to this morning when she sat with me as I worked. The helplessness she was radiating when she told me about the phone call she got yesterday... I can't even begin to understand what she must be feeling. I wish I could do something. If she'd let me, I'd be the one to tell Noah about it so she doesn't have to, but it's not my place. They might call me their family, but stuff like this I can't be part of. I can't help them. Not with this.

"Come on," I tell him, my hand on his shoulder. "She's put so much effort into dinner. We'd better go join her."

Noah nods and forces a smile onto his face as we walk into the dining room. Aria looks up, and her expression sends a pang of hurt straight to my heart. She's trying so hard to be brave, but I can see her falling apart right in front of me, and it kills me to have to pretend she's fine when all I want to do is take her into my arms and catch every single tear she's holding back.

I walk up to her and place my hand on her lower back. "Sit," I tell her. Her eyes meet mine, and I can't quite describe the moment that passes between us. It's a moment of intimacy and trust, a moment of her showing me the burdens she's carrying. She nods and sits down quietly as I fill all three of our plates.

"How was your day?" Noah asks her carefully.

Aria looks up at her brother, her shoulders tense. "Noah..."

He lifts his brows in question, and I sit down next to her, my arm on the back of her chair in a show of silent support.

Aria looks down at her lap before facing her brother again. "There's something I need to tell you, and I... I don't know how."

Noah sits up, alarmed. I can see the scenarios running through his mind, but the truth is far worse than he's imagining.

"Our lawyer called me yesterday," she says, her voice barely above a whisper. "They... They let him go on good behavior."

Noah stands up, his chair clattering to the floor loudly, his eyes wide. Agony distorts his face, and he lifts a shaky hand, pulling it through his hair. "Jack called you yesterday? Before..."

Aria looks away and wraps her arms around herself. "Yeah... that's why I got home early."

Noah walks up to her and takes her into his arms, hugging her tightly, both of them silent and lost in their grief. "I'm sorry it took me so long to tell you," she mumbles against his chest.

Noah pulls away and pats her head. "It's okay, Ari. You had more than enough on your mind yesterday."

He lets go of her and walks over to the cabinet in the corner, grabbing a bottle of scotch. Noah rarely drinks. He's too aware of what liquor does to your body, and he can't stand the thought of it.

Aria and I are both silent as he pours all three of us a glass. He empties his own and refills it instantly, emptying that too. Aria looks at me helplessly, but I don't know what to do either. There's nothing I can do to make this better.

"Jack is looking into it, seeing if there's a way to fight this."

Noah nods, but looking at the both of them, it's obvious neither believes they stand a chance at making a difference.

"Are you okay?" Aria asks carefully.

Noah nods absentmindedly. "Are *you?*"

She nods, but it's clear to me that both of them are just being brave for the other. I feel like I'm intruding on what is clearly a private moment of grief, and I rise to escape to the guest room. I only manage to take one step before Aria grabs my hand.

"I'm exhausted," she says, her voice soft, her hand tightening around mine as she turns to face her brother. "Will you be okay, Noah?"

He smiles at her and nods. "Go. Go to bed, little one."

Aria glances back at me before letting go of my hand, her gaze pleading. I nod at her, my heart filled with affection. I'm strangely honored that she trusts me to take care of Noah in a situation like this one.

She's only just rounded the corner when my phone buzzes in my pocket.

Aria: *If I stay, he'll want to console me. He hates being vulnerable around me, and he needs to process this news without worrying about me. Will you be there for him?*

Grayson: *Always.*

Noah inhales shakily and pours himself another glass as I put my phone away. I sit down next to him and take the scotch he hands me.

We both sit in silence, making our way through half the bottle before Noah speaks again.

"I can't imagine the day she had yesterday. Fuck."

I nod. Now, more than ever, I'm glad I punched that asshole in the face. "What about you, though? You all right?"

Noah shakes his head and runs a hand through his hair. "I knew this day was coming, but I thought it'd be another ten years from now. I don't get it. This guy killed our parents and now he gets to go free? Our lives are destroyed, Gray. My sister smiles all the time, but you know as well as I do that every single one of those smiles is fake."

He sniffs, as though he's holding back tears, and a hollow laugh escapes his lips. "She's the one that found them, you know? I never told you this, but Aria walked into the house just minutes after the burglary. She found our parents in a pool of their own blood, their eyes wide open. She didn't speak for months. It should've been me. Between the two of us, it never should've been her that went through that. It took months of therapy for her to even say my name, and to this day, she's never spoken to me about what happened. She spoke to the police, but never to me. If not for the case files, I'd never have known what she saw. At the time... fuck. I thought I'd lost her too."

He grabs the bottle and brings it to his lips, gulping far too much down. "After all that, she's concerned about *me*. Her heart is fucking broken, but she still worries about me. Gray, what the fuck do I do? I just want her to be happy, and all this shit that's happening. Fuck. She deserves so much more. I fucked up, man."

I shake my head and take the bottle from him. "You didn't, Noah. The woman she is today, the strength she portrays? You had a part in that. Even though you two lost everything, you ensured that she always knew she had you. You two remained a family, and that's the best thing you ever could've done for her."

He shakes his head. "It's not enough. She's lost so much in the span of twenty-four hours. Her job, her boyfriend, and now this..." Noah looks at me, his expression serious, and I instinctively sit up. "When you told her she'd always be welcome at your firm, did you mean it?"

I nod. "I wouldn't have offered if I didn't, Noah. You know that."

He looks at me in a way I can't decipher. He's usually an open book to me, but tonight I can't tell what he's thinking.

"Take her with you. I might not know much about what you do, but I know Aria is good. She's always studied hard, and all she needs is a chance. Please, give it to her. For years, Aria has been the one that took care of me, when our roles should've been reversed. Even now, she's in so much pain, but she left the room because she thought that's what I needed. She's always put me first, Gray, and I've failed her. I didn't pay enough attention to her happiness. I didn't step up when I thought Brad wasn't right for her, and I haven't helped her chase her dreams, because I was too busy following my own. She deserves the world, Grayson. I don't want to see her lose more of her spirit trying to find a job, and I think she needs a fresh start."

He looks at me with such faith that I have to look away. "I'll ask her again tomorrow. If she accepts, I'll happily give her a job."

Noah shakes his head and stares me down, his expression serious. "I want you to take care of her, Gray. I know you love your space, but Aria is far more fragile than she lets on. Even if it's just for the first few weeks, please..."

I blink, confused. "You want her to stay with me?"

Noah nods. "Cali will be such a big change for her, and I have no idea how she's going to cope with the break-up and the betrayal. I need you to look after her in my stead. I need to know that she's okay, that she's moving on with her life instead of letting this ruin her. You didn't see her a few years ago... Aria...

she's got enough demons chasing her. I don't know if she'll be able to take the additional stabs at her heart. I need you to keep an eye on her and step in if it looks like she isn't doing okay."

I look away. I've not lived with anyone in years. The one week a year that I stay with Noah is the closest I ever get to having someone in my personal space. I've not shared my home since I finally made enough money to have a place of my own.

"Promise me, Gray. Promise me you'll take care of her the way I would."

"I promise," I say, without a second thought. He doesn't even need to ask. I'll always look out for Aria. "But I can't guarantee that she'll take me up on my offer."

Noah smiles. "Oh, she will. She admires you far more than she lets on."

Aria admiring me? Somehow, the thought of that warms my heart. I wonder what it'll be like to have her living with me. Somehow, the thought of having Aria in my home doesn't seem so revolting.

Chapter Twelve

GRAYSON

I stare at my phone, feeling unsettled. Something is wrong with Nyx, but I can't tell what it is. She hasn't replied to any of my jokes, keeping our communication strictly professional. Usually she'll be sarcastic with me when I attempt to flirt with her, but in the last couple of days, things have felt different.

Nyx: *Found video footage that shows him getting into his car a few minutes after the time of death. He couldn't have made it to the crime scene in time from work.*

Ash: *I'll have the media members circulate it so we gain enough attention to stop his execution. Once the media digs into this our chances will be much higher.*

Nyx: *Okay, I'll leave it to you.*

Ash: *Seriously, Nyx... are you okay?*

I wait for her reply, and just as I've decided she's going to ignore me, she responds.

Nyx: *I went through a bad breakup recently and I'm not really myself right now. I'll be okay. This case gives me something to focus on.*

My thoughts immediately turn to Aria. Was Nyx in the same state Aria was in? I can't imagine a woman like Nyx crying over any man, considering how amazing she is. But then again, Aria did, and she's no less wonderful.

I try my hardest to think of something to say that might make her feel better, but I come up empty. In the end, I decide to throw a lame, flirty line at her, hoping it might at least make her smile.

Ash: *All I'm reading is that the illustrious Nyx is single. So I've got a shot, huh? I'd better bring my A-game. I'll win you over.*

Nyx: *Shot? The only shots involved are me shooting you down.*

I smirk. That's more like my Nyx.

Ash: *Nyx, do you happen to have a Band-Aid? 'Cause I scraped my knees falling for you.*

Ash: *Hey, Nyx? I'd like to take you to the movies, but they don't let you bring in your own snacks.*

Nyx: *...Where are you getting these from? I can't decide if they're awful or cute.*

Ash: *Cute, of course. Google taught me.*

Nyx: **face palms* Of course you googled your pick-up lines. I knew you had zero game.*

I grin, enjoying our exchange. She sounds far more like herself now, and I can't wipe the smile off my face. When did I even start to care about her so much?

Ash: *But did I make you smile?*

Nyx: *Maybe...*

Ash: *That's all I wanted.*

I put my phone away, trying my hardest to focus on my work. I've already fallen behind on everything that needs to be done.

I have no idea how long I've been working when my concentration is broken by a flash of yellow in my peripheral vision. I look up to find Aria handing me a bright yellow mug filled with peppermint tea. I take it gratefully and smile at her.

These kind gestures of hers always throw me off. I'm not used to anyone doing stuff like this for me, or even remembering which tea I like.

"Morning," she murmurs. "How long have you been up?"

I stare at her, taking in her bloodshot eyes. "Not as long as you," I say, my voice soft.

Aria grimaces and raises her hand to her face, her finger tracing over the bags underneath her eyes, and I instantly feel awful.

"I... I didn't mean it that way. I just meant that you look tired and I assumed you didn't sleep well. You're always beautiful, Aria. Always."

Her cheeks redden and she looks away, her lips tipped up ever so slightly. "That's a lot of words so early in the morning. Note to self: bribe Gray with tea and he might speak."

I chuckle as she sits down next to me. "I always speak to you, Ari. Yet somehow you're convinced I don't."

She leans in to glance at my screen, before looking up, her hair brushing against my chin. "I guess I just remember the way you were when I first met you," she says, her voice soft. "You guarded your words like they were your greatest treasure, and I made it my mission to uncover your thoughts, to make you voice them."

I look into her eyes, mesmerized by the specks of gold mixed in with the brown. How have I never noticed how unique her eyes are? She's so close, and it makes me strangely nervous. She smells like freaking cupcakes or something. Is it vanilla? I don't know, but she smells far too good.

"I'm no longer the guy you met over a decade ago, Aria."

She nods, her eyes on mine. She's no longer the little girl she used to be, either. Far from it.

"May I?" she asks, and I nod without thinking.

Aria smiles and turns my laptop toward her. Her fingers fly over my keyboard, and my first instinct is to panic. I hate it when people touch my work, and Aria has little to no work experience. I tense, but before I can even stop her, she runs the script. She runs it... and it doesn't crash.

"What the fuck?"

I grab my laptop and stare at the screen, analyzing each line of changes she made. I'm in fucking awe. I knew she was good based on what I saw in Brad's software, but this is something else. Some people are good coders so long as you tell them what they need to do, but they aren't always good problem solvers. Aria... she's an out of the box thinker. I suspected it when I saw her work, but damn.

Something about her way of coding looks familiar. I had the same thought when I saw Brad's software. It feels like holding a puzzle piece that doesn't fit anywhere. Something doesn't add up.

"What the actual fuck," I repeat, and she chuckles.

"You're welcome, Gray," she says, a blush tinting her cheeks.

I grab her hand and squeeze. "Come work for me," I tell her.

Aria's eyes widen and she looks away, wrapping her arms around herself almost protectively. When I first told her there'd always be a place for her at my firm, I didn't think much of it. All I thought was that she wanted to work for my company and that I was in a position to make it happen. But now? Now I *need* her to work for me. It isn't even about Noah asking me to help her have a fresh start. This is pure selfishness. I'd be a fool not to hire talent like hers.

"I mean it, Aria. I've been working on this shit for close to an hour now. You barely glanced at it and fixed it instantly. You're good. I'd pay top dollar to poach you from whoever you're working for. Let me make you an offer you can't refuse."

She stares at me as though she's trying to gauge my sincerity, and I throw all my charm at her. "I'll offer you a position as a senior software developer in my elite team, and you can stay with me while you settle in. The views from my penthouse are stunning, and you'll love it. It's also absolutely massive, with a home gym and a rooftop heated pool. I'll give you a signing bonus too. One that's large enough to repay Noah's med school bills."

"You're serious, aren't you?"

I nod. "I'm dead serious, Aria. I want you."

She smiles at me, her brows raised. "You *want* me?"

I freeze and Aria bursts into laughter.

"I like it when you get all wordy with me," she says, and I shake my head, feeling oddly flustered. "Gray," she murmurs, her smile melting away. "I'd be beyond honored to work for you. Honestly, if you told you you're taking me on as an unpaid intern, I'd jump at the chance. What you're offering me... it's too much. Considering I have no relevant work experience, it's too much, but you know I can't say no."

I smile at her and lean back in my seat. "So that's a yes, then? I'll get HR to draft you a contract. I'm flying back tomorrow, but I don't expect you to come with me so soon. I imagine you need some time to pack."

Aria's expression hardens and she shakes her head. She glances out the window, her mood dropping. "I'll come with you. Tomorrow."

I nod, my own excitement waning. I hate seeing her hurting and I'm worried that moving with me so suddenly means she won't get the closure she needs.

"Stealing my sister away, are you? I feel like you should probably pay *me* a poaching fee," Noah says. Aria and I both jump in surprise. Neither one of us noticed him standing in the doorway.

He walks up to us and sits down next to Aria, his arm wrapping around her. "Congratulations on the new job," he says. "A fresh start is exactly what you need, and I won't have to worry about you if Gray is looking out for you."

She drops her head on his shoulder and nods. "Will you be okay by yourself? I know we don't see each other as much as we used to, but if I move away, we won't even be able to have weekly dinners."

Noah chuckles and presses a kiss on top of her head. "I'm a big boy, Ari. I can take care of myself. Besides, you know how much I work. If you're with Gray, then at least I know you won't be alone all the time. I won't have to worry about you so much."

Aria nods, but I can tell she's feeling conflicted. I wonder if it might actually be better for her to have Noah around. I hope this move will be good for her, but I can't help but worry.

"It's done, then," Aria says. "We leave tomorrow."

Chapter Thirteen

ARIA

I'm anxious as Gray and I make our way through the airport. I can't control the way my thoughts are spiraling and I hate that I'm doing this to myself. I'm second-guessing everything.

I can't believe I'm really doing this. I can't leave Noah behind like this. We've never lived far away from each other, and now there'll be a five-hour flight between us. He's the only family member I've got left, and leaving makes me feel like I'm losing everything.

"Aria."

I look up to find Gray staring at me the way he sometimes does, as though he's analyzing me.

"You okay?"

I nod, forcing myself to be brave. The job Gray offered me is a dream come true. Besides, this might just be what I need. I lost my job when I foolishly walked out, and I already know that I won't find anything even remotely as good as the job at Aequitas.

"Yeah, I'm fine," I tell Gray.

His eyes roam over my face, as though he's assessing the truthfulness of my words. Eventually, he nods and grabs my hand, holding it in his. "I might not be Noah, but I'll try my best to look out for you the way he does. It doesn't come naturally to me, Ari, but I'll try. You won't be alone."

My heart warms, and I can't help but look away. Gray... he's something else. "I know," I tell him, and I do. I know he'll be there for me, and that makes it just a little easier to see this through.

"Come on," he says, keeping my hand in his as he pulls me along. I glance at our joint hands, feeling oddly flustered. Noah grabs my hand all the time — especially at stoplights. He's held my hand every time we cross a road for years, and he still does it instinctively. It always makes me chuckle, and it's become a bit of a running joke between us.

I've never really thought much of it, but having Gray hold my hand like this feels different. I can't help but notice how large his hands are compared to mine, and I wonder what we look like together. Do people think we're a couple, or do they think I'm his little sister? I'm not wearing make-up and even when I do, my height makes me look like a child.

Gray lets go of me to grab his passport and boarding card, and I reach for my own absentmindedly. I freeze when I look at my ticket. It says Business Class.

Gray booked my ticket for me, and I didn't think much of it, because I figured I'd just pay him back afterward, but there's no way I can afford this. Sometimes I forget Gray is no longer the boy that used to have dinner with us because sharing grocery costs was more affordable. He's the CEO of his company — a highly successful company.

I'm nervous as we approach our seats. It'd take me forever to save up for this ticket. I should've paid more attention when Gray booked it.

"Aria," he says, snapping me out of my thoughts. "It's just a company perk. Sit down."

My cheeks heat and I drop into my seat, buckling myself up in a rush to hide my embarrassment. Was I that transparent?

Gray smirks, and I involuntarily glare at him, which just turns his smirk into a laugh, exposing the dimples in his cheeks. Gray rarely laughs, and it's a shame because he looks so much more approachable when he does.

I tear my eyes away from him and glance around me curiously. I've never sat in an airplane seat this big, and I've never seen so many buttons either. I'm feeling strangely intimidated and out of place. I feel like it's obvious that I'm out of my depth, and I'm both embarrassed and tempted to touch every single thing out of fear that this might be my only chance to do so.

Gray leans back in his seat next to mine and stares at me over the partition. He's so large that it does nothing to separate our seats. "Go on, do it," he tells me, and I raise my brows, earning myself another chuckle. "I know you want to press all the buttons."

How does he know? How?

Gray sits up and leans over me, pressing one of the buttons. It moves my backrest, and I giggle. He smiles and looks into my eyes, and I suddenly realize how close he is.

"This one moves your seat," he tells me, his voice soft. His upper body is hovering over mine, and he's ditched the jacket he brought on board with him, giving me a clear view of his muscular arms. His T-shirt is plastered against his skin, every single one of his muscles outlined. I tear my gaze away, feeling guilty for even noticing him that way.

"And this is for the footrest. It's my favorite thing."

My feet rise and I smile. "Does that even help you at all?" I ask, and he shakes his head, his eyes on mine.

"Nope. I'm too tall to fit in these seats, so I never lift my footrest all the way up. But you? You fit just fine."

I laugh as he presses all the other buttons on my seat, one by one. "So, what is it like up there?" I ask, teasing. "Doesn't sound like being tall is all that beneficial."

He smirks, his eyes roaming over my face, dipping down to my chest for a split second. "Oh, but the view is nice."

I look into his eyes, my heart skipping a beat. Gray pulls away when the seatbelt lights come on, and I breathe a sigh of relief. It's been years since he and I have really hung out together, and I forgot how charismatic he is.

The air hostess goes through the safety demonstration, and I stare at her, my mood dropping as I allow my thoughts to drift. I grip my armrests tightly as anxiety kicks in. There's no going back now. I spent years building a life in Miami. I spent years doing everything I thought I should. For a while, I was certain I had achieved all I wanted. I had a stable job and a boyfriend that I thought adored me. That was as close as I was going to get to being just a regular girl. I should've known better, though. I should've known that life can't be that good. That I can't be that lucky.

I bite down on my lip as my thoughts turn to Brad. I can't help but wonder if he's with Britney now. Does he love her? Did he ever have feelings for me at all? I was ready to settle down with him. I would've said no to Gray's job offer just so I could stay with him.

I can't believe I missed the signs. He was always on his phone and he was working late so often, when realistically, he could've worked late from his laptop at home. There wasn't much of a reason for him to stay late at the office, but every single time I had any doubts, I made excuses. I'd tell myself that it was just easier to focus at the office, or that he didn't want to take his work home with him.

My eyes flutter closed as one thought after the other assails me. Would he have stayed if I'd worked harder to please him in bed? Was it the nightmares I have? Was my past too hard to overcome? I don't know where I went wrong. I can't figure out why I wasn't good enough.

Chapter Fourteen

GRAYSON

Aria is staring out the window as the cab pulls up in front of my apartment, but the excitement I expected is missing. Noah told me she's always dreamed of working in Silicon Valley, and I hoped that accomplishing that would be enough to take away her sorrow.

"You're quiet. Tired?"

Aria turns to glance at me and forces a smile, but it doesn't reach her eyes. "Yeah," she murmurs, before looking away again.

She seemed fine as we boarded the plane, but she was lost in thought from the second we took off, and she hasn't snapped out of it. The pain in her eyes tells me she's thinking of Brad, and I hate that there's nothing I can do to make her feel better, to make her see that he isn't worth her heartache.

Aria barely realizes we've come to a stop, and she jumps in surprise when I open the door on my side of the car. I walk around to open her door, but she's already stepped out before I reach her.

She rushes to get her luggage from the trunk and I follow her, placing my hand on her shoulder when she attempts to lift her suitcases. They're half her size, and not exactly light.

"Let me," I tell her. She looks up at me gratefully, and it guts me. She's so used to taking care of herself that it didn't occur to her I'd carry her suitcase? She dated that asshole for a year... surely he was at least a little chivalrous?

The thought of Aria with him angers me all over again, and I grit my teeth as I lead her into my building. She deserves to be treated right, and I despise that he got to have a year of her life. A year she'll never get back. A year that might just leave her scarred, when she's already been through so much.

I step aside to let her into the house, suddenly feeling nervous. When I left, I didn't expect to be coming back here with Aria. Not that it matters. Everything is spotless. Yet somehow, I'm a little uncomfortable. I wonder what she'll think of the place I call home these days. It's nothing like her apartment. It's devoid of color and character, and I'm not sure she'll like it.

"Wow," she whispers, her eyes on the floor to ceiling windows. She walks past me and straight to the windows that are currently portraying a stunning skyline. She places her palms against the glass and I smile as I leave our suitcases in the corner. I walk up to her, stopping in my tracks when she turns to look at me, a beautiful smile on her face.

"This is amazing," she says, and my heart overflows with a feeling I can't quite name. It's relief, I guess. Relief to see that spark back in her eyes. Aria has always loved and appreciated the simple things in life, and it's what I adore about her most. She didn't notice my crazy expensive interior, or the art on my walls. No. It's the view that captivates her.

"Come on," I tell her. "I'll show you around. Your bedroom has the same view too."

Her eyes widen, and the excitement I see in them has me feeling such intense relief. I've been worried about her... about the responsibility Noah handed me. I don't know if I'm able to watch over her the way he expects me to.

"No way," she mouths, her lips tipping up into a smile.

I chuckle and grab her hand, pulling her along. I show her every room in my home, and every gasp that leaves her lips delights me. She's giddy as I show her the rooftop pool and my boxing ring, but it's mostly the view that excites her.

Eventually, I pause in front of my guest room. I've had a guest room for years now, but other than Noah, no one has ever stayed in it.

"This is your room," I say, leading her in.

Aria looks around wide-eyed, and I follow her gaze, trying to see my home through her eyes. I spent two years picking the perfect place, and then almost another year renovating it. It's got everything I always wished I had growing up. A lot of space, a stunning view, and every amenity I could think of, everything I used to see on TV and thought I'd never be able to afford. My home... it's a fulfilled promise to myself, and I think Aria gets that.

She looks far more lively than she did on the way here, and I realize Noah was right. Asking if I'd let her stay with me was the right choice. Every time she has a moment to herself, she's lost in thought, her expression betraying her heartbreak. Aria is one of the strongest women I know, but I have to admit I'm worried about her.

She turns to face me and smiles. "Thank you, Gray," she says. "For the job, for letting me stay here, for everything. I promise I won't bother you for too long. I'll try to find a place to stay soon."

I shake my head and gently pat her head. She's in flats today, and I love how small she is. "No need, Ari. I'm happy to have you here. I'm always alone, you know? It'll be nice to have you around. You make me feel like I have a family of my own."

She smiles at me, her gaze filled with understanding and affection — and that's what I love about her. She never looks at me with pity in her eyes.

"I'll leave you to settle in," I say, and she nods.

I'm smiling as I walk out of her room and across the hallway, into my own room, my thoughts on Aria. I usually dislike people intruding in my space, but I'm glad to have her here. I'm glad I get to watch over her, and I have a feeling I might genuinely enjoy having her around.

I'm still smiling by the time I get into bed, and my smile only widens when I realize Nyx texted me. She's never texted me first.

Nyx: *I'm a Sagittarius*

I chuckle, surprised at the random text. Before I can even reply, another one comes in.

Nyx: *You asked me to tell you something about myself a while ago, so... this is it.*

I smile at my screen like some sort of lunatic, unable to help myself. Nyx has me curious as hell. I want to know who this incredibly clever woman is. I have my suspicions, but I'm unable to confirm them. I want to know more about her; I want to know what makes her tick. What she's built is nothing short of admirable, yet she always seems so down to earth and funny.

Ash: *I'm honored. I'm a Leo, by the way.*

Nyx: *Figures...*

I laugh to myself, knowing she's about to say something strangely and uniquely Nyx.

Nyx: *Did you know Leos are usually theatrical and enjoy the spotlight?... ringing any bells Mr. I'll-Take-On-Any-High-Profile-Case?*

I smirk. She's not wrong, but I've done all of that anonymously. I can't help but wonder what Nyx would think if she knew who I am. I have no doubt she can easily find out, so maybe... just maybe, she already knows. I doubt it, though. She's never once given me any indication that she knows, and stuff like that usually slips.

Ash: *You know what else Leos are? We're passionate. You ever been with a Leo, Nyx?*

I'm oddly nervous as I await her reply. Nyx and I have been friends for a while, and it isn't until recently that I've started to be playful and flirty with her. I enjoy teasing her, but so far she's not given me any indication of whether she's receptive to it, or whether I'm crossing any boundaries.

Nyx: *Can't say that I have. Sounds an awful lot like you're overcompensating, though...*

Ash: *Come spend a night with me and I'll prove you wrong, Nyx. I'll have you moaning my name over and over again.*

I worry I've overdone it when she goes silent. I wasn't joking when I said I was going to steal her heart. Nyx is my dream woman. I don't even care that I've never seen her before... though I'm starting to suspect that I *have*. I have a feeling she might be much closer to me than I initially thought, but I'm not sure yet.

Nyx: *You wouldn't want to. If you ever meet me, you won't want me. Not in that way.*

I stare at my phone, a dull ache in my heart. Nyx has single-handedly helped hundreds of people over the last couple of years, all people that were let down by the justice system. She's ridiculously smart, and she clearly has a heart of gold. There's no way a woman like that isn't beautiful. If she is who I think she is, then she's downright breathtaking.

Ash: *I might just have a thing for bearded beauties. Beardarella, is it? Seriously, though, Nyx... you're beautiful, I just know it. It sounds lame as fuck, but looks truly do fade. You're an amazing person, and meeting someone that's smarter than me is a huge turn-on alone.*

Nyx: *Such a Leo response...*

I laugh because she's right. I did just make that about myself.

Ash: *Fine, let's just say that you've had me hard more times than you think, and that's all without ever seeing you. It's the mere thought of you, your kindness, your intelligence, your sense of humor. I have a feeling that looking into your eyes is going to be mesmerizing.*

Nyx: *You say that as though we'll ever actually meet*

Ash: *We will. Talent like yours isn't easily hidden. One day, I'll come across you.*

Nyx: *But how'd you know it's me?*

Ash: *I'll shout Beardarella, and if you smile, I'll know it's you.*

Nyx: *You're crazy. Don't go shouting that at random people, Ash. I have a feeling you're already a bit of a nut job... don't add to what I'm sure is already a heavily tarnished reputation.*

I smile at my screen, wondering who she is. Is she lying in her own bed as she's messaging me?

Ash: *Where are you?*

Nyx: *As in, location?*

Ash: *Never mind. Stupid question. Someone like you must be in Silicon Valley. Fuck, I bet I've come across you already. Maybe we even work together.*

Nyx: *You won't find me, Ash. If you can't hack into my platform (and I can see you trying multiple times a day) then you're just not skilled enough to find me ;)*

I laugh. This woman. She's not wrong, but I wonder if she'd still act the way she does if she knew who I am. It's surreal to me too, but my company is one of the largest software engineering firms in the world. We make so many corporate solutions that I lose track myself.

Ash: *Here's another lame saying for you, Nyx... where there's a will there's a way.*

Nyx: *Okay, psycho. You go ahead and shout Beardarella at random people. Let me know how that works out for you. In the meantime, I'm going to bed. Tomorrow is a big day for me.*

Ash: *I know you won't tell me what you've got going on, but I'm wishing you the best of luck with whatever it is. Goodnight, Nyx.*

Nyx: *Thank you, Ash. Not just for the well wishes... for everything. Night.*

I stare up at my ceiling as I lock my phone. Nyx... she's always been so cold and distant, but tonight was different. I'm not sure what prompted her to reach out to me, but I'm glad she did.

Chapter Fifteen

ARIA

I should be excited, but instead I'm exhausted. I couldn't sleep last night, and before I knew it, my alarm clock went off. I spent all night twisting and turning, my thoughts drifting from Brad to my new job, and everything in between. I'm so anxious that I'm struggling to breathe.

I'm worried that I won't be good at my job here, and that Gray will regret offering me this job. I keep imagining everyone knowing I'm a pity hire. I imagine my new colleagues gossiping about how I came in through connections and never would've made it in by myself, and they'd be right.

I'm scared I'll let Grayson down. He probably wouldn't even say anything. He'd try to hide his disappointment, but I'd know.

On the other hand, I probably won't be working with Gray directly. He's the CEO, and I'm about to become yet another of his countless employees. I've been dreaming about working for Aequitas for years now. I know how many floors his building has, how many departments there are, and who their biggest clients are. The chances of us working together are slim to none, and I'm not sure if that puts me at ease or worries me even further.

"You're up early."

I jump, spilling coffee over the white blouse I spent hours selecting. It stains the front of my top, making it stick to my chest, and I stare at it in dismay.

"Oh shit, I'm sorry, Ari," Gray says, his tone panicked. He grabs a kitchen towel and dabs it on my shirt, the back of his fingers grazing over my breast. I can feel my cheeks heat and my embarrassment only increases when Gray suddenly pauses, his eyes widening.

He pulls his hand away abruptly and clears his throat, looking away. "I... um, I don't think that's going to come out," he tells me, running a hand through his hair, his eyes on the wall behind me.

"I... I'll go change. Give me a minute," I manage to stammer, before rushing off, flustered.

I lean back against my bedroom door the second I close it behind me, my heart racing.

Gray... he treats me like a child. I understand he sees me as family, but I'm still a woman. The way he touched me just now, his fingers against my breasts...

My eyes drop to the mirror in my bedroom, and I stare at myself. The coffee stain looks ridiculous, and I don't know what I was thinking picking this outfit. I shouldn't be wearing a skirt this tight. It only highlights how thick my thighs are, but I don't look much better in suit trousers.

My eyes roam over my reflection, and I hate what I'm seeing. My only redeeming asset is my long dark hair. Other than that, I'm too small and too fat. I understand why Gray doesn't see me as a woman, and I shouldn't even want him to.

I drag my eyes away and unbutton my blouse, letting it fall to the floor. I grab a plain loose-fitting black shirt and put it on, not bothering to look in the mirror again. This'll do. I don't know why I even bothered spending all that time selecting an outfit. It's stupid.

My mood is ruined by the time I walk back into the kitchen. Gray smiles at me, and I try my hardest to smile back at him. I don't want him to worry about me more than he already does. He tries to hide it, but his concern is obvious.

"Let's go," he tells me. "Or we'll be late on your very first day. How are you feeling? Excited?"

I nod, lying to him. I should be excited... this job is all I've been thinking about for years. Yet now that I finally get to make that dream come true, all I want to do is crawl back into bed. I want to be covered in blankets and grab a good book, so I can lose myself in some fictional story, a story that'll allow me to experience moments of happiness that elude me in my own life.

I follow Gray down to his garage, feeling more out of place by the second. He glances at me and smiles sheepishly as he leads me to a car I'll probably never be able to afford in this lifetime.

"Be honored," he tells me. "You're the only woman I've ever allowed into this baby," he says, holding the door to his bright red sports car open for me.

"Why is that?" I ask as I step into his car. "Did you only just buy it?"

He chuckles, a guilty expression on his face. "Last month."

I shake my head as he closes the door. Gray walks around the car and my eyes follow him through the window. He's wearing a suit today, and it makes him look... powerful. Powerful and incredibly sexy.

Gray sits down and turns toward me. He leans over to grab my seatbelt, and his scent washes over me. He smells like peppermint, just like he always has. To this day, I can't have peppermint tea without thinking of Gray's obsession with it.

"I can do it, Gray," I tell him, as he clicks my seatbelt in. His eyes meet mine, and when he smiles at me, those dimples of his making an appearance, my heart flutters. I look away, startled by my own reaction. He's so attentive, and part of me can't help but wonder what it'd be like to be with him, to be loved by him. I bite down on my lip and look away, flustered.

"I'll show you around when we get to the office. I'll give you a whole tour."

I look at him, panic gripping me, and shake my head as I turn in my seat. "No, Gray. You can't. I know I didn't really get this job because I earned it, but I was hoping no one would know. I really want a chance to prove myself."

Gray glances at me briefly and nods. "I see. All right. I'll drop you at the HR department instead, okay? They'll get your employee pass made and show you around. You probably won't do much on your first day. It's mostly just paperwork, meeting your colleagues and getting up to date on our current project. Your manager will fill you in."

I nod, the nerves truly kicking in now. He parks the car in what appears to be his designated spot and turns to look at me. "Aria," he says, his expression tense. "I need you to promise me you'll tell me if you're struggling. Tell me if you need help. Hell, tell me if someone is being a dick to you. I promised Noah I'd look out for you, and I have every intention of keeping that promise."

His sincerity startles me. I know Gray's loyalty to Noah knows no bounds, but I've never had his intensity directed at *me*.

"I promise," I whisper, my heart racing.

Gray looks into my eyes, his gaze unwavering. He seems to have found what he's looking for because he nods resolutely. "Very well," he says. "Let's go, shall we?"

Chapter Sixteen

I'm overwhelmed in all the best ways by the time I'm led to what is about to become my very own desk. The six screens that have been set up at my desk almost bring tears to my eyes. This... this is what I've always imagined. I can barely believe this is real.

"Your department has been dubbed The Elites," Sam tells me. Until I met her, I was convinced that every single person who works for Human Resources is useless, but she proved me wrong.

"In reality, it's called the Developmental Operations Department. No one knows what you guys actually do, to be honest."

She chuckles and I can't help but smile. "Let me introduce you to your manager," she says, nodding at the guy that's walking up to us. I try my hardest to stay calm, but I'm failing.

"Hi," he says, holding out his hand for me. "I'm Riley."

"I know," I blurt out. My cheeks heat rapidly, and I'm mortified. But Riley merely smiles, some of the ice that was previously present in his eyes melting. I clear my throat awkwardly and shake the hand he's still holding out for me. "I'm Aria," I manage.

I can't believe I'm shaking Riley Paulson's hand. I've admired his work for a while now. He developed a social media app that has become a household name. The algorithms behind it are stupidly innovative. The way he's managed to keep people on the platform, and the way he monetized it... it's crazy. When Grayson hired him, it ended up becoming front-page news, primarily because no one has been able to figure out why a guy that rich would want to work for someone else.

"I wasn't aware we'd be hiring anyone new until Grayson informed me this morning. Here's the thing, though. I can't find anything about you. No notable accomplishments, not even an impressive illegal digital footprint. Every one of us here was hired because of something we did that no one else could... but you? Tell me why you're here."

I panic. I didn't think this far ahead. I thought I'd just prove myself through my work, that I'd just work hard and keep my head down. I didn't think anyone would ask me outright what makes me think I deserve to be here.

"Questioning my decisions, Riley? When did I grant you the authority to do that?"

I turn to find Gray leaning against the doorframe of what appears to be his office. I didn't think Gray and I would even be on the same floor, but it looks like we are. So much for keeping my distance from him at work.

Riley looks at Gray, a silent exchange occurring between the two of them. When he looks back at me, his expression is unreadable. "Let me introduce you to the rest of the team," he says, before turning and walking away. I rush to follow him, and when he stops by the desk nearest to mine, I almost crash into him. I don't remember the last time I embarrassed myself as thoroughly as today.

My eyes widen when I recognize yet another person I idolize. "Elliot Evans," he says, rising to his feet to shake my hand. This time I manage to keep from blurting out that I know exactly who he is. But the amused look in his eyes tells me I'm not doing a great job at hiding my adoration. Elliot is one of the best system hackers that I know of, and I can't make sense of what this team even is. The developer of a famous social media platform and now a system hacker?

I follow Riley as he moves to the next desk, and this time I manage to hide my excitement a bit better, even though I've been cyber stalking the tall blonde standing in front of me for years now. "Laura," she says. I nod, praying my cheeks aren't flaming the way I think they are.

"Laura is our machine learning engineer," Riley tells me, moving along before I even have a chance to shake her hand. He's gone before I manage to say anything to her, and I'm at a loss. Is the introduction done?

"Follow him," Laura says, winking at me.

I'm flustered as I do as she says. This team... these are some of the smartest minds. The stuff they could do together, it's unreal. What was Gray thinking, having me join them?

Riley leans against my desk, and I hesitate before taking my seat. The way he stares tells me he isn't happy with my presence, and I can't blame him. I don't deserve to be here.

"Grayson has never done this before, so I'll choose to trust him for now. If I find out the only reason you're here is because you're fucking the boss, I'll fire you. Grayson won't be able to stop me, unless he's willing to let me walk away."

I glare at him, disappointment washing over me. I've looked up to Riley Paulson for years, but he's... a dick. "If you speak to me that way again, Grayson won't have to fire you," I tell him. "HR will do it for him."

Riley's eyes widen, and then he laughs, startling me. "You might just survive," he tells me as he leans over to grab my mouse.

"Here," he says, opening a document. "Finish this script. I didn't get to interview you, but that doesn't mean I won't test you. Grayson might have given you a way in, but that doesn't mean you'll get to stay."

I nod in understanding and turn to look at my screen. My

heart sinks when I realize the magnitude of the task. It will take me all day. "Good luck," he tells me as he walks away.

I see Elliot and Laura exchange glances, and I'm already feeling left out. I don't belong here. These people worked their ass off to become part of this team. They proved themselves, and they have notorious reputations. I'm a nobody compared to them.

Insecurity almost renders me unable to work, but as it always does, coding takes my mind off everything. In a world I can't make sense of, the one thing I have control over is everything binary. I work on autopilot, pausing only to stretch my fingers every once in a while.

I don't stop even when my colleagues leave for lunch. I can't afford to take a break now. Not when they're blatantly testing me. The code Riley asked me to finish is a mess, and I bet he's hoping I won't be able to do it, or that I'll ask him for help.

The office quietens, and I lean back in my seat, glancing around the empty space. I can spot Grayson hard at work through his open door, but the office is empty otherwise. I can't believe I made it here. Riley is right. Unless I prove myself, there's no guarantee I'll be able to stay. But then again, all I needed was a chance.

I bite down on my lip and grab my phone, hesitating before deciding to text Ash. I'm not even sure why I'm reaching out to him, but somehow, I *miss him*. Today is tougher than I imagined, and Ash is bound to make me smile somehow.

Nyx: *Hey, how's your day going? I'm having a bit of a rough day and I just thought of you randomly.*

Ash: *I see my pick-up lines worked. You're falling for me already, aren't you? Do I have you addicted to me yet?*

I laugh, the sound breaking the silence in the empty office.

Nyx: *Maybe. Maybe I'm feeling a little down because I didn't get my dose of Ash.*

Ash: *Hey Nyx, is your middle name Google? Because you're everything I've been looking for.*

I giggle. I can't help it. His pick-up lines keep getting worse and I love them.

Ash: *I made you laugh, didn't I? I'm sorry your day is shitty, babe. I hope it gets better.*

Nyx: *I'll admit it. You did make me laugh. Thank you, Ash. I hope your day is amazing.*

Ash: *It is now.*

I put my phone away, filled with renewed motivation. I barely realize what time it is when Riley walks up to me again. "Let's see what you accomplished," he says. The rest of the team rises in unison, their faces filled with amusement, and I hate that it hurts. I shouldn't expect them to welcome me so easily, yet having them so blatantly attempt to push me out on my first day hurts.

I rise to my feet and let Riley take my seat while the rest of the team surrounds us. "Go ahead," I tell him. There are many things I'm bad at, things I'm insecure about, but this isn't one of them.

He runs the script and then scrolls through the code, up and down as though he's triple-checking that what he's seeing is real. "You finished it?" he asks, his disbelief apparent.

"Well, yes. I'm still working on removing some inefficiencies and random loops, though. I don't know who coded this, but it's a bit of a mess."

Laura bursts out laughing and lifts her palm. "Don't leave me hanging," she says, and I high five her awkwardly, somewhat confused. "Riley coded it," she says. "And he's spent a week trying to finish this, but he was unable to."

I blush self-consciously when Elliot nods in approval. Riley looks up at me, suspicion distorting his face. "Who are you?" he asks.

I smile, a small burst of pride coursing through me. "The type of person who leaves no traces," I tell him, reaching for my handbag.

I didn't even realize that Grayson was watching our entire exchange until I hear him chuckle from behind me. I turn to find him leaning against the wall, his arms crossed.

"Good girl," he says, his eyes radiating pride. "Come on," he adds, pushing off the wall. "I'll give you a ride."

I nod and follow him out, leaving my team staring at my screen. Laura and Elliot are admiring my work, while Riley is still staring in disbelief.

Chapter Seventeen

GRAYSON

I can't wipe the smile off my face. "She was fucking amazing at work today," I tell Noah, gripping my phone tightly. "She's so goddamn talented, man. I can't believe I've been missing out. She should've started working for me years ago. Fuck, I probably won't be able to keep her for long. Talent like hers doesn't stay at one company. She'll get poached. I need to double-check the non-compete in her contract."

Noah laughs. "She won't leave you, Gray. Aria has wanted to work for you for as long as I can remember. You might not have been aware, but I know my sister better than she thinks I do. Honestly, I wanted to ask you to offer her a job months ago, but I didn't think Aria would be receptive to it. Part of it was also self-ishness, though. I knew she'd leave if she chose to work for you, and I was worried. I was worried sick that something would happen and I'd be too far away."

I fall silent and sit down on my bed, running a hand through my hair. "You know I'll keep her safe, don't you? I'll do everything in my power to protect her, to take care of her."

Noah sighs. "I know," he tells me. "How is she anyway, outside of work?"

"I'm not sure. I haven't really spoken to her much today. She actually told me to stay away at work. Can you believe that?"

Noah bursts out laughing. "And you managed to keep your word?"

I clear my throat guiltily. "Well, I watched her from afar."

"Typical Gray," Noah says, and something about his tone rubs me the wrong way. Is he misunderstanding what I just said?

"Noah, I..."

Before I can finish my sentence, he interrupts. "What's Aria cooking? I know what she's like, and she won't stay with you without trying to repay you one way or another. I'm guessing she'll want to cook for you and do chores."

I smile. He really does know his sister better than I thought. "Yeah, she did insist on cooking. I'm not sure what she's making, though. Whatever it is, it smells good."

Noah groans, his envy apparent. I know how much he's always loved Aria's home-cooked meals. "You'd better go join her for dinner, then," he says. "I don't think she should be left alone, to be honest. I'm worried she'll just overthink things."

I nod. "Yeah, me too."

"Thank you, Gray. Thank you for taking care of her in my absence."

His words make me feel awkward somehow. It doesn't feel like I'm doing much at all, yet it seems to mean so much to Noah. His words are still ringing through my head as I walk into the kitchen. I should remember that it's Noah's role I'm being asked to play. I should look after her the way her older brother would... but lately I struggle to see her as Noah's little sister. She's quickly becoming more than that. Maybe she always has been.

I find Aria standing in front of one of the cupboards, her back to me. Looks like she's wearing nothing but an oversized T-shirt that looks more like a dress on her. There's nothing inappropriate about it, considering she's swimming in it, but it still grates on me. I clench my jaw, irrational anger washing over me. Does she miss Brad so much that she sleeps in his T-shirt? After everything he's done, she still wants to be surrounded by something that's his? I hate seeing his T-shirt on her. Even the smallest trace of him surrounding her is too much.

Aria reaches for something high up and can't reach it. She jumps up and still fails to grab the jar she wants, and it's ridiculously cute. I need to get her a stool or some shit. I walk up to her and wrap my hands around her waist, startling her.

"Grayson," she breathes. I lift her up easily, her feet dangling in the air. She grabs the jar she wanted and I lower her back to the ground.

She turns to face me the second I put her down, her cheeks flushed. "I'm not a child, Grayson," she snaps. "Don't lift me up like I am one. I'm not a toddler."

Her eyes are flashing with anger, and she's breathing hard. Those flushed cheeks of hers... damn. I swallow hard and nod, my hand lifting to her face without even realizing it. I push her hair behind her ear gently.

"I know," I murmur. "I know you're not a child, Aria."

I take a step back and turn to walk away, confused by the way my heart is racing. "I'll start setting the table," I tell her, trying my best to hide how thrown I am.

I can't believe she thinks I see her as a child. What? Just because she's tiny? Nah. Nothing about Aria is childish. She's far too fucking beautiful. I need to start seeing her as a kid sister or something, though. I have to.

I'm agitated when she joins me at the table, and I can't quite figure out why. I'm annoyed, and seeing her in that large black T-shirt irritates me even further.

"Forgot to bring pajamas?" I ask, my tone biting.

Aria's eyes widen and she glances down at her clothes, a blush spreading across her cheeks. "Ah, that... I just, I don't know.

When I know that I'm about to go through a stressful time, I find that having something from home helps me a lot. The closest thing to home for me is one of Noah's T-shirts. It makes me feel a little less alone. Besides, it's huge and comfy."

I'm a fucking asshole. The T-shirt is *Noah's*. Fuck. I clear my throat awkwardly and serve her some of the stir-fried vegetables she made us. I shouldn't even care whose clothes she's wearing. It's none of my business.

"How was your first day?" I ask her, my tone far more gentle.

Aria smiles at me. "I loved it, but Riley is a bit of a dick."

I burst out laughing and nod in agreement. "He's brilliant, but yeah... he's an asshole."

"I can't believe he was testing me today. Do you think I should've pushed back more?"

I shake my head. "You were perfect today, Aria. Utter perfection. I wish I'd taken a photo of the exact moment you told him his coding was garbage. Man, I fucking loved it."

She turns beet red, and I grin, wanting to tease her a little more. "And what was it you said? You're the kind of person who leaves no traces? Fucking badass."

She looks away, but I catch the smile she's trying to hide. She's flustered, and I love it. "So, tell me, Ari... who are you?"

She looks at me and grins. "You'd never believe me if I told you."

"Hmm... I love a good challenge. I'll undo you, Aria. Layer by layer."

She looks into my eyes, her breathing quickening just a little, that blush of hers turning her cheeks rosy. She licks her lips, and my dick stirs. She's far too fucking stunning. Those lips of hers... They're what fantasies are made of.

I drag my eyes away, willing my heart to stop beating so quickly. This is Aria. I can't lust after her. Not her. What the fuck is wrong with me?

She shoves a big bite of food into her mouth, chewing slowly, but it doesn't help hide her embarrassment. She eats in silence, and all the while I can't stop thinking about how beautiful she is, in every single way.

I need to get myself under control. I'm supposed to take *care* of Noah's little sister — not take advantage of her.

Chapter Eighteen

ARIA

I'm nervous as I sit down at my desk. I'm still feeling out of place, and it's clear that this is a very close-knit team. I should've asked Gray why he hired me to work in this specific team, but I haven't had the courage. I'm scared he won't have an answer for me, that it's all just a favor to Noah.

My phone lights up at my desk, and I smile when I see Noah's name.

Noah: *How are you doing, Ari? New job okay?*

I grin as I type my reply. I miss him. It's only been a few days, but I'm worried about him.

Aria: *I'm good! The new job is great! How are you? Are you eating? Sleeping enough? Please don't forget to function like an actual human being!*

I almost facepalm myself. That's way too many exclamation marks. He'll know everything isn't as good as I'm saying it is, but it's too late now.

Noah: *Yes, Ari. Don't you worry about me. I'll call you later, okay? I want to hear all about the new job.*

I'm about to reply when someone slams a cup of coffee down on my desk, making it spill over the edge. I look up to find Riley standing next to my desk. I'm not sure about his expression, though. Is he... smiling? It looks more like a grimace, and it freaks me out a little.

"Your work yesterday wasn't awful."

I relax in my seat and bite back a smile. "It wasn't awful?" I repeat slowly.

He crosses his arms and shakes his head. "Some might actually say it's good."

"Some... but not you?"

Laura walks past my desk and shakes her head. "This is painful to watch," she says, grabbing her headphones from her bag.

Riley ignores her and looks away, seemingly hesitating. "It was, uh, it was good. Look, I was wrong. There, I said it. Happy now?"

I cross my own arms, mirroring his posture. "What makes you think I care about your opinion at all?"

Laura chuckles and I realize she might be wearing her headphones, but they clearly aren't plugged in.

Riley sighs. "Will you let me take you out for a drink and make it up to you? I feel like we're starting off on the wrong foot, and we'll be working together for the foreseeable future. I should've known Grayson wouldn't have hired you if you weren't a good fit for the team."

I'm surprised, and Laura is staring at us in surprise, too. Before I can make up my mind, a heavy hand drops down on my shoulder. Gray leans over me and puts down a cup of English breakfast tea before grabbing the cup of coffee that Riley made me. Gray hands the cup back to Riley, and he takes it reluctantly.

Gray's grip on my shoulder tightens as he stares Riley down, towering over him. "She doesn't drink black coffee," he says, his tone clipped. "And I don't pay you to stand around chatting shit. Get to work."

Riley tenses, his eyes dropping to mine before he nods and turns to walk to his own desk. I'm instantly nervous. It's only nine and I know I'm not slacking, yet I suddenly feel like I am.

Gray leans against my desk, his eyes roaming over my face and down to my blouse, almost as though he's checking me out. He straightens abruptly and turns to face the rest of the team.

"Since Riley spent all day wasting Aria's time yesterday, I'd better take charge myself."

Elliot and Laura rise from their seats and walk up to us, forming a little circle around my desk. But Riley stays seated, looking guilty and uneasy.

"I formed this team specifically for high budget projects," Gray says.

"Visionary type of shit," Elliot chimes in, and I smile nervously. Finally. I finally get to find out what they actually do here.

Gray walks up to the glass board on the wall and places his hand on it. It isn't until that that I realize it isn't just a fancy whiteboard. It's a screen of some sort.

"We've been commissioned to create a type of facial recognition software that'll integrate with most operating systems, except it won't just be used to unlock phones. Our job is to make it so secure that it'll replace biometric scanners altogether. It'll be used for banking, identification at airports, you name it. Our list of demands is high. One of the client's top priorities was ensuring our facial recognition can assess distress, in case someone is forced to unlock something under pressure. If it can be hacked in any way, then that might be the end of Aequitas. This project is high-risk, and I think you might be the missing piece, Aria."

I tense, suddenly nervous. "Me?"

Gray smiles at me. "You have a unique way of coding, Aria. You make everything better, but you also see ways to tie all our codes together, something we've been unable to do. We're all good at our specific specializations, but we need someone that can actually put all the pieces together. Since this project is highly confidential, we can't work with a big team. We have countless developers working on smaller elements, but only this small team touches the core of the project. Your prime focus is going to be on building the interface that ties everything together flawlessly. I'll have you coordinate with everyone and I want you to personally go through every bit of code every single person in this room writes, including myself. All the while, Elliot is going to assess your work for weaknesses."

I nod, my heart racing. This is it. This is what I've always wanted. I'm about to start working on software that'll change the world.

I look at Gray, and he smiles at me. Why does he trust me so much? Is this all just a favor for Noah? I doubt myself in many ways, but my skills as an engineer aren't something I doubt. I'm confident that I can do this, but how come Gray is? He's crazy to be risking my involvement. For all he knows, the code I finished for him the other day was just a fluke.

I need to make sure I don't let him down. The type of opportunity he's given me only comes along once in a lifetime.

Gray pulls up different sets of data, showing me the project timeline and some of the work that's already been done. I'm both giddy with excitement and terrified. This is the biggest challenge I've ever come across and the stakes have never been higher.

"Make sure you all help Aria settle in as soon as possible," he says. "We're on a deadline, after all."

He swipes across the screen, and it turns itself off. He turns to walk away, and Laura smiles as she follows him. He glances at her and shakes his head, a grin on his face. Their silent exchange somehow makes me uncomfortable.

My eyes follow them until they both disappear into Gray's office, the door closing behind them. The way they looked at each other... there was intimacy there. A woman like Laura, yeah. That's probably the type Gray goes after. Tall, blonde, thin, and intelligent beyond compare. She's just like Britney.

I drag my eyes away from Grayson's closed office door when

Elliot walks up to me. He grins at me, a knowing look in his eyes. "I fucking knew it," he says, hopping onto my desk. He glances around us, and then he smiles. "Nyx, in the flesh. You have no idea how long I've wanted to meet you."

I freeze, fear running down my spine. My identity has always been a secret that I've guarded with an iron fist. I should've known I'm no match for Elliot Evans, though. Not in terms of security testing.

"Chill," he tells me. "I'd never tell anyone about you."

I cross my arms and lean back in my seat, trying my best to exude confidence when I don't even remotely feel it. "Skaterboy," I say, and his eyes widen at the mention of his username.

I smile. He's good, but I'm not half bad either. I've never breached the privacy of the platform's members, but Elliot made it far too easy to guess who he is through our correspondence. We've worked on half a dozen cases together, and while I'm nowhere near as close to him as I am to Ash, we *have* spoken to each other a few times.

"What are you even doing here?" I ask him. He's so good at what he does he doesn't need to be working for anyone else. No one on this team needs to, yet they're all here.

Elliot smiles and looks away. "It's because I owe Grayson. Some time ago, some asshole made my boyfriend cry. Lucian's brother wanted to make him disappear, but Lucian is too kind-hearted. He asked his brother to let it go, and that dumb shit actually did. I wasn't about to let that happen. You don't make the love of my life cry and get away with it... but I don't have the right connections. I might be good behind my computer, but real-life stuff like that? I don't know how to do that. Grayson does. I asked him for a favor, and he called it when he created this team."

I stare at Elliot in shock. "Gray made someone disappear?"

Elliot nods. "Grayson isn't as simple as you think he is. He's rougher than most of us are, more heartless. That man... I don't know what he's seen, but it can't have been pretty. His past seems complex and best left hidden."

I nod, partially in disbelief. Grayson is one of the best men I know. Could he really do something like that?

Elliot walks away, and I try my hardest to focus on my work, but I keep catching myself glancing at Gray's door. There's so much about him I just don't know... and I want to find out. I want to get to know the parts of Gray he keeps hidden. I shouldn't wonder about Grayson. I shouldn't, but I do.

Chapter Nineteen

Aria

I hesitate before pressing enter. When I created this platform, it was because Noah and I had been let down by the justice system. Because our parents' killer nearly went free. I couldn't stop thinking about what would've happened if we lost the case, and that eventually led to wondering about all the people that *did* happen to.

I've put so much work into making sure this platform doesn't lose its focus. Justice. That's what it's all about.

Yet here I am. Listing my parents' killer on the Nemesis Watchlist. I'm feeling conflicted about it, which is why it's taken me *weeks* to do it. Initially, I wanted to do it during my first week here, and then I kept telling myself I'd do it the week after, until an entire month flew by. I still can't let it go, no matter how hard I try.

I know if he's been let out, he's paid his dues in the eyes of the law. I shouldn't be listing him at all, but I can't help it. I can't rest easy without eyes on him. I need to know that what he did to my parents won't happen to anyone else.

My phone buzzes, and I jump, startled out of my thoughts.

Ash: *Did you see the new anonymous watch list entry? I assume you approved that?*

I hesitate, feeling guiltier by the second. Being on the watch-list means our members will trace his every transaction, his every move, every job application. Anything he does, I'll know about. I've never allowed watch list entries for anyone that isn't a confirmed criminal on the loose.

Nyx: *I did.*

Ash: *That reminds me. Our death row case was picked up and escalated by the social media team. They pushed it for weeks, until it was picked up by the major news outlets. His execution has been put on hold due to the media pressure, and they're reinvestigating. I believe that means you owe me a favor, Nyx.*

Nyx: *You got it, Ash. You worked so hard on this case. Thank you for everything you do.*

Ash: *You do realize none of this would be possible without you and the amazing platform you've built, right? Thank you for being you.*

I freeze, surprised. Ash has a habit of saying things that throw me off. Sometimes it's weird puns and lame pickup lines, and sometimes it's stuff like this... stuff no one that really knows me would ever say.

I want to reply, but I don't know what to say. I end up typing a dozen texts, and delete every single one of them, giving up in the end. I put my phone away and climb into bed, my thoughts whirling. I can't help but overthink my choice, and my mind automatically drifts back to the burglary. Now that I'm older and the wounds aren't as fresh... I don't know. I still can't forgive him, but the gun that killed my parents was their own. It wasn't an armed robbery. That doesn't make it right, but I'm also not sure it warrants putting him on a watch list.

My phone buzzes again, and I reach for it, welcoming the distraction.

Ash: *I forgot. Compliments turn you into a turtle.*

I laugh, startled out of my thoughts. Trust Ash to do that to me.

Nyx: *A turtle? What?*

Ash: *Yep. Compliments make you retreat into your shell. I imagine you like a little turtle, your head disappearing the second someone voices their appreciation of you.*

Nyx: *Are you hiding in my room somewhere? Are you creeping on me, Ash?*

Ash: *I wish. Oh, to be in your room, Nyx. I can totally imagine myself in your bed, your body against mine. I bet I could win you over if I spent a night with you.*

Nyx: *You're that confident in your skills in bed, huh?*

Ash: *I actually meant that I'd love to talk to you all night, tell you lame pickup jokes that Google taught me, and make you smile. I'd lie there with you, looking into your eyes, learning what makes you tick... But yeah, in case that fails, there's always my dick. He's never let me down before. If I can't win you over, he can.*

I laugh out loud, my heart skipping a beat. How does he do this? How does he make me smile even when I'm having a rough night?

Nyx: *You refer to your dick in the third person... of course you do. Does he have a name?*

Ash: *He doesn't... I should probably name him.*

I giggle and almost drop my phone on my face.

Nyx: *Let's name him Asher. Because, you know... Ash and Asher... he's the Asher version of you.*

Ash: *Wow, you need Google. I'm telling you, Google's pickup lines aren't half bad. Yours... yours are terrible.*

I laugh, wondering if he's in bed, smiling at his phone, too.

Nyx: *I don't know what you're talking about... I like Asher.*

Ash: *Hmm, you like my cock, huh? Because that's what it is, and that's what we're calling it.*

Nyx: *Look at you, being all cocky. Cock-y, get it?*

Ash: *Wow. That's bad. That's truly dreadful, baby. If I were* *in bed with you, I'd be keeping that mouth of yours busy, distracting you from your terrible puns.*

Nyx: *Oh yeah, what would you do?*

Ash: *Your choice... my lips on yours or my cock in your mouth. Either way, you won't be thinking of puns.*

Nyx: *Truthfully, I'd choose Asher. I've never gone down on a man before, and I've always wondered if it's something I might enjoy. I like the idea of driving someone crazy.*

Ash: *Nyx, you aren't a virgin, are you?*

I smile to myself, my heart twisting painfully. I'm not, but despite that, I've never had truly fulfilling sex. I've never even orgasmed with a man, but that's probably got more to do with me than them... I'm not the type of woman that'd turn anyone on, that'd make someone want to put effort into my pleasure.

Nyx: *No, I'm not.*

Ash: *There's something sexy about getting to be your first, Nyx. Knowing my dick is the only one to have ever touched your lips... fuck yes.*

I squirm underneath my sheets, my heart racing. The thought never appealed to me, but somehow a small part of me wants to bring Ash to his knees.

Nyx: *I wonder what Asher would taste like... I kind of want to find out.*

Ash: *Ok well, you managed to kill my boner and revive it within two seconds flat. We're not calling it Asher. We're not. I won't be able to get it up if you do.*

Nyx: *I'm adding impotence to my list, right along with over-compensating.*

Ash: *Baby, I can't wait to prove you wrong.*

I smile to myself, surprised at how quickly Ash managed to turn my night around. We've known each other for years, and part of me wishes we'd gotten closer a lot sooner. I wonder what he'd think of me if we ever met in person... would he be disgusted by me the way Brad was? Online I can pretend to be whoever I want, but would Ash ever be interested in me in real life?

I doubt it.

Chapter Twenty

GRAYSON

The lights are on in the house when I walk in, and I wonder if I'll ever get used to that. It's been a little over a month, and it still surprises me to find Aria waiting for me at home. Will I ever get used to having someone to come home to?

Aria pops her head into the hallway and I smile. She looks cute as hell, and when she smiles at me, my heart constricts in a way it's never done before. "I thought I heard you," she says, walking up to me.

She grabs my hand and pulls me along. "Come on, I'm starving."

I let her drag me through the house until she all but pushes me into a chair in the dining room.

My eyes follow her through the room as she sets down bowls of salad and pasta. She's wearing another oversized T-shirt that she's swimming in, and I wonder if she realizes how sexy she looks in it. It's shapeless and doesn't remotely mold to her body, but it just makes me wonder what's underneath even more. I shouldn't be thinking about Aria like that, but it gets harder to push those thoughts away with each passing day.

She's always here, always in my space, her presence filling my every thought. She's at work with me, dazzling my team, and then she's at home with me, dazzling *me*. I find myself seeking her out when I shouldn't, and every day, I look forward to going home and getting to have her to myself.

"I can help, you know?" I say. "You don't have to do everything yourself, sweetheart. Besides, you definitely shouldn't be waiting for me to eat. Sometimes I get so lost in work and meetings I lose track of time."

Aria smiles and shakes her head. "It's okay, Gray. I enjoy this. It makes me feel like I'm not just freeloading here, you know? If you won't let me pay rent, then you have to at least let me do this. Besides... you've done so much for me. I don't know how to repay you."

"You don't need to repay me. I don't keep score." And if I did, Aria would always come out ahead. She has no idea how much she's changed the trajectory I was on. Seeing her work so hard at being happy and building a future for herself when she was just a teenager inspired me endlessly. It made me want to work harder and dream bigger. She's always meant more to me than she realizes, and she always will.

"Try this," she tells me, filling my plate.

I do as she says, unable to keep my eyes off her. She grins at me and leans in, and my eyes drop to her chest. Is she not wearing a bra? I tug on my tie, pulling it loose. She's beautiful, and she doesn't even realize it.

"Do you think it's possible?" she asks, and I blink. Her expression falls, and I realize I just missed what she was saying, lost in thoughts of her.

"I'm sorry," I say. "What was that?"

She shakes her head, biting down on her lip. "It's nothing," she says, falling quiet as she finishes her dinner.

I think back to what she was talking about, drawing a blank. Was it something about work?

Aria is quiet as she clears the table, and I rise from my seat, intercepting her before she disappears into her room. I walk up to her and wrap my arm around her waist, pulling her closer. She stumbles and presses her hands against my chest to stabilize herself. She looks up at me wide-eyed, and this time I'm sure. That's attraction in her eyes. The way her cheeks flush and her lips part... yeah, she's as affected by me as I am by her, but I'm not sure she's even aware of the way her body betrays her. She and I have gotten more comfortable together recently, and every once in a while, I catch her looking at me with an interest that wasn't there before. I enjoy that look in her eyes far more than I should.

"Tell me. What was it you said? I was just absentminded, Aria. I wasn't ignoring you. I'll never do that to you."

She leans in, her chest grazing against mine. I want her fully pressed up against me. I want to know what she feels like, whether she'll fit into me as well as I think she will.

"It's nothing," she murmurs. "I was just asking you for some advice about some of the work I'm doing. I hit a wall, and I'm not sure how to resolve it."

"Okay, let's take a look," I tell her, twirling a strand of her hair around my finger. She smiles at me, and my heart... my fucking heart.

"Really?"

I nod, and Aria grabs my hand with both of hers. She pulls me along to the sofa and grabs her laptop. I watch her as she sits down and pulls her legs up, making her T-shirt ride up, revealing her thighs. I force my eyes away, but the one glance was enough to make me wonder how soft her skin will be, whether she'll gasp if I were to open her legs and kiss her inner thigh.

I shrug off my suit jacket and remove my cufflinks, placing them on the table before unbuttoning the top few buttons on my shirt. I pause when I feel Aria's gaze on me.

Her eyes meet mine, and the way she looks at me instantly has me hard. This woman...

I sit down next to her and grab one of the cushions that magically appeared in my apartment, livening up my otherwise bland, boring space. I place it in my lap to hide how she affects me, and she's so fucking clueless... so clueless, that she places her laptop on top of the cushion, as though I intended to use it as a table or some shit.

She sits next to me on her knees; her face far too fucking close to mine as she runs me through the issues she's facing. All the while, all I can't think of is how I want her flat on her back, my lips on hers and my cock buried deep inside her. I want my name on her lips.

I want what I'll never have.

Chapter Twenty-One

ARIA

"Didn't you used to work for Torsis, that little boutique firm?" Laura asks, sounding excited. I'm surprised she walked up to my desk at all. In the last couple of weeks we've only spoken a handful of times. She always keeps to herself. I initially thought she just didn't like me until I realized she doesn't hang out with the rest of the team either. It's only Gray she ever really speaks to.

I frown and nod at her. "I did."

She laughs and hands me her phone. "You got out just at the right time, then. Some dude named Brad single-handedly caused the demise of your old firm. Did you know him?"

I nod, reading through the article in shock. Torsis is on the brink of bankruptcy and facing multiple lawsuits due to the delivery of faulty software. Looks like they managed to trace it all back to Brad.

Impossible. I worked on a lot of these projects, and I know everything was working flawlessly when I left. What happened?

My hand is shaking as I hand Laura back her phone. "What a moron," she says, laughing. "Such a large-scale scandal is rare. I can't believe how lucky you were to leave when you did. That Brad guy must be a moron."

"He is," I say, my eyes turning toward Grayson's office. He *is* a moron, but I worked closely on many of the projects named in the article. This couldn't have happened unless it was orchestrated. I watch Gray through his open office door, my heart starting to race as I think back to his bruised knuckles the day after Brad broke my heart. Could it be?

I smile at Laura and rise from my seat. "Excuse me," I tell her, my legs barely holding me up as I walk to Gray's office, hesitating in his doorway.

He looks up at me, his lips tipping up in a smile. "Aria."

I walk in and close the door behind me, my hands shaking. Gray rises from his seat and walks toward me, meeting me halfway. "What's wrong?" he asks, his voice tinged with worry.

"Did you hear?" I whisper. "About Torsis?"

Something flickers in his eyes, and my heart starts to hammer in my chest. I swallow hard as I gather my courage. "Was it you?"

Gray tenses and raises a hand to my face, his expression unreadable as he brushes my hair out of the way before cupping my cheek, his thumb tracing over the edge of my lips. When he looks at me this way, my heart can't help but race.

"Yes," he says, taking a step closer to me, and I place my palms on his chest. Gray raises his other hand to my face and cups the back of my head, his fingers threading through my hair. The way he's holding me... it's intimate, yet his body is barely touching mine.

"Brad was a fool to mess with you," he tells me, his thumb stroking the edge of my lips. "A fucking fool. When I saw those tears in your eyes... there's no way he was going to get away with what he did. No fucking way. No one hurts you and gets away with it. No one. Not on my fucking watch. I will never sit there and watch your heart break, Ari."

The way he looks at me, the intensity in his eyes... no one has ever made me feel as special as Gray unknowingly does. I never asked him to do any of this for me, and I never would have expected it. He took my pain and avenged me as if it were his own, never even telling me how much he's done for me.

I rise to my tiptoes, Gray's hand slipping away as I press a kiss to his cheek, my lips lingering. His hand wraps around the back of my neck, his thumb resting on my throat as my body melts into his. He turns his face just a little, and my lips brush against his.

I swallow hard and pull away to look into his eyes. The way he's holding me, one hand around the back of my neck and the other wrapped into my hair... I doubt he realizes how that affects me, how intimate it is.

"Thank you," I whisper, barely able to hold his gaze. The intensity he's looking at me with has my body responding in ways it shouldn't.

I slide my palms up, enjoying the feel of the muscles underneath his shirt as my arms wrap around his neck. I lean in to hug him, my body pressed against his. Gray holds me tightly, and I can't help but wonder if this feels the same to him.

"Would you have told me if I hadn't found out?" I murmur against his shirt, my forehead resting against his chest.

Gray tightens his grip on me and rests his chin on top of my head. "No."

I chuckle. I can't help it. "Grayson," I whisper. "You're amazing. I don't know how you did it, but I'm grateful. I shouldn't be. I shouldn't be so vicious... but the thought of Brad and my manager not getting away with how they treated me makes me breathe easier."

He presses a kiss on top of my head, and I lean back to look at him. His eyes find mine, and I wish I knew what he's thinking. Sometimes, when he looks at me this way, I could swear there's more between us... that I'm not just his best friend's little sister.

I take a step away, Gray's hands falling away. "I'll get back to work," I murmur, and he nods. I feel his gaze on me as I walk away, and I'm giddy as I head back to my desk.

I catch Laura staring at me, her gaze moving between me and

Gray's office, her curiosity apparent. I can't help but blush, and she smiles as she looks away. I hope I didn't just start false rumors about Gray and me. I have a feeling he wouldn't appreciate that at all. Not just because of his private nature, but also because of who I am.

Chapter Twenty-Two

GRAYSON

It took me close to a week, but I finally found the time to check out the latest watchlist entry on the Nemesis Platform, and part of me wishes I hadn't.

It's him. The guy that killed Aria and Noah's parents.

He might have been listed anonymously, but that's too many coincidences. The bad breakup. Nyx telling me she had a big day coming up right before Aria's first day at work. And now this.

I can't ignore it any longer. I can't keep lying to myself. I've suspected Nyx's identity for a while now, and if I'm truly honest with myself, I knew from the moment I saw her finish a query using patterns I'd only ever seen in two places before: in Brad's software, and on the Nemesis Platform.

Fucking hell... is this some sort of joke? A twist of fate? I don't know what it is, but what I do know is that Aria and Nyx are the same person. The girl of my dreams... is my best friend's little sister.

I've been fantasizing about her, fuck. Some of the shit I've said to her, telling her I wanted her lips around my cock, that I'd make her moan my name. Shit.

I tense when Aria walks into the living room, another one of her big T-shirts on, a towel raised to her wet hair. "Hey, Gray," she says, walking up to me, and I click away the information I found.

Should I tell her? I should say something, but what? The things I've said to her as Ash, damn. She'd be horrified if she knew it was me. The idea of her looking at me with disgust in her eyes has me gritting my teeth.

Besides... I'm not a hundred percent sure, am I?

Aria sits down on the sofa beside me and grabs her laptop. She doesn't even notice me staring at her. Could she be Nyx? If I'm honest, I've been imagining Aria's face every time I think of Nyx. Part of me already expected it to be her, wanted it even.

Lately, our conversations have gotten more and more inappropriate, and there's no going back. There's no way for us to pretend it never happened, that she didn't turn me on, that I didn't tell her I want to fuck her.

My phone buzzes, and I jump. My heart races when I realize it's a notification from the Nemesis Platform.

Nyx: *I have a pun for you. It's a good one this time. Are you ready? Ash... you're my density.*

I glance at Aria to find her staring at her screen, a small smile on her face and a twinkle in her eyes.

Nyx: *Get it? Destiny? Density? It's a nerdy pun for you.*

Aria laughs, and my heart skips a beat. "What's so funny?" I ask her. She freezes, as though she's only just remembering that I'm sitting here.

"Oh Gray, it's nothing," she says, a faint blush staining her cheeks pink. She looks beautiful, sitting on the sofa with me, her hair still wet, not a trace of makeup on her face. She's fucking breathtaking, and she's so far out of reach. I can't ever go there with Noah's little sister... but Nyx... I could have the part of Aria that is Nyx.

Aria looks back at her screen and bites down on her lip. I see the impatience in her eyes, and it tugs at my heartstrings. All this time I've been wondering about Nyx, wondering if she enjoys our conversations as much as I do. Now I know.

I glance down at my phone as I type a reply, a faint smile on my face. I'm feeling conflicted, but I can't resist either. I'm addicted to Nyx.

Ash: *Baby, how do you keep getting worse at this? Seriously, try Google. It's the only thing that can save you at this point.*

Aria giggles, her eyes meeting mine briefly before she looks down at her screen. "Sorry," she murmurs, before she starts to type.

Nyx: *...that WAS from Google.*

Ash: *Wow. I have no words.*

Aria bursts out laughing, and I move closer to her. She slams her laptop closed before I get close enough to see what she's up to, and I lean back beside her, my thigh grazing against hers. She tenses, and I wrap my arm around the back of the sofa, over her head.

"What's got you giggling like that?" I ask, part of me wondering if it might just come up. I'm not a superstitious man, but tonight I'm looking for a sign. Do I tell her, or not?

Aria turns to look at me, her face flushed. "Oh, I was texting a friend. It's really nothing," she says, a hint of guilt in her eyes.

I nod, my eyes roaming over her face. She's stunning, and those lips of hers... yeah, they've starred in all my recent fantasies of Nyx. Lately, things have been different between us. We haven't crossed any lines, but there's definitely an attraction. Is she feeling conflicted about it the way I was? I felt guilty texting Nyx while imagining Aria, and maybe she feels the same way.

"How has work been? Have you adapted well?" I ask, trying to find something to talk about; a way to explain why I suddenly moved closer to her. Besides, we've barely had time to talk lately. We've both been far too busy with work. Aria and I try to eat together at night, but usually we're both sitting at the dining table with our laptops out, and more often than not, she disappears into her bedroom straight after. I guess that's what made it easier to miss the signs.

Thinking of her lying in bed just a few steps away during all the late-night conversations we've had recently, fuck.

Aria looks up at me and smiles, making my heart skip a beat. "It's honestly been so great," she tells me. I lean in and brush a wet strand of hair out of her face, and she bites down on her lip, looking a little flustered. "I can't thank you enough. A fresh start is exactly what I needed, and it couldn't have come at a better time. I'll work hard, Gray. You won't regret hiring me."

I smile and shake my head. "I know I won't, Ari. I wouldn't have hired you if I thought you would disappoint me."

She nods, her gaze solemn, and it fucking guts me. Sometimes I think there's more, but right now? Right now she's looking at me like I'm nothing more than her brother's best friend, as though I'm merely her boss. I shouldn't want her to see me any differently, but now I know who she is, I want more. I want her smiles, her laughter, her passion.

I want everything she gives Ash.

Chapter Twenty-Three

ARIA

My hands tremble as I read through the information Nemesis members found on Peter Simmons.

He found a job. He applied for over fifty, but in the end, he got a job at a small convenience store not too far from my old house. In the months that we've been tracking him, he hasn't committed a single crime. Based on his phone records, all he seems to be doing is trying to contact his daughter, who won't speak to him.

I bite down on my lip and send out a request for his financial records dating back the last twenty years. I've spent so many years being angry that I've never wondered *why*. I've only ever been concerned with making him pay for what he did.

His rationale won't matter. Nothing will ever make his crimes forgivable. But now that the anger has turned into a dull pain, I'm wondering why. Why did he rob us? Why did he kill my parents?

I click the window away before the memories have a chance to claw at me. I don't want to let the anger consume me all over again. I can't.

I close my laptop and push it further down my bed. I grab my phone instead, hesitating for only half a second before deciding to text Ash.

Nyx: *You know how you always tell me you want me in your bed? Tonight I find myself wishing you were in mine.*

I didn't expect him to reply immediately, but he does, and he sees straight through me.

Ash: *What happened?*

Nyx: *It's nothing... I just feel a little lonely, a little hurt. Memories overwhelm me tonight, making it just a little harder to breathe.*

Ash: *Is this about your ex? That douchebag never deserved you, Nyx.*

Nyx: *It's not. It's some other stuff. It's not important.*

Ash: *Hmm, what can I do to make you feel better? If I were with you, I'd take you in my arms and kiss you until I'm all you can think about... but since I can't be with you, I'll have to settle for more puns.*

Nyx: *Oh no, not the puns*

Ash: *We make a great pear.*

Nyx: *Oh wow, that one is kind of cute. So your mind isn't all filthy, huh?*

Ash: *Tricked you! What do a cock and a Rubik's cube have in common? I'll tell you... The more you play with them, the harder they get :)*

I laugh and shake my head, my mood lifted. He always does this to me. Every single time I'm down, he cheers me up, and he does it with ease.

Nyx: *I have one for you... I cherry-ish you*

Nyx: *Seriously, you're amazing, and I'm so glad to have met you*

Ash: *Me too, baby.*

The sound of knocking on my bedroom door startles me, and I nearly drop my phone. I walk up to the door and open it, finding Gray standing in front of me. He's wearing a T-shirt that does nothing to hide his muscles, and I love seeing him like this, so undone.

"Hey," he says. "I can't sleep. Do you want to hang out? I don't know, we could watch a movie or something?"

I smile and nod at him, trying my hardest not to ogle him. Those gray sweatpants have me licking my lips. "I couldn't sleep either," I murmur, slipping out of my bedroom, my phone in hand. Gray grins at me and wraps his arm around my shoulder, pulling me along to the living room.

He pulls me on the sofa with him and hooks his arm around me, my head on his chest. I should probably pull away, but I don't want to. Being in Gray's arms like this... it's exactly what I need tonight.

He turns the TV on and pulls me closer as he changes the channel, putting on some late-night news show.

I pull my legs up on the sofa and turn, so I'm closer to him. He looks at me and smiles, his eyes dropping to my phone. I didn't even realize I was clutching it so tightly. A tinge of guilt has me unable to meet his eyes. Just a few minutes ago I was texting Ash and enjoying every second of it, but now that I'm sitting here with Gray I realize there's nowhere I'd rather be. Ash and I have been getting closer and closer, but then there's Gray. Lately things between us have been different... I can't quite put my finger on it, but there are little touches that didn't use to be there, and some-times he looks at me as though he knows what I'm thinking, as though he can see straight through me.

Grayson frowns and leans in, taking my phone from me. "None of that," he murmurs. "When you're sitting here with me, I want your attention."

My eyes widen, and Grayson smirks. He leans in and brushes my hair out of my face, his gaze lingering. His eyes drop to my lips, and my heart starts to race.

"Why couldn't you sleep?" he asks.

I drag my eyes away and shake my head. "It's nothing... I was just thinking of my parents, that's all."

He nods and opens his arms wide. "Come on," he says. "There's nothing a hug won't make better."

I blush and lean in, wrapping my arms around his neck. Grayson tightens his grip on me and shifts on the sofa, lying down and pulling me along, so I end up on top of him. He places one hand on my lower back while the other finds its way into my hair.

My heart starts to race, and I bury my face in his neck. This is just a hug to him, but to me... it's so much more. The way his body feels against mine, big and hard against my soft curves. Gray has no idea how stupidly handsome he is, how he affects me.

"Ari, you've grown into a woman they'd be so proud of. You're beautiful, clever and kind. You're everything they could want you to be."

I nod, my eyes falling closed as Gray plays with my hair. He smells so good, and being in his arms is a strange experience... it's got me feeling excited and peaceful all at once.

"You'd have loved my Mom," I tell him, my voice soft. Gray tenses underneath me, and I smile as I tell him all about her. The way she used to walk me to the playground no matter when I wanted to go, the stories she'd make up for me before bed, the way she'd pretend to have random illnesses so Noah could diagnose and cure her. I lie in Gray's arms as I tell him all about Mom, the memories making me smile instead of cry for the first time in years.

Chapter Twenty-Four

GRAYSON

I glance at Aria from my office, my eyes roaming over her. She looks beautiful today, and I'm not the only one who notices. So far, Riley has dropped by her desk seven times. Seven times, and it isn't even noon yet.

Every time he interrupts her work, she smiles at him, without a trace of annoyance. I watch as he walks up to her yet again, his tablet in hand. I have no doubt he's asking some complete bullshit questions. I never would have hired him if he needed this much help. Nah. It's Aria's attention he's after, and she doesn't even realize it.

I watch as his eyes drop to her chest and I grit my teeth. I loved that blouse on her this morning, but right now, I love it a little less. The possessiveness I feel toward her is unreal. She was only ever meant to be a responsibility, so why is she rapidly becoming more? The way I held her in my arms last night... I shouldn't have, but I couldn't resist. I wanted to feel her against me. Knowing she couldn't sleep, that she was sad... I wanted to be the one to take her pain away. I told myself I'd stay away, but I can't.

I want her eyes on me, and no one but me. I want her smiles, her laughter, I want *her*. I want her to myself. I breathe a sigh of relief when Riley finally walks away and grab my phone.

Ash*: I'm having a hard time focusing today, Nyx. All I can think about is you. I was just thinking... If you were a vegetable, you would be a cute-cumber.*

I watch as Aria picks up her phone, smiling as she unlocks it. She bursts into laughter, and I smile to myself.

Nyx: *Google, again?*

Ash: *Guilty, but let's just say that you don't want to know what's truly on my mind.*

Nyx: *Mean. Now you know I have to find out. Tell me.*

I smirk as I type my reply.

Ash: *I'm wondering what you'll taste like. I want your lips on mine, but that's not all. I want to know how soft your skin is, how your voice will sound when you moan my name... and I want to know what your pussy tastes like.*

I watch Aria tense, and I wonder if she's pressing her legs together the way I imagine she is. I might not be able to say any of this to her, but I can say it to Nyx. I can't walk in and steal her attention away from Riley the way I want to, but Ash can.

Ash: *I dreamt about you last night, and it's all I've been able to think about since. You were smiling at me, your hands pressed against my abs. I pushed you up against the wall, making you feel how hard you make me. You moaned, and I buried my hand in your hair, pulling your face to mine as I kissed you. The way you kissed me back... fuck. My hands roamed over your body and I slipped them underneath your dress, my fingers tracing over the edges of your underwear.*

I watch as Aria glances around the office, her cheeks bright red. She hesitates, and then starts typing.

Nyx: *Then what happened?*

I grin, loving the way her cheeks are flaming, the way her

breathing seems to quicken. I wonder if she's getting wet reading about my fantasies. I want to walk over to her and pull her out of her chair to kiss her. Fuck.

Ash*: I pushed aside the lace you were wearing, my fingers sliding straight into your hot pussy. You were soaking wet for me, Nyx. Such a wet pussy... fuck. You told me you wanted me, your hands undoing my suit trousers. I wanted you naked, but you weren't patient enough. No, you wanted me deep inside you. So I gave it to you, baby. I gave it to you hard, loving the way you moaned my name. I fucked you from every angle I could think of, until I found one that made your moans a little higher, your pants a little quicker. I fucked you like that, until you came all over my cock, your lips falling open and a beautiful blush on your face.*

I watch her as she reads my text, her eyes wide. She swallows hard, her body tense. Yeah, I've got her turned on.

Nyx*: Okay, wow. That's... that's pretty hot, Ash.*

Ash*: It was, but the real thing will be better. Just thinking of you has me wanting to wrap my hand around my cock so I can come to the thought of you. Tell me, baby, are you wet for me? Tell me you're as turned on as I am. Tell me I'm not the only one going crazy.*

Nyx*: You're not the only one, Ash. You've got me squirming in my seat, wondering what it'd be like if you touched me like that in real life. I want to find out what your lips will feel like against mine. Will you be able to make me moan the way you tell me you will?*

She runs a hand through her hair, her cheeks blazing. I've never seen her blush this badly, and I love it. She rises from her seat, her phone in her hand, and I frown. She glances toward the bathrooms, hesitating before taking a step away from her desk. No fucking way. A strange burst of jealousy settles in my stomach, and it makes no sense whatsoever. But I don't like the idea of her touching herself because of *Ash*. I want it to be me.

"Aria?" I call as she walks past my open office door. She pauses, and when she turns to face me, her expression is anguished. I smile at her and tip my head to the side, indicating for her to come in.

The frustration in her eyes brings a smile to my face. It's about time our roles reversed... she's been driving me crazy for weeks now.

Aria walks into my office, and I take her in. She's wearing a short pencil skirt today, combined with a white blouse that's failing to hide how hard her nipples are. She either isn't wearing a bra, or she's wearing one of those super soft useless ones, my favorite kind.

"Come here," I say, my voice gruff. "Take a look at this."

Aria nods and walks around my desk, a flash of guilt in her eyes when they meet mine. Is she thinking of the way I held her last night?

It's me that gets to hold her, the one she confides in... but it's Ash that's got her wet. I hate this, and I hate that this mess is all of my own making.

I pull up some random unfinished script and Aria bends over my desk to look at it, her skirt riding up. She starts to type, unaware of the view she's presenting me with. The way her skirt wraps around her ass... damn. What would she do if I push her down on my desk and bury my face between her legs? I want my teeth wrapped around her panties and drag them down.

I sit up and lean in, making her ass brush against my chest. Aria turns around, flustered, and I wrap my hands around her hips. She's leaning back against my desk, and I turn my office chair so she's standing between my legs, barely any distance between us.

"Oh, I'm so sorry, Gray," she says. She looks at me, her gaze heated. My eyes drop to her hard nipples, and the way her chest moves up and down, her breathing accelerating by the second... it's making me even harder than I already am.

I let go of her and shrug out of my suit jacket, draping it over her shoulders. My fingers brush against her nipples as I pull the jacket closed, and a small moan escapes her lips.

"You must be cold," I whisper, pulling my fingers away. I've already crossed far too many boundaries today, but I can't help myself. Not when it comes to her.

Aria looks away, her cheeks bright red, her blush extending down her neck. I want her naked, so I can find out if the rest of her body reddens like that, too.

"I, um, yes," she says, flustered. She clutches the lapels of my suit jacket, unable to face me. I'm a fucking asshole. How the fuck am I jealous of myself?

Chapter Twenty-Five

ARIA

I twist and turn in bed, my mind replaying the way Gray was looking at me today, the way his fingers brushed against my breasts as he draped his jacket over my shoulders.

Thoughts of him are all that's keeping me sane. It's my ammunition against the niggling feeling that something might be wrong. I've barely been able to sleep lately, and every day my anxiety gets worse.

Tonight, I'm battling a sense of paranoia I used to experience every night, and not even thoughts of Gray keep them away.

I sit up in bed, my heart racing. Countless scenarios run through my mind, each worse than the one before. I try my hardest to resist the compulsion, knowing how irrational I'm being, but I can't help myself.

I know no one is going to break into Gray's house. There are too many checks to get through first. There's security at the front door, the elevators are linked to key cards, and then there's the actual front door itself, which has physical locks and an alarm system. Despite all of that, I can't resist the urge to check that the doors are truly locked. That we're safe.

It's a routine I went through every single day after the robbery. It took a lot of therapy, but eventually I managed to stop checking every single night, and then the time in between my checks became weeks before they turned into months. I can feel that tonight is one of those nights, though... one of those nights where I know I'll lose.

I swallow hard as my feet hit the cold floor, a sense of dread washing over me. I don't want to do this, but that niggling feeling won't go away until I see for myself that the door is locked. I won't be able to sleep. I won't be able to fight the nightmares.

I know it's because I keep thinking of Peter Simmons. Every time I get another notification, I feel more conflicted. Just today, he donated some money to a charity named Brady. I looked it up, and it appears to be a charity against gun violence. Is it a way of repenting? I can't help but overthink things. If my parents hadn't owned the gun he managed to get his hands on, would they still be alive? By the time I walked into the house, it was too late. The gun was on the floor, and my parents were bleeding out. What if the gun hadn't been there at all? Based on the police investigation, it appears he was surprised by my parents coming home earlier than expected. He seemed to have struggled with them for the gun, shooting my mother during the battle, and then my father once he got his hands on the gun. It's why he couldn't be put away for first degree murder. The best thing we could do was felony murder. The fact that he was unarmed is the only reason he's a free man before completing his time.

I feel sick to my stomach as I slip out of my bedroom. I hope Gray is fast asleep already. The last thing I want to do is alert him to my weird behavior. I can't even imagine what he'd think. He's been seeing the worst parts of me lately. He spent hours with me last night, letting me talk about my parents until I fell asleep in his arms. I don't want him to think badly of me. I don't want him to feel like I'm a burden. If he finds out I can't sleep again, he might feel so bad that he spends another night with me, and I don't want to do that to him, no matter how much I need him tonight.

I breathe a sigh of relief when I reach the door and rest my palm against it, dropping my head to the cold wood. I hate this. I hate that I can't fight it. I hate that the memories assail me every time I try. Even as I'm standing here, I'm trying to keep myself from unlocking and re-locking the door, but I can't. I'm weak. I know it's all in my head, yet I can't fight this.

I inhale deeply as I unlock the door, the sound loud in the silence of the night. I turn the lock, and when it clicks closed, a rush of relief washes over me. I drop my forehead to the front door, feeling as helpless as I always do after having done this.

I turn to walk back to my bedroom and freeze in my tracks when I find Grayson leaning back against the wall, his arms crossed. He's staring at me, the moonlight coming in from the windows illuminating his silhouette. He's in nothing but black boxer shorts, and I can't help the way my eyes roam over his body. He's far more muscular than I imagined, and I force my gaze away, startled by my own thoughts.

He walks up to me, and my heart starts to race. Gray pauses in front of me and raises his hand to my face, pushing a strand of hair behind my ear. His gaze is searching, and it makes me feel bared to him. I should be coming up with an excuse, a way to hide the vulnerability I'm feeling, but instead I find myself staring into his eyes. What I find there isn't curiosity or confusion. It's understanding, tinged with a hint of concern.

He cups my cheek, his thumb tracing over the edge of my lips. "You set off the silent alarm, Ari. This house is a fortress. It's as safe as it's going to get, sweetheart. You can't even open the door if you haven't turned the alarm system off first. Usually I'm the first person up and the last one to go to bed, so I never thought to show you. I'm sorry."

I try my hardest to push down the sense of shame I feel and look away, my arms wrapping around myself without even realizing.

I'm about to come up with an excuse when Gray suddenly leans in. He lifts me into his arms and carries me to the living room, rendering me speechless.

"Grayson," I whisper. He looks at me and smiles, making me forget about the excuses I'd come up with. He sits down on the sofa with me in his lap; our position the same as the night Brad broke my heart.

"When I can't sleep, I'll sit here and stare out the window. The view is so astonishing it melts away my worries. Tonight is the first night I don't have to be alone as I sit here."

His arms wrap around me, but his gaze is on the skyline in front of us. I relax in his arms and rest my head against his shoulder, my knees drawn up to my chest. We sit there like that, the two of us finding solace in the silence of the night.

"I can't help it," I whisper.

Gray tightens his grip on me, and I squeeze my eyes closed.

"I've done it ever since my parents were taken from me. When I get these feelings, I can't go to sleep unless I'm sure the doors are locked. I can't help it. I don't want to do it, but if I don't, I can't keep my destructive thoughts at bay. I'll worry that someone will break into the house, that we'll get hurt. And I just keep thinking I could prevent it if I make sure the door is locked."

Gray exhales shakily and pulls me closer, his lips settling against my temple. He presses a gentle kiss to my skin, and I try my hardest to blink away the tears that are gathering in my eyes.

"The way I grew up... not every house I lived in was as safe as I wished it was, so my home is outfitted with countless security measures. You're safe here. But if that isn't enough, know that you'll always be safe in my arms, too. I'm here, Ari. I'll help you keep those thoughts at bay."

I swallow hard and throw my arms around him, hugging him tightly. Noah and I are both lucky to have Grayson in our lives. I rest my forehead against his shoulder, creating some distance between us. Having our bodies pushed together like this...

I lift my face to find him staring at me, his gaze intense —

heated even. I force myself to smile through the thoughts that I shouldn't be having. I shouldn't be wondering what his lips might taste like. Just a few months ago, I thought I'd spend the rest of my life with Brad. Yet here I am. I'm a hypocrite. How could I be thinking about Grayson when my heart is still bleeding?

I lean in, my lips brushing against Gray's cheek, and press a lingering kiss to his skin. I allow myself that much. One friendly kiss.

And then I flee. I jump off his lap and walk away, leaving him sitting in the living room, my heart in disarray.

I've only just calmed my raging heart when my phone buzzes, the Nemesis App lighting up my phone. My guilt only intensifies as I reach for it, knowing that there's only one person who I've got my notifications turned on for.

Ash: *Nyx... hypothetically, what would you recommend I do if I'm left with blue balls by someone who doesn't even realize what she does to me?*

My eyes widen as I re-read his text, and I can't quite explain why my heart tightens the way it does. I bite down on my lip, pushing down the sudden heartache I have no right to feel. I've found myself in Grayson's arms twice in a row now, and I enjoyed being in his embrace. I have no right to be jealous now.

Besides, I should've known that Ash was just joking around with me. I made the exact same mistake I made with Brad. With him, I also assumed he was flirting with me when I couldn't have been more wrong. I swallow hard as I type my reply, my chest constricting painfully. I'm still the same fool I was then.

Nyx: *Hypothetically... you should let her know. Whoever she is, she probably doesn't even know what you think of her. Maybe she's second guessing herself, wondering if you're flirting with her or if she's reading too much into things. Maybe all she needs is to hear those words.*

Somehow, it hurts to think that Ash has someone he's after. It hurts even more to know that once again I let myself be fooled into thinking someone might be into *me*. Of course he can't be.

He doesn't even know me. He has no idea what I look like, and while I don't know who he is either, I can tell he's naturally charismatic. I wouldn't be surprised if flirting is in his very nature. He probably doesn't even realize he's doing it.

Ash: *I am. Nyx, I am flirting with you. I wish I had the balls to do something about the blue balls you keep giving me (appreciate the pun?)*

I stare at my phone, confused. He was talking about me? I can't figure out what he's after, but he must have some sort of endgame. Is it my platform? He can't want me because he doesn't know me. Am I just a challenge to him?

Nyx: *Very punny*

I put my phone away, unable to stop overthinking everything. My thoughts keep turning to Grayson and the way he's been making me feel lately. Tonight, simply texting Ash has me feeling guilty... and it shouldn't because there's nothing going on between Gray and me, is there?

Chapter Twenty-Six

GRAYSON

My mind is on Aria as I walk into the kitchen to make breakfast. The way she fits into my arms... I shouldn't think of her the way I do, but fuck. I want a taste. I want her lips on mine and my body on top of hers. I want to hear her whisper my name. Everything I tell her I want to do over text... I want it all.

"Morning, Gray," Aria says, sounding tired. I tense when she walks into the kitchen, carrying with her the smell of my soap. Fucking hell. The thought of her in my shower, her body wet and slippery.

"Morning," I say, trying my hardest to hide how hard I suddenly am. She looks beautiful today, and I force myself to look away, when all I want to do is drink her in.

She pours herself a cup of tea, and I struggle to keep my eyes off her. She's truly stunning in that red dress, and the way it clings to her body is straight up sinful.

"Where are you going?" I ask, a tinge of jealousy settling in my chest. She looks gorgeous, and I'm instantly worried she's going on a date. It's been a few months, and she's bound to move on at some point. Besides, I see the way men around her look at her, the way Riley keeps asking her out. She might not be as clueless about it as I thought she was.

Aria leans back against the kitchen counter and shakes her head. "I don't know," she says, her voice soft. When she looks up at me, there's vulnerability in her eyes. "I couldn't sleep last night, but I don't want to let that ruin my weekend. I might go for a walk or something. I haven't really explored Cali yet, and I want to. Do you have plans for today?"

My first instinct is to say that I do. Having her around has been driving me crazy. It's in the little things she does and says. It's in how wickedly smart she is, the way she smiles, those lips of hers. The way she cares about me and the vulnerability she won't show anyone but me. I thought I knew what to expect when I offered her a place to stay, but I was wrong. So wrong.

She smiles at me, and I know I'm lost. "No, I don't have plans," I tell her, regretting it instantly. The last thing I need is to spend more time with her, but I can't stay away. Not when she looks at me that way. "How about I show you around?"

The way her eyes widen in delight has my heart racing. "Really?" she asks, and I know there's no going back. I nod, and she straightens, her fatigue replaced by excitement. "I made a list of things I want to see," she says, reaching into the top of her dress. My eyes widen when she pulls her phone out. What the fuck? Aria's cheeks redden when she catches me staring, and it only makes her look more beautiful.

"Oh, um... I have this bad habit of putting my phone in my bra when I don't have pockets," she explains, and I nod absent-mindedly, trying my hardest to tear my gaze away from her breasts.

I clear my throat awkwardly. "Ah, if you've got a list then I'll be of no use."

She chuckles and walks up to me, her hand reaching for mine.

"No way. I need you to accompany me. I want to see this city through your eyes. You're from here, after all. We've both been so busy lately, and I just want to finally take some time to relax."

She looks far happier than she did when she first got here. It's only been a couple of months, but she no longer looks like her heart is irreparably broken. I see the change in her smile, in her attitude. When she first got here, she spent all of her weekends in her bedroom, reading and watching TV, but now she actually wants to go out.

I entwine our fingers and raise my hand to her face, brushing aside her hair. Does she have any idea how beautiful she is? Somehow, I don't think she does.

"Okay, fine," I tell her. "Let me get changed."

Aria frowns, her eyes running over my body. "Why? You look hot like this."

I tense, surprised, and glance down at my outfit. I'm wearing an old white T-shirt and gray sweatpants. She thinks that's hot?

She smiles. "You're usually in suits, but this T-shirt really showcases your muscles. You look great," she says, her fingertips grazing over my bicep.

I smile tightly and nod, taking a step away from her. "Can't go out in sweats, Ari," I tell her, walking away, my heart beating far louder than it should.

I get changed in record speed, but I keep the same T-shirt on. I shouldn't, and I know it. I shouldn't want to wear something she likes, but fuck it. No harm, right?

Aria smiles at me when I walk up to her, and I notice she's got a handbag now. I raise my brows and look at her, but I know I shouldn't be asking the question that's on my mind.

She laughs when she catches me looking at her breasts, and she shakes her head. "It's in my bag now. I promise I won't embarrass you by fondling myself in public."

I smirk at her and tip my head toward the door. "Yeah, I'd rather you kept that a private show."

Her cheeks redden as she walks past me, and I bite back a smile. I'm enjoying teasing her, and I shouldn't. I'm crossing the line, and I know it.

"Okay, tell me where we're going first," I say as I step into the car.

Aria smiles at me sheepishly, looking far too adorable. "The Tech," she tells me.

I freeze, my hands on my steering wheel. "That's a kids museum, Ari."

She shakes her head. "It's not! It'll be fun, I promise. They have some cool stuff we can do there. Did you know they have a bird simulator type of thing? We can go experience what it's like to fly, Gray!"

I glance at her, amused. "Ari, there's an indoor skydiving experience right next to the office, and you want to go put on a 3D mask and pretend to fly instead?"

She looks at me open-mouthed. "Shut up!"

I shake my head. "How about I take you there?"

She places her hand on my thigh and nods. "Oh my god, *yes*."

Her excitement brings a smile to my face. Scratch that. Aria brings a smile to my face. She always does.

She's buzzing by the time I park my car and her seatbelt is already unbuckled by the time I reach her door. I grin as I offer her my hand.

I entwine our fingers as I pull her along and into the building. She squeezes my hand tightly, her hand slowly getting clammy.

"I'm nervous, Gray. I don't know."

I turn to her and raise my hand to her hair, my eyes on hers. "We don't have to do this, babe. It's safe, and I think it'll be fun, but if you'd rather go to The Tech, we can."

Aria shakes her head and takes a step closer to me, her palm flat on my chest. I don't think she quite realizes what all these little touches are doing to me. She's driving me insane, and she doesn't even know it.

"No," she says. "I want to do this. If it's with you, then I'm sure it'll be fine."

I cup her cheek and nod. "I'll be there, Ari. It'll be fun."

Chapter Twenty-Seven

ARIA

I'm still smiling hours later, my heart racing. "Wow, that feeling of floating and flying, it was insane."

Grayson laughs at me and shakes his head. "All you did was lie on your belly," he says, looking amused.

I side-eye him and cross my arms. It was obvious Gray wasn't new to indoor skydiving. All of those flips he did... It was crazy. I can't believe how good he was. I had no idea he was an adrenaline junkie. There's so much about him I don't know and I'm enjoying discovering new sides to him.

"Come on," he says, grabbing my hand. He interlaces our fingers, and I smile up at him. He does this a lot... grabbing my hand like that. Does he even realize he's doing it?

Brad never used to hold my hand. We always walked side-by-side, like the strangers we were. Gray isn't even mine. He never will be, yet he treats me better than Brad ever did.

"Table for two, please?" Gray asks as he leads me into a bar with a truly astonishing view, his hand tightening around mine.

The waitress barely notices me, she's far too busy checking

131

Grayson out. A twisted sense of satisfaction courses through me when her gaze pauses on our joint hands. She looks at me then, and I wonder what she sees. Do I look like I could be his girlfriend?

She seats us outside, our table giving us an unobstructed view of the beautiful skyline. It's stunning, but it pales in comparison to the view from Grayson's living room. When I glance back at him, he's already looking at me. His gaze makes my heart skip a beat. I've known Gray for years, yet it feels like I'm only just getting to know him.

He barely takes his eyes off me as he places his order, and he's got me feeling flustered. This feels a lot like a date, even though I know it isn't.

I'm distracted as I order a cocktail, my eyes lingering on Grayson's T-shirt. He really does look good in it, and I can't help but remember what he looks like without it. Those well-defined abs, his arms. I swallow hard and bite down on my lip. The way his body felt underneath mine, so strong and big. My mind fills with images of him on top of me, sinking deep inside me. What would it be like to be with him?

"What?" he says, his eyes twinkling.

I blush, realizing I've been caught staring. I shake my head and smile. "Nothing," I tell him, praying my expression doesn't give me away. "Today was just perfect, that's all."

"I'm glad," he says. "Today is the most fun I've had in a while, too. If not for you, I'd likely have spent all day working."

I look at him with raised brows, a question I don't want to voice coming to mind. Since I'm a sucker for punishment, I decide to ask anyway. "You'd really have worked all day? Surely a man like you has a hot date every week."

"A man like me?"

I nod, my cheeks flaming. "You know... intelligent, hot, CEO of an amazing company."

Besides... he must do. He disappears for a few hours every Sunday. Sometimes he stays away all day, and sometimes he's back within hours. It's obvious he's seeing someone, and the thought of it makes me uncomfortable. I try my hardest to ignore it, but the way I see Gray has started to change. The feelings I have for him... they're far from sisterly.

He grins at me and leans in, his forearms on the table. "Most people just think I'm some sort of nerd. Besides, I really enjoy my alone time. I don't go on dates very often."

I bite down on my lip, instantly feeling bad. "I'm sorry, and thank you for coming out with me today. I'm already asking so much of you by staying at your house, and now I'm taking up your time. I wasn't really thinking."

I shouldn't have asked him to entertain me, when he already does so much for me. I know what it's like to need a bit of time to yourself, just to recharge before you're able to tackle another week filled with socializing. It must be even worse for Gray, since he has so many employees he oversees.

He shakes his head and reaches out for me, his hand settling on top of mine. "Don't be sorry, babe. I had a great time today. I like hanging out with you, Aria. I like having you around. Don't ever think otherwise."

I stare at him, trying to assess his sincerity. I've gotten so comfortable with Gray over the last couple of months that I might be overstepping unknowingly. It doesn't even feel like it's been such a short amount of time. It feels like I've always been with Gray. I've never experienced this with anyone else. I've never felt so comfortable so quickly.

"How have you been enjoying living here? Do you enjoy Cali?"

"It's been great, thanks to you. I'm not sure I could have even gotten through my first few weeks here if you hadn't been there."

Gray's expression falls and he looks away. "Are you still thinking about Brad? He isn't worth your time."

I shake my head and look down. I was heartbroken when I walked into my apartment to find Brad in bed with someone else. I thought I'd never get over it, and while the pain is still there, it isn't tied to him. It's the deception that hurts me, that plagues me. It's the betrayal of trust that broke me.

"No," I tell Gray. "I won't lie to you and tell you it doesn't hurt anymore because it does. But you're right... Brad isn't worth my tears. He's not worth my time. I'm not even sure I loved him, you know? I don't miss him. I'm just hurt he cheated on me. I hate wondering where I went wrong, why I wasn't good enough."

Grayson tenses, and I know he's about to try and reassure me, but I don't want him to. I don't want empty compliments or attempts to make me feel better. "Did you know?" I ask him. "Did you know he wasn't right for me that night you came over for dinner?"

Gray looks away. "I didn't know he was cheating, no. But I did think you could do better. I'll always think that, Aria. In my eyes, no one will ever be good enough for you."

I stare at him with wide eyes, wondering if there is any truthfulness to his words. He can't mean that... can he?

Everything about Grayson confuses me. When I'm around him, I don't feel broken. I feel like he sees the real me, every single part I keep hidden... He sees it all, and he makes me feel like I have nothing to be ashamed of. When I'm around him, my heart isn't hurting.

Ash has that effect on me too, but it's mostly because he doesn't know who I am, because I get to show him the best sides of me. Grayson, on the other hand... he sees *me*, the real me, and he never makes me feel like I'm not enough, or like I'm too much.

He doesn't even realize how much he affects me, and it's best that he doesn't. I don't want to burden him with my fractured soul. It's not his responsibility to put me back together, yet that is exactly what he's doing.

It isn't what he signed up for, though... And I'd better remember that.

Chapter Twenty-Eight

ARIA

I stare at my screen, unable to focus. This rarely happens to me. No matter what's going on in my life, I'm always able to lose myself in my work. But not today. Today all I can think about is Gray.

"So, has he figured it out yet?"

I freeze, my head turning toward Elliot, who is leaning against my desk. I was so deeply lost in thought, I didn't even notice him walking over.

"What?" I ask, a hint of fear making my voice high.

Elliot grins. "Riley. Has he figured out who you are?"

I breathe a sigh of relief and shake my head, my eyes roaming around the room to ensure that this conversation is private.

"No, and he won't."

He chuckles and shakes his head. "You do realize he's spending a few hours a day trying to trace you, don't you?"

I frown. "What? Why?"

Elliot laughs and glances at Riley, drawing his attention. "He's obsessed with you. Both sides of you." My eyes widen, and he smiles at me. "You don't see it, do you?"

"See what?"

Elliot shakes his head. "Never mind. You'll find out."

He leans in, reaching for my keyboard. "Found some security threats in last week's work," he tells me, running me through them.

I bite down on my lip, frustrated. I can't believe I missed that. I've been so distracted this past week, and it's unacceptable. My thoughts have been on last weekend and on Gray, when I should've been focusing on work. This project is too important. I can't let my team down like this.

"Hey," Elliot says. "This is literally my job. I'd hate it if I didn't find anything. It's okay."

I nod and grab my tablet to take notes while Elliot talks me through his concerns and potential fixes. It's going to take me a few hours to resolve this, and it shouldn't have happened in the first place. If I'd just been more focused, I wouldn't have so much work to do now, causing delays.

Elliot looks up at me, a kind smile on his face. "We've been moving so much faster since you joined the team, Aria. You're doing really well. We're back on track to hit our deadline now, and when you joined, we were three months behind. Keep doing what you do. We're lucky to have you."

His words startle me in the best way. I can't believe Elliot Evans just said that to me. I've been admiring his work for years now, and here we are, finally working together in real life.

"I know you've been busy, but did you see the new case that popped up on your platform?"

I frown and shake my head. I haven't even opened the app in two days now. Every time I want to, I'm reminded of Ash. Lately Gray and I have been getting closer, and it's making me feel guilty. Even though I know I'll never be with Gray, I've found myself pulling away from Ash out of guilt.

"Check it out. It's right up your alley. I signed up to join the case, and I reckon you'll want to be involved too."

He winks at me and walks away, and I grab my phone. I check the case logs and indeed, there's a cold rape case. My heart breaks as I read through the files. This woman has been let down by the system repeatedly, and all her hope is officially lost.

I'm not at all surprised when I see Ash has already signed up to work this case, but I'm hit with renewed admiration for him. The number of cases he's contributed to rivals mine. I click on my notifications hesitantly, pulling up my chat with him.

Ash: *Did you see the new case? It's been a while since one as tough as this one popped up. I signed up. You know we make a power couple, Nyx. You should join.*

Ash: *Hey, I haven't heard from you in a while. Is everything okay?*

I can't help but glance at Gray's office. His door is open, and I can see him sitting at his desk, his face hidden behind his screen.

Nyx: *I saw the case. I'll check it out :)*

My phone buzzes, but before I can check my messages, Riley walks up to me.

"Was Elliot just talking trash about me?" he asks, his eyes narrowed, and I frown. I guess curiosity won. I knew he wouldn't let it rest after he saw Elliot laughing and looking at him.

"The world doesn't revolve around you, Riley."

He crosses his arms and grins at me. "Do you want to bet I can rock your world, though?"

I mirror his posture and stare him down. "Do you want to bet I'll report you to HR if you so much as try?"

His smile drops, a hint of frustration in his eyes. "Are you still mad about the way I treated you on your first day here?"

I stare at him, annoyed. I don't get what his deal is. "No, I'm not," I tell him honestly. "I'm just busy. We're on a deadline, Riley."

He looks away, and all of a sudden I'm worried that I was too harsh. I've become quite friendly with both Laura and Elliot, and

I'll often have lunch or coffee with them, but I guess I must've been harboring at least a bit of a grudge because I rarely hang out with Riley.

"I'm sorry," I say, feeling worse by the second. "I was just about to go grab a coffee down the street, actually. Elliot and I took some notes that I need to think through. Would you like to come with me?"

He looks at me in disbelief, and then he smiles. "Huh, so you don't hate me. I have some work to do, so how about we grab lunch together soon? There were some front-end issues I wanted to discuss with you anyway," he says.

I nod. I feel like I'm losing control of everything, like I'm falling behind, like I'm not on top of things as much as I should be. I need to work harder.

I might not be able to control the feelings I'm developing for Gray, but this I can control.

Chapter Twenty-Nine

GRAYSON

Aria has been quiet and distant all week, and I can't quite figure out why. Last weekend was perfect, but she's barely spoken to me since. She's been hyper-focused on work lately, and I can't even fault her for it.

I thought we were making progress, though, I thought she was feeling what I was feeling. The way she was looking at me as she was sipping her drink... I thought she wanted me, that things were starting to shift between us.

I sit down on my sofa and stare out the window. I've always loved my space, so this house has never felt lonely, but tonight it does.

I've come to expect hanging out with Aria, watching TV together, eating together. They're all mundane things, but they're the best part of my day, and I didn't even realize it until Aria started to hide in her room.

It's not just me she's hiding from, though. It's Ash, too. Her responses are short, and I can't tell what's wrong. Last weekend

changed things for me, but they seem to have changed for her too
— in the opposite direction. She seems further away than ever.

I don't want to intrude either, especially because she seems
okay at work. She's been working hard, and I've seen her smiling
at Riley multiple times. Just today he asked her out at least half a
dozen times, but she doesn't even seem to realize it. Just before
she left the office, he asked her if she wanted to join him for a
drink. I saw her hesitate, as though she considered saying yes. The
mere idea of her with Riley annoys me.

I grab my phone and open the Nemesis app. My finger hovers
over the instant messaging function and I hesitate for a split
second before deciding to text her.

Ash: *You're being quiet lately. What's up?*

Her replies have been late recently, even when I know she's
got her phone on her. I'm not sure what's going on, but something is up.

Nyx: *I just have some stuff on my mind, that's all.*

Ash: *Will you tell me? I'm a pretty good listener, if I do say so
myself.*

She goes quiet for a couple of minutes, and I wonder if I've
lost her attention. Just as I've decided that she's put her phone
away already, she texts back.

Nyx: *It's nothing, but I did find you a funny pun.*

I purse my lips and look out the window, wondering why
she's being so off with me.

Ash: *Oh no. tell me.*

Nyx: *What does a whale say when he's confused? I'll tell you.
Could you please be more Pacific? Lol.*

I stare at my phone and shake my head. Her puns are awful.
Truly awful. But I bet she's sitting in bed, grinning like a fool.

Ash: *I don't know what to say, other than that I'm o-fish-ally
enchanted with you.*

She goes silent, as she has been doing all week. She's been
friendly, but she doesn't respond to any of my flirty lines, and I
can't tell what happened. Did I do something?

A pang of disappointment runs through me as I walk to my bedroom. My thoughts are all over the place as I underdress for bed. I miss her. I miss hanging out with her, I miss the way she makes me feel like I'm the only one that truly knows her, the only one she confides in.

I miss the little touches. Throwing my arm around her on the sofa, holding her hand in mine whenever I think I can get away with it. I miss that. She's right here, but it feels like I haven't seen her in ages.

I run a hand through my hair, frustrated. I'm driving myself crazy. This is all fucking insane. I can't have her either way, so what does it all matter?

I twist and turn in bed, forcing myself to think of anything but her, when a bloodcurdling scream snaps me out of my thoughts.

I sit up, instantly panicked. It takes me half a second to realize it's Aria, and another ten seconds to reach her room. My heart is pounding as I push her bedroom door open.

I find her lying in her bed, fast asleep, tears running down her face. "No," she whispers repeatedly, her tone pleading. She thrashes in her sleep, trapped by her bed covers.

"Aria," I say, leaning on her bed with my knee. I call for her repeatedly, but it doesn't wake her. Instead, she claws at her sheets desperately.

I grab her sheets and pull them out of her grasp, but it doesn't even remotely calm her. I've never seen her like this. I don't know what to do. I sit down on her bed and place my hands on her shoulders, shaking her gently but firmly. It doesn't wake her. She's so deeply lost in her nightmare I can't pull her out.

I lie down on the bed and pull her into my arms, holding her close to stop her from hurting herself. She kicks at me, and I hold her tighter, my hand tangling in her hair. I feel her tears against my chest, and it kills me.

"Mom," she whispers, and I swallow hard. My heart fills with sorrow as her movements calm a little. I don't know what she's seeing in her dreams, but I know it must be tearing her apart.

Aria wraps her arms around me, and I wonder if she's hugging her mother in her dreams. Is she experiencing losing her Mom all over again?

"I've got you, babe," I whisper, my hand running over her hair soothingly. "You're safe with me, Ari. You'll always be safe in my arms."

She inhales shakily, her body relaxing in my arms. She's so small, yet she fits into me perfectly. I rest my chin on top of her head, her lips pressed against my throat. Her breathing evens out, and I exhale in relief.

"Grayson," she breathes.

I tense. I thought she'd fallen back asleep, but I must've woken her up somehow. Aria tightens her grip on me, hugging me tightly.

"Thank you."

"Anytime, sweetheart. I'll hold you and keep your nightmares at bay, okay?"

She nods, her nose brushing against my neck. I hold her like that until she falls back asleep, my heart breaking for her.

Chapter Thirty

Aria

My mind keeps replaying this morning's scene. I woke up in Grayson's arms, our legs tangled together, his erection pressing against my thigh. I swallow hard, unable to forget the feel of him. I should've known that he'd be big, considering how tall and wide he is... but I wasn't expecting *that*.

I was so startled that I didn't dwell on my recurring nightmare the way I usually would've done. Normally it would've ruined my entire day, but today I'm distracted. Today the nightmare is in competition with thoughts of Gray. I've been trying to stay away from him, reminding myself who he is... but these little things he does make it impossible. It's impossible to resist him.

The way he held me, never once questioning me. The way he whispered my name, telling me I'm safe in his arms. No one has ever been able to pull me out of that nightmare. Not until Gray.

It always goes the same way, a perfect replica of the day I lost my parents. I'm on my way home, excited to tell Mom that I aced my English test. When I get there, the front door is open. I walk in, and the house is eerily silent. My heart starts to race, a small part of me aware that something must be wrong. Just when I've gathered the courage to call for my parents, I see them. Both of them on the ground, a metallic smell filling the air. Dad's arm is wrapped around Mom, but his eyes are on the ceiling. It takes me a while to register that he isn't blinking.

I kneel beside Mom and her eyes find mine, her hands covering her stomach as redness pools onto the floor beside her.

"Aria," Mom whispers.

"No," I murmur, repeating it over and over again, panic and disbelief rendering me immobile. Even though I can't make sense of what's happening, I know I'm losing my mother. I start to cry, and Mom shakes her head.

"I love you," she whispers, her eyes falling closed. I grab her hand and hold it tightly, my eyes roaming over the room. I spot the house phone and jump up, rushing to grab it. I press the buttons with shaking fingers, and just as I lift it to my ear, I see him.

Black clothes, bright blue eyes, and hands stained with blood. He freezes and I drop the phone, my every instinct telling me to run.

He takes a step toward me, and my cries turn into sobs. I take a step back, my back hitting the wall, and that's where both my dreams and memories end. The last thing I remember before everything went black was him turning his back to me as he walked away, leaving my life in pieces.

"Aria?"

I look up to find Riley standing by my desk. His expression tells me he must've been standing here for a while now, and I immediately feel guilty.

"I'm sorry," I tell him, but he shakes his head.

"Are you okay?"

"Yes, of course," I say, my tone defensive. Riley smiles at me, but I see the worry in his eyes, and I hate that. I've worked so hard to leave my past behind me, yet every time I have one of these nightmares it feels like I'm still that little girl, helpless and alone.

"Would you like to join me for lunch?" he asks, glancing around uncomfortably. I pause, my eyes roaming over the empty office. I didn't even realize everyone had left. How long has Riley been standing here?

"I... um." I don't know what to say. I feel like Riley has disliked me from the second we met, and it's making me uncomfortable that he's trying so hard to hide it just because he's my manager. "Sure."

He tips his head toward the door, and I grab my purse to follow him. The silence between us is awkward, and I'm not sure how to deal with it. I'm surprised when he leads me out of the building and not to the company cafeteria.

"Where are we going?"

Riley smiles at me. "You'll see."

I hate surprises, but I have a feeling that telling him that would just result in more tension between us.

He leads me into what appears to be a huge garden, with a dozen picnic tables spread around. "Wow," I whisper, following him to one of the tables. "This place is incredible."

Riley grins in satisfaction as we sit down. "I'm sorry," he says. "The way I acted on your first day of work was unacceptable. We've not really gotten along ever since, and it's all my fault. Honestly, I'm surprised Gray let me get away with it at all. I guess he knew you'd be able to meet any challenge I could set, and you've really proven yourself over the last couple of months."

He looks away, glancing at the menu instead. "You were right. You're untraceable. I've been trying to track every single digital footprint of yours for weeks now, and I can only find the most mundane things. There's not even any porn, and we all watch porn."

I chuckle, caught by surprise. Riley grins, but there's something more than humor in his eyes.

"Your record is too clean, Aria. The information about you is too carefully controlled, and that's what gives you away."

I grin. "Does it? You still know absolutely nothing about me."

Riley smiles as he places his order and waits for me to place mine. He rests his elbows on the table the second the waitress walks away.

"No, but I'll find out. I have a feeling you're hiding more than tentacle porn, and I'll find out what it is."

I burst out laughing. "Tentacle porn?"

Riley nods, dead serious. "You seem the type. Quiet, beautiful, smart. You're definitely watching some fucked up porn."

My smile drops, and I look away. Not because of his porn comment, but because he called me beautiful. Is he trying to flatter me or is this one of those things you say when you feel bad? I don't get it, but it reminds me of Brad. This is how it all started with him. He'd take me out for lunch, and he'd say stuff that made me think he was flirting with me, when all along he just wanted to use me.

I look into Riley's eyes, distrust making me sit up straight. "Tell me honestly, Riley... what is it you want from me?" I ask, unable to help myself. I can't go down this road again. I can't let myself believe someone is being friendly when they have ulterior motives. I can't figure out what he wants, but it's something.

Riley looks startled and shakes his head. "I'm sorry, Aria. It was just a joke, the porn thing."

I look into his eyes, trying to assess his sincerity, knowing that I'm not capable of doing that. Brad lied straight to my face for months, and I never realized it.

"So why did you ask me out for lunch? It just... it seems strange to me."

Riley frowns. "Why is it strange? I genuinely wanted to get to know you better. You're intriguing, Aria. I've never met anyone that continues to show me up the way you do. You're brilliant, and I'm just a little curious about you, I guess?"

I hate that I distrust him without good reason. He's done

nothing to warrant it, yet I can't shake the feeling that he wants something from me. I don't want to be this person. I don't want to second guess everyone and everything around me, but I can't help it. I can't help but think that in part, I was to blame for the way I was deceived. This time, I have to ensure I keep my eyes wide open.

Chapter Thirty-One

ARIA

I'm exhausted by the time I walk into Gray's apartment. I haven't seen him all day, and part of me is relieved. I managed to slip out of bed before he woke up, avoiding awkwardness between us. He was gone by the time I walked out of the shower, and I'm scared to face him. I'm scared he'll have questions I can't answer. Besides, things have been awkward between us ever since we went out for drinks.

I've been feeling conflicted. I'm falling for Grayson, and there's nothing I can do about it. I can't stop it. Every day, my feelings grow. It was easy to ignore at the start, but now? Impossible.

I'm startled when I find him standing in the kitchen, staring at a box of eggs. He looks up at me and the helplessness in his eyes guts me.

"What's wrong, Gray?"

He walks up to me and grabs my hand, pulling me toward the kitchen counter. Before I realize what's happening, he's got his hands wrapped around my waist and he's lifting me on top of the counter.

"Tell me how you do it," he says. "How do you make your scrambled eggs so magical? I've made them hundreds of times, Ari. But they never taste like yours."

I chuckle and shake my head. "That's what's got you so worried?"

He stares at me, expecting an answer, and I can't help but laugh. "It's a mixture of green chili, ginger and garlic, Gray."

He looks outraged, and my heart flutters ever so slightly. He's adorable.

"It's that simple?"

I nod, and he stalks toward the fridge, in search of green chili, I assume. He returns with the ingredients, looking triumphant, and I just about manage to suppress a giggle.

"So, I guess we're having scrambled eggs for dinner?"

Gray pauses and looks up at me. "I'm sorry," he says. "I should've asked what you wanted. I just... I don't know. Usually when I have a rough day, scrambled eggs make it better. It's stupid, now that I'm saying it out loud. I just wanted to do something nice for you, I guess."

I look at him with wide eyes. "This is for me?"

He walks up to me and places his arms on either side of me, leaning in. "Yes."

I wrap my arms around his shoulders instinctively and hug him. I must have startled him because it takes him a couple of seconds to hug me back, but when he does, he holds me tightly. I've been trying my hardest to stay away, to remind myself that he's Noah's best friend, but it's too hard. Staying away from him is too hard.

"I'd ask you if you were okay, but I know you'll just lie to me," he murmurs.

I smile and rest my head on his shoulder. "I'm sorry," I tell him. "I didn't mean to wake you, but I'm so grateful you were there last night."

Gray buries his hand into my hair and sighs. "Sweetheart, there's nowhere I'd rather have been last night."

He pulls away to look at me, his hand still tangled in my hair. "Would it help you if I sleep with you?"

My heart skips a beat and I feel heat spread across my cheeks, even though I know he doesn't mean it that way. He notices my blush and smirks.

"I mean... I can do that too, if you want. Might help you sleep," he says, teasing me. My mind can't help but go there. He felt so hard and big against me this morning, and I can't help but wonder what he'd feel like inside me. I push the thought away, annoyed with myself for even thinking it. This. This is why I'm staying away from Gray. Because I find myself wanting more of him than he'll ever give me. I look away and bite down on my lip.

"All jokes aside," he says. "I'd be happy to. You seemed to calm down in my arms. If you think it'll help, I'd be happy to."

I look into his eyes, wondering if he's just saying that because he thinks it's the right thing to say, but I can't find a trace of insincerity in his eyes.

"You don't think it'd be weird?"

Gray lifts his free hand to my face and brushes my hair behind my ear. "I don't think so. It wasn't weird last night, was it?"

I shake my head.

"Then it's done."

He takes a step away and starts to chop the chilis and garlic while I try my hardest to still my racing heart. He's truly certain that spending the night with me wouldn't affect him in any way, isn't he?

I push down the unwarranted resentment I feel. I'm being ungrateful, and I can barely make sense of my feelings. Gray has always treated me like family, and I've never had an issue with that. I shouldn't want anything else from him.

"So I noticed you went out for lunch with Riley?"

I look up at him, startled.

"The two of you walked into the office together, looking awfully chummy."

"Chummy?" I repeat. That's not quite how I'd put it. It was awkward at best. I'm still embarrassed about the way I acted during lunch. I should've hidden my concerns and suspicions better. For all I know, he was just trying to be friendly.

"He's a nice guy. Clever, too."

"He thinks I watch tentacle porn," I blurt out.

Gray freezes, spatula in hand. "He what?"

I laugh and try my best to explain the story, expecting Gray to find it funny. Instead, his expression becomes entirely unreadable.

"Oh, so you two were flirting, huh?" he says, his tone... *off*. "That's nice."

I blink, confused. "What? No. Not at all. I think he was just joking because he can't seem to find much dirt on me."

Gray turns the stove off and empties the contents of the pan onto a plate without much care. He stares at the plate and then pushes it toward me.

"I'm not hungry," he says. "You have this."

He turns and walks away, leaving me sitting on top of the counter, confused as to what just happened.

I eat my eggs in silence, replaying our conversation in my mind, wondering what I might have said to annoy him. I'm worried that he thinks I'm not taking my job seriously. I don't want him to think I'm going around flirting or anything like that.

I'm still thinking about it when I get into bed later that night. Gray disappeared after making me eggs, and I'm not sure what to think of it. He seemed angry, or maybe disappointed is a better way to explain the look in his eyes.

I shake my head and reach for my phone, trying my hardest to stop thinking about him. I absentmindedly scroll through the notifications on the Nemesis Platform, freezing when I realize what I'm reading.

It's the historical information I requested on Peter Simmons. I scroll through it, my heart squeezing painfully.

He was laid off a few months before the robbery, and two weeks before that fatal day, his house was repossessed. I scroll through all the transactions, the mounting debt, the eventual homelessness. The payments he kept up with the longest were the ones related to his daughter. School fees, piano lessons, tutors.

I read through all the data, slowly connecting the dots. His daughter attended the same school as me. Is that why we were the target?

I still remember his eyes when he saw me standing in the living room. He looked as scared as I was, and at the time I couldn't understand why he had stacks of my clothes in his hands. But it's starting to make sense now. His daughter is the same age as me. Is that why he was robbing us? Did he need something for her?

I inhale shakily as I read through the countless messages he's tried to send her; all of them ignored. I've spent years hating this man for taking my parents from me, but it's starting to look like Noah and I aren't the only ones whose lives were destroyed.

Peter's regret is in everything he does. It's in the anti-gun violence charity donations, the unanswered messages to his daughter, the mundane notes his parole officer is taking.

He's out of jail, but he continues to pay for his crimes. Every unanswered message and every donation he makes will always remind him of what he took from me.

I've been receiving notifications for months now, and never once has he done anything to indicate he might turn to crime again. If anything, his actions betray his regret.

A tear rolls down my cheek and my hands tremble as I will myself to do the right thing.

That has to be enough. It has to be. I can't lose sight of who I am. I can't continue to abuse my own platform. He's paid his dues, and I... I'll need to accept that.

I have to let this go. I have to finally give my heart a chance to heal. I hesitate and inhale deeply, my finger hovering over the removal button.

I gather my courage and click it, removing Peter Simmons from the Nemesis Watchlist. Months. I kept him on there for months, and there isn't even a hint of a crime. I need to stop. I have to.

I sniff loudly as I put my phone away, a sense of loss overcoming me. I've spent so long hating him. Some days it's all that kept me sane. And now? Now all I'm left with is sorrow.

I curl into a ball, a sob tearing through my throat. Memories of my parents assail me, and hot tears start to stream down my face.

Devastation unlike anything I've ever felt before fills me, and I give in to it, I let it consume me, allowing myself to cry the way I should have done back then.

I tense when strong arms wrap around me and turn in his embrace. "Grayson," I whisper, choking on my sobs.

He holds me tightly, one hand in my hair, the other wrapped around my waist. He doesn't say a word — he just holds me the way I need him to.

Chapter Thirty-Two

GRAYSON

I hesitate in front of Aria's bedroom door, still battling my annoyance. I said I'd sleep with her tonight to help keep her nightmares at bay, but I can't stop thinking about her with Riley.

She denies flirting with him, but what she told me definitely was *something*. That was more than just friendliness. Riley has been hitting on her for months now, and she can't be so clueless that she doesn't realize it.

I drop my forehead to her door, tensing when I hear a muffled sound. Is she *crying*?

I walk into her bedroom, finding her curled up in bed. I'm hesitant as I walk up to her. She doesn't even notice me, she's that lost in her pain.

I slip into bed, wrapping my arms around her and pulling her close. Aria tenses and turns in my embrace, pressing her face against my neck.

"Grayson," she whispers, her voice laced with heartache. I thread my fingers through her hair, my free hand running over her back, consoling her as best as I can.

It fucking kills me to see her cry like this and having no idea what happened.

Aria stills in my arms when her tears dry up, her lips pressed against my throat. "What happened?" I ask, my voice soft.

She shakes her head and tightens her grip on me. "Memories of Mom and Dad," she murmurs. "I'm fine most of the time, but some days are tougher than others."

I nod and press a kiss on top of her head. There's nothing I can do or say that'll take away that pain, so I just hold her, praying it's enough.

"What are you doing here?" she whispers.

"I told you I'd sleep with you. Do you still want me to?"

Aria nods and snuggles in closer. I'm glad I get to hold her tonight. I might not be able to mend her heart, but I can hold her as she falls apart. I can catch the broken pieces of her heart.

"I don't know if this will help, Ari. But know that I'm here, okay? No matter what you see when you close your eyes, know that I'm here."

I roll onto my back, taking her with me so she ends up lying half on top of me, her head on my chest. She's quiet as she lies in my arms, her breathing uneven. My eyes flutter closed as the minutes pass, but Aria is restless.

"Tell me something about you that no one knows," she whispers. "I can't keep my thoughts from going to that day, and I don't want to think about it, Gray. Distract me."

I'm a fucking asshole because my dick hardens at those words. My thoughts immediately turn to all the ways I'd love to distract her, and I grit my teeth.

I twist a little in bed, trying to hide how she turns me on and feeling fucking awful about it. Aria tightens her grip on me and her lips brush against my throat. My cock fucking jerks, and I bite down on my lip.

"I used to cage fight. I still do boxing matches every once in a while. That's why I have a fully equipped gym with a ring set up upstairs."

"Cage fight? What? Why did you used to cage fight? This is the first I'm hearing of it."

I tighten my grip on her hair and inhale deeply. "When I told you I grew up in a rough environment, what I meant is that I grew up in the system, Ari. Always moving from one house to another. Most foster parents are in it for the money they get from the government, and honestly? They didn't treat us that well. They're all good at passing all the checks, and no one really listens to the problem kids. At most, we get moved to a different house if we complain, but the kids that are forced to stay? They become victims. Sometimes it's emotional abuse, but sometimes it's physical. I learned how to fight to protect myself and others."

Aria falls silent, and I worry I said too much. The violence in those homes, the crimes I committed ... Aria doesn't need to know about that. That part of my past needs to stay where it is.

"Your turn."

She snuggles closer to me, her lips right below my ear. "I decided to study software engineering because I've always looked up to you. I didn't know about your past, Gray. I only knew that you didn't have a family, but I selfishly never stopped to think about why or how. Regardless of your childhood, you grew up to become my role model. You still are."

I turn us over onto our sides, in part because her leg keeps edging closer to my cock, but more so because I want to look at her. She looks flustered, her cheeks rosy, and she's never looked more beautiful. I lean in and press a lingering kiss to her forehead, wishing I could take more, wishing I could take her lips.

"You're better than I am, Aria. You're a better person, you're stronger, you're smarter. Don't look up to me. Look in the mirror."

My words render her speechless, and she looks away, the edges of her lips tipping up into a smile. She buries her face in my neck to hide her flaming cheeks, and my heart skips a beat. I chuckle and tighten my grip on her.

I'm done for. The way she makes me feel... yeah. There's no point in fooling myself any longer.

I'm falling for my best friend's little sister.

Chapter Thirty-Three

GRAYSON

I wake up with Aria pressed against me, my cock throbbing. Fuck. This woman... she has no idea what she does to me, draping herself all over me like that. She's got her leg hooked around my hip and her breasts pressing against my side. Just a little higher, and her thigh would be pushing up against my dick. How would she respond if she knew how hard she constantly makes me? She doesn't seem to have a clue how beautiful she is, how the men around her respond to her. Part of me wants to roll her over and show her how she makes me feel, just to see her lips fall open and her cheeks redden.

Aria shifts in my arms, pulling herself closer, and I swallow hard. She fits into me perfectly, and all I want to do is hold her tighter. She sighs, still fast asleep, her lips settling against my neck. She kisses me, and I bury my hand in her hair, holding onto my sanity as best as I can.

A soft moan escapes her lips, and I tighten my grip. What is she dreaming of? The thought of her thinking of anyone but me has me seeing red. What if she's fucking dreaming of Brad while she has her body pressed against mine?

She groans and hooks her leg up higher, moving more of her body on top of me, until my dick is nestled right between her legs. My eyes fall closed as I pray for patience. I'm not even religious, but she's got me praying. When she moves her body against mine, grinding up on me, I abandon the idea of praying and start reciting the digits of Pi instead. It doesn't stop my cock from throbbing, and it doesn't keep the thoughts of what I want to do to her at bay at all. I should've known Pi isn't powerful enough when it comes to Aria.

She sighs and drags her nose across my throat before pressing a lingering kiss to my skin. I swallow hard. Fucking hell. Useless fucking Pi. All I can think about is how it's going to feel when I sink my cock deep inside her. Aria is a fucking spitfire, and I just know she'd be soaking wet, her pussy squeezing me tightly.

Damn. The thought of her face, her expression, the look in her eyes. I bite down on my lip and throw my arm over my face. It's taking all of me not to push my hips against her, to move so my cock glides against her the way I want it to. I need her to wake up soon, because I'm pretty sure I'll actually go insane if she keeps moving against me the way she does, her lips teasing me as much as the rest of her body does.

She whimpers, and her hand finds its way underneath the T-shirt I'm wearing. Her fingertips graze my abs, and I tense underneath her touch. "Gray," she whispers, and I tighten my grip on her hair. Fucking hell. She's dreaming of *me*.

She whimpers again, her body tensing on top of mine, and I realize I must've held onto her hair too tightly and woken her up. Fuck. She lies on top of me, completely still, probably trying to assess whether I'm awake or not.

"Dreaming of me, baby?" I say, my voice sleepy and husky.

Aria groans and buries her face deeper into my neck. I can't help but chuckle and pull her closer, one arm around her waist and the other still buried in her hair.

"When I said I'd sleep with you, this isn't quite what I expected... I'm pleasantly surprised."

She squeaks — there's no other way to describe the sound she makes, and I chuckle, wanting to tease her the way she just teased me. "Tell me, baby... what did I do to you in your dreams? Did I kiss your neck the way you just kissed mine? Or did I do more than that? Did I get to have those sexy lips of yours? Maybe I pushed my cock deep inside you... tell me, were you hungry for me in your dreams?"

"Gray," she whispers, her tone needy. She squirms against me, pushing her thighs together. But that just makes my dick nestle deeper against her.

"Aria," I groan, struggling to make her name sound like the warning it's meant to be.

"I'm so embarrassed," she murmurs, her lips moving against my ear with every word. I'm so fucking hard, and all I want to know is if she's wet for me. I want my fingers between her legs, my name on her lips. I want her to look at me as I make her come.

"Don't be," I tell her. "I'm enjoying this... it seems like you are too, considering you're still lying on top of me, my cock nestled between your legs."

Aria gasps. "Gray!" she whisper-shouts, admonishing me. She pushes away from me, and I finally catch sight of her face. She's beet red, and she looks fucking stunning. She avoids my gaze as she jumps out of bed and makes a run for her bathroom. So fucking cute.

I'm tempted to stay in her bed and wait for her to come back out, but I won't do that to her. I love teasing her, but I don't want to embarrass her.

I grin as I get out of Aria's bed, my dick still painfully hard. Fucking hell... I haven't even had her naked and this is probably the most turned on I've ever been. I'm going to need to take care of this because there's no way that's going down. Not after the way she just touched me.

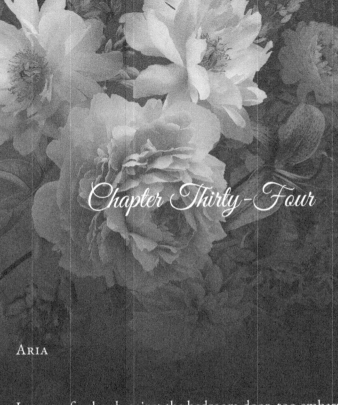

Chapter Thirty-Four

ARIA

I rest my forehead against the bedroom door, too embarrassed to leave. I know I'll have to face Gray at some point... but I'd like to avoid it for as long as possible if I can. My stomach doesn't agree, though. I'm starving.

I jump at the sound of knocking on my door, and my already flaming cheeks get even hotter when I hear Gray laughing on the other side. He has this effect on me. I was heartbroken last night, but waking up in his arms made that pain lose its grip.

"Ari... you can't hide forever. You're hungry, aren't you? I have croissants and I even bought you that sugary coffee crap you like but can't ever finish."

I perk up, intrigued. "A caramel macchiato?"

"Yup."

I place my hand on the door, hesitating before I pull it open. I find Grayson standing in front of me, wearing nothing but workout shorts. My eyes roam over his chest and down... and *down*. I can't believe I climbed on top of him last night. I'm so embarrassed. If Gray knew what I'd been dreaming about, he'd never look at me the same.

"Up," he says, and I blink in confusion. "My eyes are up here, babe. You keep staring at my dick like that and I'll give you something to look at."

Oh God. I try to push my door closed so I can hide, but Gray isn't having it. He leans in and picks me up, throwing me over his shoulder as he carries me to the kitchen. "Gray!"

"Nope," he says. "You're eating."

I glare at him when he puts me down by the dining table, but he ignores me and sits down opposite me, his torso on display. I take a bite of the croissant, but I can barely take my eyes off him. "Boxing training?" I ask, knowing full well that's what he does every Saturday morning.

"Yeah," he says, grinning at me. "Somehow, I'm feeling a little frustrated this morning, unsatisfied, if you will. I've got some extra energy to expend."

I'm sure my face has been bright red all morning, but if it wasn't, it is now. "Gray, I'm so sorry," I tell him. "You were trying to keep my nightmares at bay, but I ended up becoming one for you. I didn't mean to make you uncomfortable. I truly am sorry."

He frowns at me, his gaze searching. "Aria," he says, drawing out my name. "I don't know... I'm a little concerned, to be honest."

I gulp, my heart racing. I had this coming. He has every right to berate me.

"Baby, did you not feel how hard my cock was? I don't know, I mean... I'm pretty sure my dick is above average, at least, but if you didn't feel it pressed up against your pussy, then I may just be wrong."

I choke on my croissant and cough, reaching for my coffee. I gulp half of it down before I'm even able to speak again, and all the while Gray looks at me, amused.

"I... I mean... I don't," I stammer.

"You don't what? You don't think my cock is big?"

I look at him wide-eyed and shake my head. "No, it's huge. I mean, no, not huge. Like, not abnormal or anything. It's the biggest I've ever felt, but like not in a strange way? It's perfect, actually."

I clamp my lips together and hang my head in shame. What did I just say? What is wrong with me?

Grayson bursts into laughter, and my eyes fall closed. Oh God. What have I done?

"It's perfect, huh? But how do you know, Ari? You haven't seen it yet. You haven't felt it inside you yet."

I can't even look him in the eye. I truly wish the ground would just swallow me whole. It'd be best for everyone involved.

Gray chuckles and rises to his feet. "Come on," he tells me. "Since you left me frustrated this morning, you'd better make it up to me with a sparring session."

He pulls me out of my seat before I can object, his hand wrapped around mine. "That's probably not a good idea," I tell him, and he turns back to look at me.

"Why? You don't think you can keep from throwing yourself at me?"

I groan in embarrassment and Gray chuckles as he pulls me along to his rooftop gym that houses his boxing ring.

"I'm in a dress, Gray," I tell him, and his eyes roam over my body, lingering on my chest.

"I know," he says, turning to grab boxing pads. "I'll show you a routine, all right?"

I nod, trying my best not to notice the way his muscles ripple as he moves. For a while, I do just fine. For at least a couple of minutes, I get into it. I manage to do as he says, reciting the sequence in my mind.

Jab. Jab. Right hook.

I recite it over and over again as Gray has me perform the same sequence in rapid succession. But then he drops the pads and smiles at me.

"Okay, come on," he says, tilting his head toward the ring behind us. "Let's spar."

He grabs my hand and pulls me into the cushioned area, a wide smile on his face.

"Try to hit me."

I grin and dive toward him, aiming straight for his face, but he moves out of the way easily and I almost lose my footing. I glare at him and try again, but he keeps evading me with such ease that it angers me.

"Damn it, Gray!"

I look at him through narrowed eyes and try to trick him by moving in one direction and then jumping in the other. I manage to catch him off guard, and he loses his balance. I grin, but my smile is wiped off my face when he takes me with him as he falls back onto the thick cushions. He laughs and turns us over, his body on top of mine.

He looks into my eyes, the smile melting off his face. I feel him harden against me and I gulp. His eyes drop to my lips, and my breathing quickens. He tilts his head ever so slightly, and I lean in just a touch closer.

One taste. That's all I want.

Just as I've decided I want to find out whether he tastes like the peppermint I can smell on him, a song starts to play.

Gray freezes and drops his forehead to mine. "The system is hooked up to my phone. Noah is calling," he tells me, his eyes filled with guilt.

I nod, and he pushes away from me, pulling me up with him. "I, um... I have some work to finish anyway," I say.

I walk away as I hear Gray say "Answer call."

I hear my brother's voice as I slip out of the door, and the guilt I feel nearly wrecks me. Gray is Noah's best friend... he's someone we've both always considered family. What am I doing? What am I even thinking?

Chapter Thirty-Five

ARIA

Gray walks into the kitchen, a smile spreading across his face when he sees the poached eggs I made for breakfast. My eyes roam over his body, taking in the formal suit he's wearing. Every Sunday he dresses up, and I'm pretty sure it's a woman he's meeting, even though he tells me he rarely dates. The care he puts into his appearance on Sundays... it's not at all the same as during weekdays.

"Morning," he says, and I smile at him, a little flustered. I've avoided him after yesterday's boxing session, and thankfully, he's let me.

"Nightmares?" he asks, and I blush involuntarily. I couldn't sleep last night, because I kept wondering if he might show up in my room. My mind kept replaying the way he touched me, the way his lips almost touched mine. I don't know how much of my dream was real, but I have a feeling I might have touched him as much as I dreamt I did.

"None." I shake my head as I hand him a fork. "You look

good," I tell him, my eyes roaming over his suit. He glances down at his shirt and smiles.

"Ah... you like me in a suit, huh?"

I blush. I can't help it. "I mean... it's a nice suit. Even if it's on you."

Gray laughs and shakes his head. "I'm wounded."

"You'll get over it."

He looks into my eyes, a sweet smile on his face. "Oh, but babe, what if I don't?" he says, his voice soft. He looks away, shaking his head.

Every once in a while I'm certain Gray is flirting with me... but he can't be, can he? I'm scared I'm misunderstanding him the way I did Brad. I'm starting to want things I shouldn't even be thinking about, and I'm scared I'm reading too much into things. I'm scared of hoping for more.

Gray takes a couple of bites of his food and then pushes the plate away. "I gotta run," he says. "Will you save this for me? I'll eat it later."

I can't help but wonder where he's going, but I know I don't have the right to ask. I'm already intruding on his privacy by being here. I can't question him about his whereabouts. My stomach clenches in what I can only describe as jealousy as dozens of scenarios run through my mind.

"Hot date?" I ask, unable to help myself. I don't know why I do this. Why do I ask questions I don't want to know the answer to? A man like Gray must be dating, even if it's just casually.

He looks at me, an amused glint in his eyes. "If I'm lucky," he tells me, and my heart twists painfully. I look away and wrap my arms around myself, a pang of jealousy tightening my stomach. "Come with me."

I look up at him, my brows raised. "Come with you... on your date? Somehow I don't think your girlfriend is going to appreciate that."

Gray smirks and crosses his arms. "Ari, I'm going to church. Come with me."

I blink in confusion. "You're going to *church*?"

He nods and looks away, a bittersweet smile on his face. "I go every Sunday morning. Where did you think I went every Sunday?"

I never knew that about Gray. I've known him for years, yet somehow I keep learning more about him every day.

"Yes, I'll come with you," I say without thinking. I've not been to church in years, but I can't say no to Gray. I can tell this means something to him, and I'm honored he's including me.

He nods and waits patiently as I rush to get changed. He's standing by the door, his eyes on his phone. When he looks up at me and smiles, my heart skips a beat.

"Let's go," he says, and I nod.

Gray is quiet on the way to church. He seems nervous and I'm curious as to why, but the atmosphere is so tense I don't dare to ask questions.

He parks in front of the church, his eyes on the entrance. I turn to open my door, but Gray grabs my hand. His eyes never leave the church entrance, and his grip is tight. His expression looks more pained by the second. I can't help but worry.

"Gray..."

He looks at me, and the vulnerability in his eyes undoes me.

"Ari," he whispers. "I thought if you're here with me, I might actually be able to go in, but I can't do it."

I entwine our fingers, my thumb circling over his hand as I lean back in my seat, my eyes fixed on him.

Gray looks at me and mirrors my position, the two of us staring at each other. I'm not sure why he doesn't want to go in, but I don't think questioning him is going to help. I think he just needs me to be here for him, and that's exactly what I'll do.

I know all too well what it's like to not want to talk, no matter how badly people want you to. I don't want to put that kind of pressure on Gray.

He brings our joined hands to his lips and presses a kiss to the back of my hand, making my heart skip a beat.

"Thank you," he says. I nod at him, and he turns back toward the church, his gaze searching, his hand still entwined with mine.

He rests our hands in his lap, his grip tight, as though he's holding onto me for strength. It surprises me to see him like this. I've never seen him as anything but strong and powerful, even when he had nothing.

Even back when we'd share meals just to save some money, Gray was my hero. He was the person I wanted to be like, the person I wanted to impress. He's always worked hard, and he's always been serious. He's also always been one of the few people that believed in me. He's always encouraged me to follow my dreams, and to ensure that those dreams are big.

Today I'm seeing a different part of Gray. He's no less powerful, and if anything, the vulnerability he's showing me endears him to me further.

"This is the church my mother left me at."

I tense, a soft gasp escaping my lips.

Gray smiles, but it's bittersweet. "I keep coming here, wondering if I might catch a glimpse of her. I know she probably wouldn't have left me here if this is a church she frequents, but I can't help but hope, you know?"

He turns to look at me, a desperation in his eyes that I'm all too familiar with. "Isn't it pathetic?"

I shake my head and raise a hand to his face, cupping his cheek. "No, Gray," I murmur. "It's anything but that. I'd give the world to see my mother just one more time. Why would it be any different for you?"

He nods and places his hand over mine. "I need to know. I need to know why she left me. If it was because she couldn't afford to keep me, then that's no longer an issue, you know? I have more money than I know what to do with. And maybe, I don't know, maybe she regrets it, but she just can't find me."

I nod, wanting to keep the hope right along with him. "Does the pastor know you come here every week?"

He nods. "I've left him my business card, just in case she ever comes to ask about me."

"Then you've done all you can, Gray. So long as he knows how to reach you if she does walk in one day, then it's okay. It's okay to just sit here in hopes of a glimpse. You don't have to go in if you don't want to. I'll sit here with you every day if you want me to."

Gray turns his head slightly, pressing a kiss to the palm of my hand. "You would, wouldn't you?"

I swallow hard as I attempt to calm my raging heart. "Yeah... for you, I would."

Chapter Thirty-Six

Aria

I pause in front of Gray's bedroom, wanting to knock, yet wanting to give him space at the same time. He took me out for lunch after church, but I could tell his mind was elsewhere. He looked so somber, and nothing I did or said cheered him up.

The thought of him doing this every single week kills me. He's been alone here for years, and I don't even think Noah knows what Gray is going through. I've been here for months, and all this time I didn't know.

I've just about convinced myself to knock when my phone buzzes. I grab it, partially relieved to have an excuse not to go into Gray's room. I don't know what to say to him, and I hate seeing him hurting. Even worse, I know that even if I go in, there's nothing I can do.

I unlock my phone, frowning when I see a notification for the Nemesis App.

Ash: *If I sincerely asked for your help, would you grant it? I think I'm ready to call in my favor.*

I tense, my thoughts whirling. Ash has always been flirty and lighthearted. When it comes to cases, he's serious and hardworking, but he's never once asked for a personal favor, nor has he ever taken credit for the incredible work he's done.

Nyx: *Provided that it's within my power and doesn't go against my morals, yes.*

Ash: *Will you help me find someone?*

I freeze, my eyes widening. My hands tremble as I type my reply, and I almost drop my phone.

Nyx: *Who is it?*

Ash: *My mother. I already have a file on her, so I've got a starting point, but I keep running into dead ends.*

I swallow hard, my heart beating out of my chest as I sink to the floor, my back against Gray's bedroom door.

Ash.

Ash, the guy I've been talking to for years now, the one that continuously teases me and flirts with me...

Could it be?

I don't dare follow my thoughts in the direction they're going. I can't. Ash has been flirting with me for months now. The things he's said... telling me I've made him hard on numerous occasions? I must be misunderstanding something and drawing false conclusions.

I try my hardest to pull myself together. I need to reply. Ash has never asked anything of me, and I can't deny his request now. Especially not when it's one that's so sincere. Besides, I might be wrong. I hope I am.

Nyx: *Send it over, and I'll have a look at what I can do for you. No promises, Ash.*

Ash: *Thank you, Nyx. I'd say I'll thank you in bed, over and over again, but today has been a rough day. Instead, can I thank you with a virtual hug? Just imagine me being the big spoon.*

My eyes fill with tears and I try my best to blink them back. I drop my head to my knees and inhale shakily. My heart is breaking right alongside his, and I don't know what to do. I don't know what to say.

Nyx: *What if I prefer to be the big spoon?*

Ash: *Right about now I'd actually appreciate that. Since I can't have you, I'll settle for your help. I'm sending you the files through the Nemesis secure channel we always use.*

I don't have the patience to wait for the files. Instead, I force myself to get up and into my room, moving almost entirely on autopilot. I turn my laptop on and log onto my platform, feeling sick.

I should've done this weeks ago. Months ago, even. I keep all data on my platform encrypted and I don't have access to users' private data myself, but it isn't hard for me to unravel Ash's details.

My stomach twists violently as more and more information unveils itself, and I burst into tears when I confirm what I already know.

I can't even explain why it saddens me so much, but it does. It feels like Ash instantly became just as out of reach as Gray is.

I need to tell him, and I know that once I do, he'll stop treating me the way he does. He might even pull away altogether out of embarrassment and horror.

I sniff and try my hardest to pull myself together. I'm being ridiculous and selfish. Gray asked for my help, yet here I am, thinking about myself.

I open up his files when they come in, reading through everything carefully, forcing myself to focus on nothing but the information in front of me. My hands are shaking as I reach out to the few connections that I know can help with this. All we need is a small lead, which we might be able to find if we search databases using the data Gray already has as filters. If nothing else, it'll give us a list we can further refine.

I close my laptop the second I've sent out all my requests, as though that makes anything even remotely better. It doesn't undo what I just found out, and it won't prevent what's coming.

I need to tell Gray. I can't mislead him.

I'm trembling as I walk back to his room, my heart beating in my throat. I'm scared of his response. I'm scared whatever is left of my heart will be torn to shreds.

I pause in front of his door. Just thirty minutes ago I was standing here because I wanted to make him feel better, because it's what my heart begged me to do. Now I'm standing here, knowing things will never be the same again.

I knock on his door, my heart heavy. When he calls for me to come in, dread overcomes me. I walk into his room, stopping in my tracks when I realize he's in bed, his bedroom pitch dark.

"Ari," he says, his voice filled with an ache I didn't think him capable of. Grayson is the strongest person I know. He's without a doubt the most powerful man I know.

I walk up to his bed, pausing right next to him. He sits up, the sheets falling to his waist, exposing his bare chest. He reaches for me, and I stumble, falling into his arms. Before I even realize what he's doing, he's got me on my back in his bed, his body on top of mine.

He hides his face against my neck, his weight pressing onto me. "Just a couple of moments, Ari. Please," he whispers, and a delicious thrill runs down my spine.

I wrap my arms around him and let my eyes fall closed. "In the last couple of months you've been my solace, Gray. Now let me be yours."

He presses a lingering kiss against my neck, and I exhale shakily. "You are, babe," he whispers. "You are."

Chapter Thirty-Seven

A R I A

I wake up in Gray's arms, our legs tangled together, my head on his chest. I blink, last night coming back to me. My heart constricts painfully, and I turn in Gray's arms to look at him.

He's still fast asleep, his arms wrapped around me. His lashes flutter ever so slightly, as though he might be dreaming. I'm scared to move, scared that I might wake him. I want to stay the way we are, just a little longer. Moments like these are mine to keep.

I carefully place my hand on his bare chest, wanting to be closer to him than I already am. I can't imagine how bad his heart is aching, how much further it'll break when I tell him what I must.

He's been taking such good care of me. Every single night he checks all the locks with me, and he's taken to putting me to bed, just because he worries about my nightmares.

He's lying right here with me, yet it feels like I've already lost him. I didn't even realize how much he's come to mean to me. When did this happen? When did I stop thinking about Brad? When did Gray start to occupy my thoughts?

It isn't just Gray, either. Ash means more to me than I dare admit. The playfulness between us... it made me feel like a normal person. To Ash I was someone amazing, the founder of a platform he loves, a mysterious woman. I can't ever live up to the image Gray must have of Nyx.

Being Nyx allows me to be everything I'm not in real life. I get to be strong, fearless, mysterious, and even, admittedly, intelligent. That's not an image I can uphold in front of Gray, who's seen me get cheated on and struggling to find an entry-level job.

My heart twists painfully as I imagine the disappointment I'll find in his eyes when I tell him the truth, but it doesn't compare to the pain I feel at the thought of losing both Ash and Gray.

He tenses underneath me, and his grip on me tightens. "Aria," he whispers, still half asleep. He pulls me closer, and my heart skips a beat. There's something so sexy about him whispering my name like that.

His hands run over my body, one hand settling on my ass while the other wraps around my thigh. He pulls me closer, shifting me on top of him so that my leg is hooked around his hip.

I suppress a moan when I feel how hard he is underneath me. He pushes his hips up slightly, moving against me in the best way, and a small whimper escapes my lips.

I try to pull away so I can slip out of his bed, but his grip on me tightens. He tenses, his lashes fluttering. "Don't go, babe," he murmurs, his voice groggy. "Let me hold you, just like this."

I relax into his arms even as my heart rate skyrockets. He must still be half asleep, but I don't care. I'm knowingly fooling myself, but I don't care. All I care about is that Gray *wants* me in his arms, and while I still can, I'm going to relish in this moment.

I hook my leg up higher, wanting him even closer, and he moans. He grabs my waist and turns us both over. I swallow hard when his eyes find mine. I expected to find grogginess, and maybe even confusion, but what I'm seeing is pure lust.

He lowers his face to mine, and for a second I think he might kiss me, but then he turns his face to the side, his lips brushing against my neck. He leans in further, pressing a kiss to my throat, and a soft moan escapes my lips.

I want him closer. I want my hands in his hair and his lips on mine. But before I can do something we'd both regret, he pushes away from me. He rolls onto his back and stares up at the ceiling for a second before rising from his bed. I swallow hard at the sight of his clearly outlined erection. Feeling it was one thing, but seeing it is something else entirely. He's *big*.

Gray walks to his bathroom, and I sit up, flustered. He pauses in the middle of the room, turning just enough to look at me. The way he smiles puts me at ease, and I relax back into his pillows.

"How about I make you omelets for breakfast?" he asks, grinning. "I've been perfecting my recipe for a while now."

I nod, unable to keep the smile off my face. This happiness... I'll hold on to it just a little longer. Just a few more days. I want a few more days of Gray looking at me like that; his eyes filled with affection.

I don't know how he'll respond if he finds out who I am, and for now, I don't even want to think about it. Besides, he's got more than enough going on already. A few more days... that's all I'll take.

Chapter Thirty-Eight

GRAY

I lean back against the wall, out of sight. Riley has been chatting up Aria for a while now, and whatever it is he's asking of her, she seems to be agreeing.

Riley is grinning when Aria rises to her feet, and I tense when she grabs her handbag.

"Where are you going?"

She tenses when she hears my voice behind her. Her eyes roam over my body, taking in the suit I'm wearing today. That look in her eyes... the attraction, it sets me at ease.

"Grabbing coffee," Riley says.

I look at Aria, trying to read her. Is she going on a fucking coffee date with Riley? "Great," I murmur. "I can do with one."

She looks startled, and I wonder if she actually wanted to go out with him. She looks beautiful today in that summer dress, and I wonder if she wore it for Riley. Am I interrupting something here?

I close the distance between Aria and me, and I breathe a sigh of relief when she smiles.

"Let's go," I say, placing my hand on her lower back.

Riley looks annoyed to find his plans disrupted, but I don't give a fuck. I see the way he looks at Aria. Not on my fucking watch.

"Oh boss, we wouldn't want to intrude on your busy schedule," Riley says, and I ignore him.

Instead, I lead Aria out the door, taking in her every move and expression. She seems a little nervous, and I want to know why.

All I've been able to think about all morning is the way we woke up together. The way she pushed her body against mine, the way her curves felt... I was sure she wanted me. Yet here I am, watching her smile at Riley as though he's the only person in the world.

I'm annoyed by the time we reach the quaint little diner she wanted to go to. What the fuck am I even doing here? Aria hasn't spoken a word to me, and it's clear I'm intruding.

"Gray," she says, her eyes finding mine. "Wanna share a caramel macchiato with me? They always make me feel sick, but I really want one."

I smile. I can't help it. It's something so small, yet it makes my damn day. I see the way Riley tenses, and a petty part of me revels in it.

"Sure," I say, reaching for her. I brush a strand of hair out of her face, and the way she smiles at me makes my heart skip a beat.

Riley falls completely silent as we search for a table, and I ignore him as I pull Aria's seat out for her. She sits down next to me, and I wrap my arm around the back of her chair.

Riley clenches his jaw, and I recognize the helplessness in his eyes. I should feel bad, but I don't.

"So, how do you two know each other?" Riley asks. "I knew you personally hired her, but considering how good she is at her job, I figured it couldn't be nepotism. But maybe it was."

Aria tenses, and I tighten my grip on her chair. She looks down at her coffee, trying to hide her expression. But she's an open book to me.

"Does it matter?" I ask. "Why do you care how she came in, so long as she does her job? Come to think of it... didn't she fix the mess you left us with? The months of delay, who fixed that?"

Aria places her hand on my knee and shakes her head. "You're right, Riley. It absolutely was nepotism. Grayson gave me the chance of a lifetime, and I'm grateful for it every day. I'm working as hard as I can, every single day."

He looks away, clearly feeling guilty. I get why he's lashing out, but Aria doesn't. She thinks he's concerned about the quality of her work, this silly girl. She can't see how much her colleagues admire her. How much *I* admire her.

She takes a sip of her coffee, and some of the foam sticks to her lips. I lean in and wipe it away with my thumb before raising it to my lips and sucking it off. Aria's eyes widen, and her cheeks redden beautifully.

All the while, Riley's expression keeps turning darker. I'm not done, though. I see the way he stares at her at work. Aria might be clueless, but I'm not.

"She's an old friend," I say, wrapping my arm around her shoulder. I take her coffee from her and raise it to my lip. I smile as I take a sip from the lipstick-stained cup. "She's also my roommate."

Aria tenses, and so does Riley. "You two... you live together?"

"When Gray offered me a job, I had no place to stay," she says, and it irritates me she's trying to justify why she lives with me. Is she scared Riley will misunderstand?

He glances between the two of us, and I take another leisurely sip of Aria's sugary drink. He's about to speak up when his phone rings. He sighs and shakes his head as he picks up. "It's Elliot," he says.

Aria glances at me while Riley takes the call, and I see the questions in her eyes. I'm struggling to push down my possessiveness today. I don't know what it is, or what changed, but I'm no longer willing to risk letting her slip away. I know Noah would be furious if I make a move on her... but I'll deal with that. I'm done sitting still and watching her slip away.

"I have to head back to the office," Riley says, looking agitated. "Let's catch up soon," he adds, his eyes on Aria.

She turns to me the second he's out of sight, her brows scrunched up in annoyance. "What was that?" I feign ignorance and shrug. "Grayson," she says, her tone putting me on edge.

"What? It's not like you could've kept us living together from him forever. With the way he continuously flirts with you, it was bound to come up."

"He doesn't flirt with me," she says, her eyes wide.

I lean in and cup her cheek, my thumb tracing over her red lips. "Oh yeah? Didn't he take you out for lunch a while ago, just the two of you? Let me guess... he took you somewhere nice and romantic? And what about all the times he hangs out at your desk, pretending to need your help just so he can be near you? You're fucking clueless, Aria. So fucking clueless."

"Clueless?" she repeats, her eyes flashing with anger.

I let go of her and take another sip of her coffee, irritated. "Forget it," I tell her. "Flirt with him all you want. Date him, for all I care. I'll stay out of your business."

"Oh, so you won't care if I take him home one day, then? You won't care if I date him, or if I sleep with him?"

Rage almost consumes me at the mere thought of her with him, but I force myself to stay calm.

"I didn't realize that was on your mind at all," I tell her. "You can do whatever you want, Aria, but don't you even fucking dream of bringing him into my home. I promised Noah I'd take care of you. I'm going to do just that."

She pales and looks away. How did we get into this mess? Why couldn't I just keep my damn mouth shut? Why did I have to crash her coffee date?

"Fine," she says, and I know it isn't fine at all. I might very well have pushed her into his arms when I meant to do the opposite.

She rises from her seat, her eyes flashing with anger. Her movements are rough as she grabs her bag and turns to walk away. I'm tempted to follow her, but I've already done enough damage today.

Chapter Thirty-Nine

ARIA

I'm still angry by the time I sit down at the dining table, my laptop by my side. Usually I'd have waited for Gray so we could have dinner together, but today I don't want to.

I'm strangely upset that he doesn't care if I date Riley. Am I really nothing but a responsibility to him? All this time I thought he'd been enjoying my company, but now I'm wondering if I've been a burden to him all along.

It wouldn't be the first time I misread a situation, after all. The sound of the front door opening startles me and Gray walks in, his eyes settling on me, his expression unreadable.

He walks past me and grabs himself a plate before joining me at the table. "Did you eat?" he asks, his tone rough, and I glare at him.

"I did. Not that it's any of your business. I'm not a child, Gray. When Noah asked you to look after me, he didn't mean literally."

Grayson's expression darkens. "Seems to me like you need a

babysitter. You can't even tell that Riley wants you. Or did you knowingly ask him out for coffee today?"

I grit my teeth, anger making me lose all rationality. "So what if I did, Grayson? What if I just wanted to go on a date? What's wrong with that? It's been months. I was bound to move on someday."

He barks out a laugh, but there's no humor in it. "And you thought you'd move on with Riley? *Riley*? If you're going to spread your legs for someone, then at least choose someone better. You're not exactly picky, though, are you? You're literally going with the first man that showed any interest."

I rise to my feet, my chair clattering to the floor loudly. "What did you just say to me? Are you seriously standing there and acting like I'm some sort of slut?"

Gray pulls his tie off and throws it onto the dining table. "I'm not doing this," he says. "Fuck whoever you want. I don't give a shit."

He walks away, heading straight for the door that leads to the rooftop. I stare after him as he slams the door closed behind him.

What was that? We've never argued before, and this was... bad. It was bad.

I run a hand through my hair and inhale shakily. I'm blinking back tears, all the while angry at myself for it. I shouldn't care this much, yet I do.

I grit my teeth and walk up to the door, following Gray. I'm not surprised to find him standing by his punching bag. He's lost his clothes, standing there in nothing but black boxer shorts, his body on display.

I watch as he swings his fist toward the bag and sends it flying over and over again, the chains rattling. His muscles tense with every punch, and I hate how good he looks. I hate everything about this. I hate how much he wants Nyx. I hate that he acts like I'm a child that he needs to look after, and I despise myself for giving him that impression in the first place.

I walk up to him, and he tenses when he notices me. "Leave," he tells me, and I shake my head.

I place my hands flat against his chest, and he tenses. I glare at him and push against him, my frustration mounting when I fail to move him.

"How fucking dare you," I snap. "How dare you act like I'm seducing Riley?"

Gray smiles humorlessly. "You wanna fight, babe? We'll fight."

He lifts me up and throws me over his shoulder with ease. I thrash against him as he carries me to the boxing ring, throwing me over the ropes. I hit the thick cushions butt first and glare at him as I scramble to my feet.

"You're a fucking hypocrite," I tell him, attempting to throw a punch the way he taught me. I miss, of course. He evades me with ease. "You act like you're a saint, but I see you flirting with Laura. I know she's not the only one either. Who else is there, Gray? How many girls are you leading on? You're a fucking asshole, making people feel special when they're just one of many."

He frowns, and this time when I push against him, he loses his balance. He falls onto his back, but he takes me with him. Before I realize what's going on, he's got us turned over, his body on top of mine, our position the same as it was the last time we were here... when I thought he was going to kiss me.

He grabs my hands and pins them above my head, locking me in. "What the fuck are you talking about?" he snaps. "Laura? What the fuck?"

I glare at him, trying my hardest to hide how badly my heart is aching. "I see you disappearing for lunch with her all the time. Do you think I'm blind? I see her sneaking into your office during office hours. Tell me, Gray. Have you been sleeping with her? Office quickies, maybe?"

He blinks in confusion, and then he smiles. His body relaxes on top of mine, and he shakes his head. "No. I haven't. She's setting up a subdivision of my company, baby. That's all. The only one I've been *sleeping with* is you."

"I know I'm not the only—"

He cuts me off before I can even finish my sentence. His lips come crashing down on mine, and he moans at the same time as I do. He pushes against me, and the way he's hardening so quickly exhilarates me. He deepens the kiss, and I lose myself in him. I've wanted this for longer than I care to admit.

I push against his hands, and he lets go of my wrists just as I tangle my legs with his. I shift in an attempt to get him closer, and he moans.

"Aria," he whispers, his lips dropping to my neck. His teeth graze my skin, and I gasp. Gray chuckles and moves his lips back to mine, kissing me leisurely this time before pulling back. He rests his forehead against mine, his breathing labored.

"It was always you," he tells me. "You're the only one for me."

He looks into my eyes, and the sincerity in them kills me. It kills me, because I know he's lying to me.

He shifts on top of me, his eyes roaming over my face. He smiles at me, and my heart breaks in a way I've never experienced before.

"Am I? Am I the only one for you, Gray?"

He nods and leans in, his lips brushing against mine. "Of course you are, Ari. I've thought of no one but you ever since you walked into the house on Noah's birthday a few months ago. It's you, and no one but you."

He says it with such sincerity that I'm questioning myself, the same way I did with Brad. Grayson leans in and captures my bottom lip between his teeth, sucking on it before kissing me properly, his movements slow, as though he's been imagining kissing me, as though he feels the same way I do.

He moves lower, pressing a kiss to my neck, and I moan when he grazes my skin with his teeth, his movements rough and impatient. I'm about to pull him back to me when his stomach growls loudly.

I burst into laughter, and Gray drops his head to my chest. "Hungry?" I ask.

He nods. "Starving."

He lifts himself off me, looking embarrassed. He extends his hand and I grab it, letting him pull me up.

"Um, Gray," I mutter. "I don't think you should eat the dinner I made."

He looks at me through narrowed eyes, and I smile nervously. "I was mad at you... so I made the food really spicy." I like spicy food, but Gray hates it. "I'll eat the leftovers tomorrow."

He shakes his head and wraps his arm around me. "Let me take you out tonight, then. Let's go out on a date."

I look at him, wide-eyed. "A date?" I repeat, partially in disbelief, even after the way he just kissed me.

He grins and lifts his fingers to his lips. "Wait... did you just want me for my body?"

I can't help the way my cheeks heat, and Gray laughs as he pulls me along.

Chapter Forty

GRAY

Just having her hand in mine has me smiling. Lately I've taken to holding her hand whenever I thought I could get away with it, but this is different. Now I have the right to keep her tiny hand in mine. Now I can rightfully show her off. It's pettiness at its finest, but I don't care. She's finally mine, and I want people to know it.

"Wow," she whispers as I lead her into an Italian restaurant that I knew she'd enjoy. It's filled with rose bushes and ivy on the walls, lending it an atmosphere I thought Aria would love. On top of that, it's open air, with a stunning view. She and I both seem to have a thing for a good view.

"Gray, this is amazing."

I can't keep my eyes off her as we're led to our table. She's still wearing the same dress she wore all day, yet somehow it looks even sexier on her now. I have every intention of respecting her boundaries and going as slow as she'd like us to, but at the same time, I'm also wondering what that dress will look like on my floor.

"You're staring at me," she murmurs, her cheeks rosy, and I smile.

"I can't help it, babe. You're beautiful, and now I no longer need to steal glances. I can just stare at you as much as I want, and I have every intention of making full use of that right."

"What right?" she asks. "Who said you have any rights to me?"

I freeze, my heart rate accelerating as a burst of panic rushes through me. For a split second, I wonder if I misunderstood her. If she thinks this thing between us is just purely physical, if it's anything at all.

But then she smiles.

"Aria," I say, my hand reaching for hers over the table. "My lips were assaulted today. My innocence is forever gone. You must take responsibility for me," I tell her, my tone dead serious.

She bursts into laughter, and it's a beautiful fucking sight. I grab her hand and bring it to my lips, kissing the back of her hand. It's not something I've ever done to any other woman, but Aria has me feeling old-school.

"Your innocence is gone, huh? You're in for a surprise, Gray. You'll be forever tarnished by the time I'm done with you."

My dick hardens at the very thought of what she's insinuating. Every night I've spent with her has been pure torture.

"Is that a promise?" I say, grinning wickedly.

I see the heated look in her eyes, and I love it far too much. I want to see her looking at me that way all the damn time.

I reluctantly let go of Aria when the waitress walks up to us to take our order, and just those few moments of not touching her have me impatient and annoyed.

"So, will you?" I ask as soon as the waitress walks away.

Aria leans on one hand, her elbow on the table. She looks so relaxed, and oh so fucking stunning.

"Will I what?"

"Take responsibility."

She straightens, that dreamy look fading from her eyes, replaced by insecurity. "What are you saying, Gray?" she asks, her voice soft.

"Tell me you're mine, Aria. Tell me that from this day forward, I get to call you mine."

She stares at me, her eyes wide. "Gray," she whispers. "Don't you think we're rushing into things? It was one kiss. I'm worried you aren't thinking clearly. It was just a heat of the moment thing, and that's okay. I don't need you to suddenly... I... I get it."

I sit back in my seat and cross my arms. "I don't think you do," I tell her. "Because that question was really just a formality. You *are* mine, Aria. I'm fine with taking a bit more time to convince you, but that won't change the facts. I'm fucking crazy about you, and I have been for months. Hell... I'm pretty sure I love you."

She looks flustered, and I decide there and then that I love that look on her too. I love catching her off guard.

"Say it," I tell her.

Aria's lips tip up in a smile, and she leans forward, giving me a glimpse down her dress. Is there any part of her that isn't beautiful? I doubt it.

"I'm yours, Gray."

I smile. "Good girl," I murmur.

"But that's a two-way street, Gray," she says, her voice trembling ever so slightly.

"I'm yours, Aria. I think I may well have been yours from the second you first smiled at me. When you welcomed me into your home and showed me what family looks like, what it feels like. Over the years you've stolen more of my heart, until eventually, I had none of it left because it was entirely in your hands."

I entwine our fingers and look away. "Do with it what you will," I tell her. "It is yours to keep."

"I'm worried," she tells me, and I turn to face her. The insecurity in her eyes breaks my heart. It wasn't me who put it there, but I'll be the one to take it away.

"I'm worried that you'll leave me, Gray. That you'll get bored, or that you'll meet someone far better than me. I'm worried that we're risking everything for what might end up being nothing more than a fling."

The desperation in her voice tells me she truly believes this lunacy, and it astounds me. I wish she could see herself through my eyes. She's so perfect for me, it's almost like she was fucking made for me.

"Then we'll take it slow, Aria. Whatever you need, I'll give you. So long as you promise me you're mine, I won't ask more of you."

"What about Noah?" she asks.

I look away, a tinge of worry settling deep within me. "You're worth everything to me, Aria. I have no doubt that Noah will think I'm not good enough for you, and he'd be right... but I'm willing to prove myself. He might be mad at first, but he can't stay mad forever. It might take a few weeks, or it might take months. Either way, I'm not going anywhere, and he'll have to deal with that."

She looks at me as though she wants to believe me, and I hope she does. I don't think she'd ever be able to understand how much I'm willing to give up for her. Noah is the only person I truly consider family, and if it comes down to it... I'd still choose Aria over him. It should scare me how easy that choice is to make, but it doesn't.

Aria and I... we've been years in the making. We just didn't know it.

Chapter Forty-One

ARIA

I giggle when Grayson presses another kiss to my lips. This entire week has been perfect, and getting to touch him like this is a dream come true. We haven't done more than kiss, but even that has been perfect. I thought he'd be impatient with me, or that he'd push for more, but he hasn't. He makes it clear that he wants me, without ever making me feel bad for wanting to take it a little slow.

"We're supposed to be finishing some work," I tell him, and he smiles sheepishly, pulling me down on the sofa with him.

"I can't believe you expect me to work when you're in my arms, Ari. I can't. Do you know how long I've wanted to do this? Every night when you'd watch TV with me, all I could think about was pulling you closer and finding out if your lips are as soft as they look. I have so much lost time to make up for."

He tangles his hand through my hair and pulls me close, his lips hovering over mine. "I used to imagine this," he whispers before kissing me, tilting his head to deepen the kiss.

He pulls me onto his lap, and I moan against his lips. He

keeps one hand in my hair while the other roams over my body, settling on my ass, his grip tight.

I can feel how hard he is, and I love this. I love how blatantly he wants me. His hand slips underneath the oversized T-shirt I'm wearing today, and I tense when his fingers brush the underside of my bra.

I pull away and rest my forehead against his, my hands wrapping around his, keeping them in place. Gray tenses and moves his hands back down. "What's wrong?"

I'm scared all of a sudden. I've seen his body, I know how muscular he is. Gray is smart, he's powerful, and he's the CEO of an astonishing company. I can't even imagine what type of women he must have been with. If Brad didn't want me, how could Gray?

"Hey, talk to me, baby."

I look away, crippled by my insecurity. I don't know how to explain, and shame washes over me. "I... I'm embarrassed, Gray. It's nothing, really."

He buries one hand in my hair and cups my cheek with the other, his thumb brushing over the edge of my lips. "It's not nothing, baby. You're the most beautiful woman I've ever seen, and I swear to you, I've never wanted anyone more. Tell me how to make this better."

The way he looks at me, the sincerity in his eyes... it goes straight to my heart. He's never done anything to make me feel like he doesn't want me. Even now, I can feel how hard he still is underneath me. It's not him that burned me.

"It's nothing," I whisper, leaning in. Gray's eyes fall closed when I kiss him, and his grip on my hair tightens. He groans when my hands roam over his body. I want him. I've wanted him for as long as I can remember, and I don't want to let my insecurities hold me back. The way Gray kisses me tells me how he feels about me, and I'm going to trust those feelings.

I pull my lips away from his, enjoying the way he's panting, the subtle way he pushes his hips up against mine. I look into his eyes as I pull on the edges of his T-shirt, and he grins as he pulls it up and over his head in one swift movement.

I inhale sharply when his body comes into view. "This..." I whisper. "I've been fantasizing about getting to touch you," I tell him, and Gray's eyes darken.

His hand wraps around the back of my neck, his thumb resting against my throat. "You never did tell me what you were dreaming about that night."

I blush, thinking back to the way I touched him, the way I kissed his neck. "You want to know?" I whisper.

He nods, his breathing as labored as mine. I revel in his need for me and smile, raising my hand to his face. "In my dream, I was in bed with you, and you were lying down underneath me."

He shifts us on the sofa, and I fall on top of him. "Like this?"

I giggle and nod, pushing myself up the way I did in my dream.

"Show me what you dreamt," he murmurs, his gaze heated.

I lean in, my lips brushing against his neck, and he squirms underneath me until he's pressed right where he wants to be. A soft moan escapes my lips, and my eyes fall closed.

"I kissed you right here," I whisper, pressing a soft kiss to his neck, right below his ear. "Then I kissed you here." I move my lips a little lower and kiss him again, eliciting a moan from him.

"You didn't take well to being teased, so you buried your hand in my hair and pulled me up, your lips finding mine. You were rough with me, but I loved it."

Gray does exactly what I told him, pulling me up as he kisses me. This kiss is different, and when his tongue tangles with mine, I roll my hips against his, needing more. He turns us over, spreading my legs with his knees, and when he presses up against me, a moan escapes my lips.

"I need you so fucking bad."

His hands roam over my body, and he grabs the edges of my T-shirt, but he pauses abruptly, as if reminding himself of the boundaries I've been setting. "Do it," I whisper. "Take it off."

Gray looks into my eyes. He seems to find what he was looking for because he nods and pulls my T-shirt up slowly, revealing my body.

"Fuck," he groans.

He reaches underneath me, his hands on my bra straps, and I freeze. "I don't want to take it off," I whisper, my voice trembling. I'm scared of showing him my body. I look good in this bra, but without it? Not so much.

He drops his forehead to mine, and I'm scared I'm disappointing him already. We haven't even slept together yet and I'm already letting him down.

"I'm in love with you, Aria Grant. Head over heels. Butterflies and all that shit. I'll wait a lifetime for you if you want me to. So tell me, baby... do you want to stop? We can stop right here if you want to."

I look into his eyes, his words reverberating through my mind. He didn't even hesitate to tell me he's in love with me, and I can't help but smile. "I want you, Grayson. I've wanted you for so long that it hurts... and I, well, I'm definitely crazy in love with you too."

His eyes widen at those words, and he grins, relaxing on top of me as his hand continues to explore my body. His fingers brush over the edge of my soaking wet panties, and he bites down on his lip. He swallows hard and drops his forehead to mine.

"Fucking hell... I just knew it. I knew you'd be wet and needy, baby. How could you not be? Every part of you is perfect."

He pushes my underwear aside and brushes his thumb along my wetness, making me moan helplessly. I've wanted this for so long.

"Will you let me take it off?"

I nod, and he rises to his knees, taking his time pulling the black fabric down my legs. I can see how hard he is, and I want him. I want him inside me.

Gray lies down on his side next to me, holding himself up on his elbow, his eyes on mine as his fingers find their way between my legs.

"You don't have to do that," I whisper. No man ever has, and I don't expect it from Gray either.

He frowns at me. "Baby, you *are* going to come. Multiple times, if it's up to me."

His fingers slip into me with ease, and the way he touches me has me ready to come within minutes. He grins as I squirm, pushing my hips up against his hand. I'm getting closer and closer. "Such a wet fucking pussy," he whispers. "You want to come for me, don't you?"

I nod and thread my hand through his hair, pulling his head to mine as my muscles tighten around his fingers. "Grayson," I moan, my lips finding his as wave after wave of pleasure rocks my body.

He smiles against my lips and pulls away to look at me. I can't even imagine what image I'm presenting him with. My cheeks must be flushed and my hair a mess, but he looks at me as though I'm the most beautiful thing he's ever seen.

I smile as my hands run down his abs, pausing at the waistband of his boxer shorts. "I've been wondering what's underneath here," I whisper, slipping my hand in. I palm his dick, and his eyes fall closed.

"I want more," I whisper.

Gray runs a hand through his hair, frustrated. "Baby, I'd want nothing more... but I don't have protection. Considering the amount of confidential data in my apartment, I've never taken a woman home with me. Besides... I didn't think you'd be ready for a while longer, so I haven't bought any yet."

I smile and pull him closer. "That's okay, I'm on the pill," I whisper, pushing down his boxer shorts.

"Are you sure, Ari? I'm clean... I've never had a woman without a condom, but I still want you to be sure."

I nod, and Gray pushes my legs apart wider, settling between them. I moan when he slides up against me, pushing just the tip in before leaning in to kiss me.

I lift my hips impatiently, and he smirks as he pulls back to look at me. He looks into my eyes as he sinks all the way inside me. "So fucking good," he groans, his eyes never leaving mine as he pulls back slightly before thrusting back into me.

"You have any idea how long I've wanted this pussy."

I moan and wrap my arms around his neck, moving with him. I don't remember sex feeling this good. I've never felt this... full. The way he's stretching me out, it's almost painful, but I love it.

"I've dreamt of you, baby. For months now, you've been fueling my fantasies."

He thrusts into me harder, faster, clearly hanging on by a thread, and I love this. I love how badly he wants me. I love his expressions, his need.

"Tell me, Ari. Have you been touching yourself to thoughts of me? Because I have. Every time I wrapped my hand around my dick, it's your face I imagined."

"Yes," I moan. Even when the messages Ash sent me turned me on, it was Grayson I imagined. "Yes, Gray."

He leans in and captures my lips as he increases the pace until he loses it. "Aria," he moans, and my pussy squeezes him tightly. I've never felt this needy before. Just having him come deep inside me has me feeling so damn close to him.

Gray collapses on top of me, and I wrap my arms around him as he kisses my neck. "I'm not done with you," he whispers. "I told you I'm going to make you come multiple times tonight, and I have every intention of keeping my word."

Chapter Forty-Two

ARIA

I smile to myself when Gray finds yet another excuse to walk out of his office. He walks up to me, a stack of documents in his hands this time.

"Aria," he says, his expression serious. I turn to look at him, trying to assess whether he actually needs something this time. So far, he's asked me for help with five different queries that are elementary level at best. It should annoy me, but honestly, I'm loving it. I love how blatant he is about his affection. He isn't trying to look cool or any of the crap Brad used to pull.

The last couple of days have been so perfect that it's surreal. It feels like this might all be a dream. Like I'll wake up tomorrow to find that being with Gray is still only a fantasy. He's perfect, and I'm falling harder every second I spend with him. Grayson is more about actions than words. He shows me how much he cares about me every single day. It's not even about the dates, it's the little things. We sit on the sofa together, talking for hours, never getting enough of each other. It's in the way touches me, never pushing me outside of my comfort zone. I'm still not comfortable taking off my bra, and he never questions me about it, never pushes me. Instead, he just kisses my insecurities away, taking his time with me.

"Grayson," I say, smiling as I rise from my seat.

His eyes are twinkling, and I just know he's made up another excuse to spend some time with me.

"I was reviewing some of the ideas you sent me for the interface," he says, waving around the documents in his hands. "And this doesn't look quite right."

I suppress a smile and nod gravely. The documents in his hand aren't even remotely related to me. If I'm not mistaken, they're meeting minutes.

"I better take a look at that," I say, sounding concerned. All of these little delays during the day mean that Gray and I both have to work overtime at home, but it's worth it. These little interruptions make my day.

Gray frowns. "Oh, looks like I didn't grab all of your notes. I must have left them in my office. Why don't you come with me and we'll run through them?"

I nod, barely able to suppress my giddiness as I follow him to his office. The second the door closes behind us, he wraps his arms around me, bending down to kiss me. Even with the high heels I'm wearing, I can't quite reach him unless he leans in.

His lips crash against mine, and a soft moan escapes my lips. "Aria," he whispers, his hands running over my body. His touch is needy and desperate, reflecting how I feel. I never have to wonder with Gray, his feelings for me are obvious.

I slip my hand underneath his suit jacket, wanting more of him. He smiles against my lips and lifts me into his arms. I instinctively wrap my legs around him, and he carries me to the sofa in his office. He lies me down, covering me with his body.

He's hard, and the way he presses against me drives me insane. I can barely take it. He's been kissing and teasing me like this ever since we started dating, making my need for him overtake my insecurities.

His tongue presses against my lips and I open up for him, wanting more. He deepens our kiss and I push up against him, needing him closer.

"I can't do this, Aria. I can't function when you're so close to me. I can't stop thinking about you."

I giggle. I can't help it. I've never felt so wanted before. "But you know we'll end up having to work late," I tell him, trying my best to sound admonishing.

He grins, and I know my words are falling on deaf ears. "I don't mind working if I get to have you in my lap," he says, pressing a kiss to my neck.

"I know you don't mind, but I have to get some work done. I'm not the CEO around here, remember? I am but a measly worker bee with a manager to answer to."

Gray laughs and pulls me up, his arms wrapping around me in a tight hug. He presses a kiss to my temple and sighs. "Fine," he says. "I'd better find a way to get rid of Riley."

I burst into laughter and shake my head. "That's not quite where I was going with that," I say, shaking my head.

I kiss him, my lips lingering, before I push away. "No more kisses until tonight," I tell him, and the outrage on his face amuses me endlessly. He groans as I walk away, and I can't wipe the smile off my face as I sit down at my desk. When is the last time I felt this happy?

My happiness fades when I notice Riley approaching me, his expression stormy. "Hey, did Grayson just say something about the interface? Why didn't you run that by me?"

I panic internally but manage to smile nonetheless. "Oh, it's nothing," I say, trying to play it off. "I just had some concepts in mind for the potential application of our software."

Riley frowns, looking displeased. "I'd prefer if you came straight to me with any ideas you might have. I don't appreciate you going over my head, straight to Grayson. I doubt he appreciates it either. He wouldn't have made me your manager if he wanted to deal with you himself."

I nod, willing my face into a serious expression. If only he knew it isn't even me reaching out to Gray at all.

I notice Gray standing in front of his office, his arms crossed and his eyes on me. I've finally come to recognize that angry look in his eyes as jealousy. I can tell he's tempted to walk over here and find out what's going on, but I appreciate that he doesn't. I asked him to keep things low-key for a while, and so far he is reluctantly following my wishes.

"I understand," I tell Riley. I smile at him, and some of the frost in his eyes melts. "I didn't mean to overstep."

Riley shakes his head, smiling sheepishly. "No, I think I just overreacted. I'm sorry, I'm being a dick. With the deadline looming, I'm just a little tense. I think I just need a coffee to be honest." He runs a hand through his hair and sighs. "Can I get you one? Do you want to walk with me?"

I see Gray tense from my peripheral vision, and I shake my head, a grin finding its way onto my lips. "No, I'd better get my work done," I tell him. Riley nods at me and walks away.

Gray has been worried ever since Riley took me out for lunch. It's crazy that a man like Gray could be jealous over a woman like me. I glance at his office door, relieved to find he's actually gone back to work. I want him to myself tonight, and that won't happen unless we both manage to finish our work.

He seems so into me that my insecurities are slowly losing their hold. All but one. I grab my phone and stare at it, my thoughts drifting to Ash. He hasn't texted in a while, not even about his mother. I can't tell if it's just because Gray is preoccupied with me, or if it's something else. Does he feel guilty about all the things he used to say to Nyx now that he's dating me?

Gray tells me he's had feelings for me for a while now, but all the while he was flirting with Nyx over text. His behavior fills my heart with fear. I want to believe he's different, but I'm scared to take that risk. I didn't see the signs with Brad, but I see them now. I see them, and I'm tempted to ignore them.

I know I can't, though. I can't continue to wonder whether I truly am the only girl on Gray's mind. I can't live in ignorance. I hesitate before unlocking my phone. My fingers hover over my keyboard, and I'm nervous as I type my text. I need to know.

Things have been so perfect recently, and that on its own should be a warning sign, but even so, I'm hoping that I'm wrong to distrust Gray.

Nyx: *I think I might just take you up on all those offers to make me scream your name...*

Minutes pass, and he doesn't reply. Just as I breathe a sigh of relief, my phone buzzes.

Ash: *Just tell me when and where, babe. Just the idea of you wanting me has me hard.*

My heart breaks as I reread the text over and over again. So much for me being the only one for him.

Chapter Forty-Three

GRAYSON

I'm surprised when I walk out of my office to find that Aria is already gone. We usually go home together, and I was looking forward to getting her alone again.

I check my phone but I have no missed calls from her. Usually if she has to run an errand of some sort, she'll let me know. I sent her a text on my way out, double-checking that she really has left, but she doesn't reply.

Somehow, I'm feeling uneasy on the way home. I feel like something is wrong, but I can't quite figure out what it is. I'm surprised when I walk into the house and find it pitch dark. Aria dislikes being home alone, and she usually turns on the hallway lights as soon as she gets in. I expected to find her in the kitchen, a smile on her face and that cute apron of hers tied around her.

Instead, I find the house empty. I walk around, trying my best to calm my raging heart. I haven't felt this way since I was a little boy. This type of fear, this helplessness... It feels foreign to me, yet familiar all at once.

I walk to Aria's bedroom, hesitating before I open the door.

Relief rushes through me when I find her standing in front of her bed, and it doesn't even register that she's got her suitcase out, not until she turns to glare at me, tears in her eyes.

She looks away and starts packing. I walk up to her and she takes a step away, making me freeze.

"What's going on?" I ask, worried. I take another step toward her, wanting to take her into my arms and wipe those tears away, but she won't let me. She places her palms against my chest and pushes me away, though she barely manages to move me.

"Babe, you're worrying me," I tell her, my every instinct begging me to wrap my arms around her, to take away the sorrow in her eyes.

"Don't," she says, her voice trembling.

"Don't what?" I ask, my heart constricting painfully. I feel like I'm losing her and I can't figure out what I did wrong.

"Why?" she asks me. "Why did you lead me on? Why would you tell me I'm the only one for you when I'm not? I don't get it... am I just someone to pass the time with?"

Her voice breaks and she swallows down her sobs, trying her hardest to stop crying. She sniffs, her entire body shaking, and it kills me to see her this way. "Aria, I don't know what you're talking about. You *are* the only one for me, baby. Of course you are."

She starts to sob and drops her forehead to my chest. "Then why? Why are you cheating on me? Emotional cheating is still cheating, Gray. After everything you saw me go through... Why? Why would you put me back together only to break me like this?"

I grab her shoulders and look into her eyes, the puzzle pieces finally falling into place. I should have known.

I cup her cheeks and wipe her tears away with my thumbs. "Baby, I would never cheat on you. That would never ever happen."

Aria starts to cry even harder, and I wrap my arms around her, hugging her tightly. I lift her up and sit down on her bed with her on my lap. She pushes against me weakly, as though she thinks she should resist my embrace, but can't.

"I assume this is about Nyx?" I say carefully. "When you told me you'd take me up on my offers to make you scream my name, this isn't quite what I had in mind."

Aria freezes in my arms, and she sits back to look at me. "What?"

I bury my hands in her hair and drop my forehead to hers. "If I'd known that you were going to misunderstand like this, then I'd never let it get this far. I'm sorry, baby."

Her eyes widen in disbelief, and I see her connect the dots. I smile at her and press a soft kiss to her forehead, my lips lingering. "Baby, I knew you were Nyx from the second I saw you fix a script I'd been working on for hours. I've been trying to hack into your platform every day for months now. Did you really think I wouldn't recognize the patterns you coded back at Noah's house? I knew, but at the time I... *Ash* had a part of you that was strictly off-limits to me. I couldn't tell you. Hell, I couldn't even acknowledge it myself, because it meant losing the one part of you that was mine."

I sigh and tighten my grip on her, hugging her tightly. "Ari, the second I sent you the files I had on my mother, I knew you'd figure out who I am. I just thought that you needed more time, that you were finding your own way to tell me. I know how much this platform means to you, and I was trying my best to give you space. I guess the lines started to blur in the last couple of days, because in my mind you and Nyx are the same person."

I see her thinking through my explanation, assessing the truthfulness of my words. "You knew," she whispers, her forehead dropping to my shoulder.

I turn my head and place my lips against her neck, kissing her softly. "I can't believe you thought I'd ever cheat on you, Aria. I would never do that. You're the best thing that ever happened to me, and I'd be a fool to let you go. No one will ever compare to you, baby."

She hugs me tightly, and I can't even explain how that makes me feel. For a couple of minutes I thought I was about to lose her, and for those few moments, all I could see was bleakness. I can never go back to my life before Aria. I won't survive the emptiness now that she's shown me what true happiness is.

"I'm not perfect, Aria. I'll make mistakes, and at some point I'll probably hurt you. But I will never do it intentionally. Every mistake I make, I promise to learn from. I know you've been hurt before, and I know those scars still pain you. I promise you I will help you heal, and I will be here through it all."

Aria looks into my eyes, and she nods. "I was in the wrong here, too. I should have told you I'm Nyx the second I realized who you were. I don't want to punish you for pain you didn't cause, but that's exactly what I'm doing. You've done nothing to make me distrust you, yet I still did. I'll try to be better, Gray. I promise."

I lean in, my lips grazing over hers, before I capture her lips fully. This kiss is different, it's more emotional and tinged with desperation. Aria pushes against me and rises to her knees, her hands threading through my hair as she deepens our kiss.

I'm breathless by the time she pulls away, feelings I have never felt before overwhelming me. "Together, Aria. You and I can get through anything together. Just promise me you'll talk to me. No matter what's going on, just talk to me. I don't ever want to come home to find you gone. Don't abandon me like that," I murmur, my head dropping to her chest.

Aria wraps her arms around me and nods. "I promise."

Chapter Forty-Four

GRAYSON

I glance at Aria's packed suitcase and shake my head. "I can't believe you were ready to leave, Ari."

It hurts to know she'd have walked away from me. From us. Over what? A misunderstanding? It's one I'm at least partially to blame for, but it's nothing but a misunderstanding nonetheless.

She drops her forehead to my chest, and I wrap my arms around her, hugging her tightly. "I'm sorry," she says. "I wasn't thinking clearly... all I could think was that this couldn't be happening to me again."

"Well, since you're already packed..." I say, rising to my feet. I close her suitcase and lift it. Aria's eyes widen, a hint of panic in her expression.

"Gray," she whispers. "I'm sorry. I'm so sorry," she says, her voice breaking.

I smile at her and shake my head. "There you go, overthinking again." I grab her hand and pull her along with me, leading her to my bedroom, her suitcase in hand. I put it down by the entrance of my wardrobe and then pull her toward my bed.

"Baby, you aren't going anywhere. I'm going to keep you right by my side. I want you in my bed, Aria."

So far we've spent every single night together, yet her stuff is still in the guestroom. It's about time she properly moves into my room. "You're it for me, baby. I want a whole life with you. I want your clothes next to mine, your makeup in my bathroom. I want you to have your own side of the bed, and I want to wake up to you completely disregarding that and lying on top of me instead, driving me insane."

I thread my hands through her hair and hold her tightly. "I want every part of you, Aria. I want your wicked sharp intellect, those lips I can't get enough of... I want your every smile, your every thought."

She looks at me as though she's struggling to believe what I'm saying, and I smile. "Now don't get me wrong, I also want your body against mine. I want to sink my cock deep inside you every single day, and I want to hear you moan my name. I want all of you, Aria."

She bites down on her lip and swallows hard as she looks up into my eyes. "Take it," she tells me. "I'm yours. Every broken, damaged piece of me. Take it all."

I lean in and kiss her, tightening my grip on her hair as she rises to her tiptoes to deepen the kiss. Her hands roam over my body impatiently, and I smile against her lips. I love the impatience she fails to hide. I love that she wants me just as badly. Aria pushes my suit jacket off my shoulders, letting it fall to the floor, and I groan when her tongue tangles with mine. My movements are rough as I tug on her dress, letting go of her only long enough to pull it over her head.

"Grayson," she moans, her fingers tugging at my shirt buttons. Within minutes we're both in nothing but our underwear. I push Aria onto my bed and she lays back, her body on display for me. She looks stunning in her black lingerie, and I can't wait to get it off her.

"You're beautiful, baby."

I rest my knee on the bed and lean over her, my lips dropping to hers. She's panting by the time I pull away, and I smile when she whimpers. I drop my lips to her neck, leaving a trail of kisses down to her chest, purposely teasing her with every touch.

"Take it off," she whispers, and I tense. She's been insecure about her breasts for a while now, but when I look into her eyes, I find none of her usual insecurity. There's only lust.

I reach underneath her to take off her bra, and she lifts her chest up to give me easier access. My cock fucking jerks when it comes undone, and my hands tremble as I pull it away.

"Fuck," I groan. "What the fuck have you been on about?" I murmur, cupping her perfect tear drop tits. "This is perfection, Aria."

She moans when my tongue traces over her nipple, and I grin as I tease her. My girl is a nut job, man. How could she ever be insecure over a body as perfect as hers? She's got curves for days.

Aria's hands find their way into my hair, and she pulls tightly. The way she moves against me... so needy. I pull away to look at her, holding myself up on my forearms.

"Baby, I fucking need you so bad," I murmur. "I won't last. I can't cope. I need your pussy."

She looks into my eyes and nods. "I want you, Grayson. I want you so badly it hurts."

Just hearing her say those words... Fuck.

I rise to my knees and wrap my hands around her panties. "Up," I command, and she lifts her hips for me. I look at her as I pull the fabric down, exposing her soaking wet pussy.

I grin as I run a finger over her clit, watching the way she squirms for me. "I thought you said you needed me bad," she says, and I chuckle as I make quick work of my boxer shorts.

I settle in between her legs and bury one hand in her hair, pulling on it. "I'm going to fuck every goddamn insecurity out of you, you hear me? By the time I'm done with you, you won't ever wonder if I want you again."

I keep my eyes on hers as I sink into her. The way her pussy clamps down on me is fucking insane. She's so fucking hot, so wet. "I'll never get enough of this pussy, Aria. You will always be the only one for me. Always."

She moans when I thrust all the way in. "I will never leave you," I tell her, pulling my cock almost all the way out before thrusting into her hard, giving it to her the way she likes it. "I will always want this fucking pussy. You will always be mine, Aria. Always."

She moans and moves with me, her pants getting quicker, her moans getting higher as I fuck her with all I've got, watching her tits bounce with every move.

"So goddamn perfect," I groan. She's so fucking perfect. Her pussy is a fucking vice. I can't last long when she looks at me like that, when her pussy feels this good.

"I fucking love you," I tell her, and her muscles tighten around me. I groan, my forehead dropping to hers as she fucking milks me. I didn't expect her to come on my cock like that, but I should've known. She's my girl, after all. She's fucking perfect.

Chapter Forty-Five

GRAYSON

"Gray, where are you taking me?"

I smile and tighten my grip on her hand, pulling her along. "You'll see," I tell her, excited about the surprise I have in store. Last night is still fresh on my mind, and I know it's on hers too.

"Wow," she says, when I lead her onto the beach. I walk her to the gazebo where a dining table has been set up for us and Aria looks at me, her eyes wide. "You did this for me?"

I smile and pull her closer, bending down to kiss her. "What? I can't take my girl out on a date?"

She grins as I pull out her chair for her, and I'm relieved to see her smiling so genuinely. Last night's argument took a toll on her, and she's been quiet all day.

I'm worried she's thinking about Brad, that she's comparing me to him. I never intended to break her trust, but I should have realized she would misunderstand. I should have known the texts between us could be misinterpreted. I shouldn't have assumed we were both silently aware of who the other was.

I pour Aria a glass of champagne, lifting mine to hers. "Here's to you. To us."

She smiles and taps her glass against mine before raising it to her lips. "I'm glad it's you," she says, her voice soft.

I raise my brows in question, and her cheeks flush. She looks away, her lips turning up in a smile.

"Ash," she whispers. "I'm glad it's you."

I smile, my heart tightening in a way it never has before. "Ari, I was shocked when I found out who you were. I'd been intrigued with Nyx long before I realized it was you. That day, at your brother's dining table... fuck. At the time you had so much going on, and it didn't seem right to ask you then, especially because it was nothing more than a hunch. But the truth is I didn't *want* to ask you if you were Nyx. We'd just gotten closer over text, and it felt like I'd gotten to know a part of you that you kept hidden from everyone else. I was selfish, Aria. I knew I couldn't have you in real life, but over text? Over text, I got to say everything that I couldn't say to you face to face. I got to flirt with you, and I got to tell you how beautiful you are. I thought that was all I'd ever have of you. But I should have known... I should have known that I wouldn't be able to resist you."

Aria's cheeks turn a beautiful shade of crimson, and I can't help but fall a little deeper. I'm so caught up in her I don't even notice the waiter standing by our table. Not until Aria laughs at me and turns to look at him.

I can barely take my eyes off her as she places her order, and I'm impatient as I place mine.

"Why did you choose the name Nyx?" I ask as soon as he walks away. It's something I've wondered about for months now, and I can't figure it out.

Aria grimaces and looks away. "Nyx is the Goddess of night. I've loved her for years, because it's only at night that I come alive. After I lost my parents, living through the days was too hard. Pretending that I was okay, smiling when I felt dead inside... I went through the motions, but at night... at night is when I could be myself. It's during sleepless nights that I learned to code, and it was during a sleepless night that I met you."

She looks away, trying to hide the sorrow in her eyes, but it doesn't escape me. "I've always loved the name Nyx," I tell her. "I think I might start calling you that."

She laughs, startled. "I think I'd actually like that," she says. She tilts her head and smiles at me. "Tell me, why did you pick Ash?"

I look away, my smile melting off my face. "It's a play on my name," I tell her. "When I thought of things that are gray, one of the first things that came to mind was ash... and just like ash, I'm all that's left behind when everything burns down."

I don't see pity in her eyes, and I don't know why I expected it. This is Aria, after all. She gets me like no one else does.

"Gray," she says. "You have no idea how much I look up to you. It's because of you I taught myself how to code. If not for the way you've always inspired me, the Nemesis Platform wouldn't even exist. I can't believe I get to call you mine. You're brilliant, and your accomplishments are astounding. Despite all of that, you're the best person I know."

I look away, unsure how to reply to that. She smiles at me as though she understands, as though she knows what I'm thinking. She probably does. I reach for her, grabbing her hand over the table.

"You know," she says. "You've been doing this for a while... grabbing my hand like that."

I grin and press a kiss to the back of her hand. "I couldn't resist. Your hands are the only part of you that was accessible to me. The only part I could touch without betraying how much I wanted you."

She looks at me with wide eyes, as though it's only just occurring to her that I've wanted her for a while. I see the question in her eyes, but she wouldn't believe me even if I told her.

I'm startled when my phone rings, snapping me out of the moment. I glance at it, grimacing. "It's Noah," I say, my voice soft. I try my best to suppress the guilt I feel as I pick up the phone.

"Hey, man. What's up?" I say, and Aria tightens her grip on me, squeezing my hand. I see the same guilt reflected in her eyes and she tries to slip her hand away, but I catch her in time and entwine our fingers.

"Nothing much. I'm packing. Anything in particular I need to bring? I tried calling Aria, but she's not picking up. If she needs anything from home, I can bring it for her."

I face the ocean, feeling conflicted. I forgot Noah is visiting soon.

"No, nothing that I can think of."

"You okay? Am I calling at a bad time?"

I glance at Aria, and the anxiety in her eyes makes me uncomfortable. I don't want to lie to Noah.

"No, it's nothing. I'm just out right now."

Noah chuckles. "A date? Well, I'll be damned."

"Something like that," I mutter. My conversations with Noah have never been awkward, but today I wish I didn't even pick up.

I breathe a sigh of relief when he ends the call after minimal small talk, and I instantly feel guilty.

"What are we doing?" Aria asks. "We can't..."

I shake my head and look her in the eye. "We'll tell him, babe. Together."

Aria shakes her head. "We don't even know what this is yet. Do you really want to risk your friendship with him?"

I smile at her reassuringly. "Aria, I've never been more sure of anything in my life. I meant it when I told you I love you."

She looks at me in disbelief and I vow to myself here and now that I will make her see that she is everything, that she is worth everything.

Chapter Forty-Six

GRAYSON

Aria moans and pulls me closer, her legs wrapping around me as she leans back on the kitchen counter. "I miss you already," she whispers.

I pull away to look at her. "Nyx... we should tell him straight away."

She shakes her head and wraps her arms around my neck. "I don't want to, Gray. I haven't seen my brother in months, and I know he's not going to like this. I don't want his entire time here to be spent arguing. Let's tell him on his last day here. That way, he'll have plenty of time to be angry... *at home*. By the time we see him again he'll have gotten over it."

What she's saying makes sense, but it doesn't feel right. I've never kept anything from Noah... or, well... I've never kept *much* from him. The only thing I've ever kept to myself was *Nyx*, and I ended up telling him about her in the end too.

"Baby, he's your brother, so I'll do whatever you want me to do, but I don't think you're making the right call." She pulls me in for a kiss and I pull her closer, my dick pressing up against her. "We share a bedroom now, Nyx. How do you explain that?"

"Gray," she whispers. Her tone tells me I'm not going to like what she's about to say. "I'm moving back into the guest bedroom while Noah is here."

I frown, and she raises her hand to my face, smoothing out my scrunched-up brows. "I can't stay in your bedroom, Gray."

I drop my forehead to hers and inhale deeply. "Babe, I don't like this one bit."

"I know," she whispers. "But Noah will be worried about me, as it is. He never liked Brad, and he'll just think I'm rushing into another relationship."

I look into her eyes and brush her hair out of her face gently. "Is that what *you* think? Is this just a rebound to you?"

The thought of that fucking destroys me. I don't even want her thinking of that asshole. The fact she even uttered his name pisses me off. I should've put him in the hospital when I had the chance.

Aria shakes her head, her eyes blazing with sincerity. "It's not, Gray. You know it's not."

Except I don't. I don't know that. Things have been great between us, and the sex is fantastic... but she keeps her distance at work, and even at home she doesn't cling to me the way I've seen her cling to Brad. It's not until we get to bed that it feels like she's *mine*.

I push away from her and smile tightly. "Well, Noah is going to be here any minute now. Make the call Aria. When are we telling him? Or are we not telling him at all?"

She looks down at her feet and sighs. "Let's tell him halfway through his stay here. How about that?"

I nod. I don't like it, but I'll respect her decision. Noah might be my best friend, but he's her family.

My doorbell rings just as I take a step away from Aria, and I smile wryly. I've always been happy to see Noah, and I hate that today I'm not. I knew that getting involved with his sister would fuck shit up, but I underestimated the guilt I'd feel. He trusted me when he asked me to take care of her, and I betrayed him. I did it knowingly, and the worst thing is I don't even regret it. I'd do it all over again if it means I get to have Aria.

I open the door with far less enthusiasm than usual, and I'm oddly nervous when Noah smiles at me.

"Sup, buddy?" he says, throwing his arm around me. I freeze, and he notices. "You okay, Gray?"

I nod again and take a step back. "Yes, of course. It's great to see you," I say, my voice monotone even to my own ears.

Aria walks up to us, and Noah opens his arms wide. "Smurf!" he shouts, earning him a glare.

"Asshole!" she shouts back as she walks into his embrace. I never did understand siblings, and every time I see Aria and Noah together, I wonder what it'd be like. They insult each other, but they clearly love each other. It makes little sense to me.

Aria leads Noah into my home, and I love how comfortable she feels here. Noah chuckles when he walks into the living room and looks at me. "Nice pillows," he says, grinning.

Aria elbows him. "They're cushions, you dimwit."

"You've ruined Gray," he says. "He was a great guy before you torpedoed into his life, and now look at this place... there are orange cushions and candles in an otherwise perfect bachelor pad."

"I quite like it," I say honestly. My home had no character before Aria moved in with me. I like that she put her own touch on what I've come to think of as *our* home.

Noah sits down on the sofa and extends his legs, crossing his ankles on the table. "So, how have you been?" he asks Aria. "How is the job? Has Gray been taking good care of you?"

If only he knew how well I've been taking care of her... I had her begging for mercy at least three times last night.

I stand back as Aria and Noah catch up. She looks so happy to have him here, and I have to admit she was right. If we told him about us right now, it'd ruin his entire trip.

Hell... it might still ruin our friendship.

I turn to look at Aria. Even if somehow things don't end up working out between us, even if she someday decides she can do better... I still don't think I'd regret us. But would she?

Chapter Forty-Seven

ARIA

I lie back on the fancy outdoor bed that Gray has on his rooftop, my eyes on the pool where he and Noah are doing laps. I've been nervous all day, scared that Noah will catch on. Gray has done as I asked, and he's been keeping his distance, but the way he looks at me...

Gray swims up to the stairs at the edge of the pool, and I watch him as water drops glide down his skin. I miss him. I miss being able to walk up to him and kiss him. I want to run my hands over his body and feel him tense underneath my fingers.

It's hard to believe I get to call Gray my boyfriend now. I can't believe he's mine. It certainly doesn't feel like he is now that Noah's around.

Gray walks up to me and I rise to my knees, my cheeks heating when his eyes run down my body, taking in the skimpy white bikini I'm wearing. I grin when I see him harden in his soaking wet swimming shorts, and I can't help but giggle when he runs a hand through his hair in frustration.

"Why do you look so beautiful?" he murmurs, reaching for

the towel on the bed. I glance past him at Noah who is still doing laps and smile as I place my hand on his shorts, wanting to feel how hard I've made him. Gray tenses, his gaze heated. "Nyx," he whispers, hardening even further. "I'm going to fuck you on this bed. As soon as your brother is gone, I'm going to drag you back here and spread your legs so I can kneel between them."

I let go of him and shake my head. "Noah's walking up to us," I tell him, and his eyes widen. He glances at his swimming shorts and groans as he walks away, his back to my brother. I wish I could have taken care of that for him...

"Hey," Noah says. "Where's Gray going?"

I shake my head, unable to keep the smile off my face. "I don't know. Bathroom, I guess."

Noah looks at me, his gaze searching, and I'm instantly nervous. He sits down next to me and grabs one of the towels, drying his hair.

"How have you been, Ari?" he asks, his voice soft. "Has Gray been looking out for you?"

I look away, unable to look my brother in the eye, knowing how much I'm keeping from him. How would he respond if I tell him about Gray? Would he be disappointed? I have no idea how this might affect their friendship, and I'm worried. Good things don't last... At least not for me. At some point, Gray's going to realize he can do much better than me. Everything that right now seems like a novelty is going to become tiring. When the infatuation wears off, he'll move on with someone better suited to him. It's only a matter of time. When everything eventually falls apart, I don't want Noah to get hurt alongside me.

"He's been great. Wonderful, really."

"How do you feel? It killed me to see you so heartbroken. I know you loved Brad."

I look down at my hands, my thoughts turning to the pain Brad put me through. I barely survived that. I can't go through it again. If Gray ever cheats on me, I don't think I'll ever recover. The mere thought of him with someone else tears me apart.

"I'm not sure I did. I thought it was love, but in hindsight it wasn't him I loved... It was the thought of having a relationship, a normal life."

Noah nods, a hint of relief in his eyes. "I knew being here would be good for you. How's the job?"

I smile, a genuine smile this time. "It's amazing. I've never been happier. Working for Aequitas, the team I'm in... It's a dream come true."

"I'm glad to hear it," Noah says, looking up. I follow his gaze to find Grayson walking up to us, his eyes on his phone.

"Texting your girlfriend again?" Noah calls, his tone teasing.

I freeze, my stomach twisting violently. Girlfriend? A thousand thoughts whirl through my mind, each worse than the one before. Noah and Gray are close, and as far as I'm aware, they tell each other almost everything. Who is Noah talking about?

I grip the edge of the thin mattress, my nails digging into it deeply.

"No," Gray says, his eyes on me. "It isn't Nyx. It's just work."

Nyx?

"Aw, so it isn't the girl you're hopelessly in love with," Noah teases. Gray sits down next to me, his thigh brushing against mine. Noah grins. "You are, aren't you? You're in love with Nyx."

Grayson smiles at me, the affection in his eyes obvious. "Irrevocably."

My heart skips a beat, and I force myself to look away. Will he always look at me this way? Will his eyes start to wander?

"So, are you getting anywhere with her then?" Noah asks.

Gray looks at me, his expression pleading, but I shake my head. I'm not ready. I'm far too scared things will go wrong. I can't explain the paranoia I feel, but I can't escape it either.

Gray runs a hand through his hair, frustrated. "I thought I was," he says as he gets up and walks over to the barbecue in the corner.

Noah elbows me and looks at me with raised brows. "You know anything about this mysterious girl?" Something about his tone seems off, but I can't quite put my finger on it. I shake my head, and Noah looks away.

"Gray is a good man," he says. "I hope Nyx gets her shit together soon. Gray's patient, but he won't wait forever."

He turns to look at me, his expression serious. Does he know? He can't, can he?

Chapter Forty-Eight

GRAYSON

I stare at the skyline from my sofa, unable to fall asleep. Aria is probably fast asleep in the guest room, while I gave Noah my room. Three days. It's been three days, and everything feels fucked up. I haven't even kissed Aria, and she's given me no indication that she misses me at all.

I couldn't even focus on the game I took Noah to. Fuck. I was looking forward to that for months, but all I could think about was the guilt I'm feeling, the things I'm keeping from him. I'm betraying his trust big time.

I'm surprised when I hear a door open, and I expect it to be Noah. Instead, it's Aria. She pauses a couple of steps away, her expression unreadable. "Gray," she whispers.

"What's wrong?"

She shakes her head and walks up to me. I tense when she drops her knee to the sofa, her legs between mine. She leans in, her hands threading through my hair, and then she kisses me.

My eyes fall closed as I pull her against me roughly, making her lose her balance. She trips, and I grab her, turning us both over so she falls on the sofa, my body on top of hers.

She tangles her legs with mine and pulls me in closer, her body flush against mine. The way she moans when I deepen our kiss and writhes underneath me... it betrays how much she wants me.

"Grayson," she whispers against my lips.

I take her full bottom lip between my teeth, teasing her as I pull away. "What are you doing here?" I ask. "You've been going out of your way to avoid me."

She looks into my eyes, and I swear I lose myself in them. "I miss you," she says. "You're right here, but I miss you."

I lower my lips to her neck, kissing and biting, my movements rough. It feels like I haven't seen her in forever. I've missed her touch, her body against mine. She buries her fingers in my hair and pulls tightly. "Stop teasing me," she says, moving her hands down my body.

I look into her eyes and smile. "What is it you want? Tell me, baby."

Aria's cheeks redden, and that flushed expression of hers makes me even harder. I move so that my cock is nestled right between her legs, the black T-shirt that she's wearing wrapped around her hips.

"You," she tells me.

I grab the edges of her T-shirt and pull it up as Aria raises her arms for me. She moves to cover herself, but I shake my head. "Nyx, tits like these should never be hidden... Not from me, anyway."

It's been a few weeks, but she's still insecure. Her first instinct is still to cover herself up. I grab her wrists and push them over her head, locking her in with my left hand, using my right hand to caress her body. "You're beautiful," I tell her, cupping her breast, my thumb teasing her nipple. It hardens underneath my touch, and I smile as my fingers trail down from her stomach to her thighs. I've learned not to spend too much time on areas that Aria feels self-conscious about. Just enough to show her she shouldn't be insecure, but not so much that she'll start to overthink. She squirms when my fingertips brush over her lace panties, and she pushes her hips up.

I smirk at her as I drag my fingers down the soaking wet fabric. "That's not enough," I tell her. "What do you want me to do? Tell me... Do you want my fingers buried in your tight, wet pussy?"

Aria gulps, and then she nods. I grin as I push aside her panties, finding her soaking wet for me already. She wants me that badly, huh?

I watch her as I drag my thumb over her clit. Her lips fall open and she struggles to stay quiet. She whimpers when I pull my fingers away and I chuckle.

"On your knees," I tell her, and she obeys, turning over. "Fuck," I whisper. "Baby, your ass looks phenomenal this."

"Gray," she whispers, her tone lacking the passion I was expecting. "I have stretch marks," she tells me. "Don't look, please."

What the fuck?

I grab her hair and pull her head back. "Look," I tell her, making her face the window. It's mirroring us, and she looks sexy as hell like this. "Tell me what you see."

I push her panties down her thighs, leaving them wrapped around her knees. "You, I see you," she says. I lean over her and press a kiss on her spine.

"Let me tell you what I see, Ari. I see the most beautiful woman I've ever laid eyes on. A body beyond compare, tits that I can actually grab and an ass I'd be smacking if it didn't make so much noise."

Aria gasps when I push two fingers in, stimulating her G-spot. She moans and I reach around her, wrapping my free hand over her lips. "Quiet, Nyx. Or do you want to wake your brother up? I'm all for telling Noah, but maybe not like this."

I look at her in the window's reflection, and she's so fucking beautiful. "I need you," I tell her, and she nods. I grab her hips and align my cock, watching it slip into her, inch by inch.

I will never get enough of her. The way her pussy clamps down on my dick is unreal, and the view she's presenting me with is almost too much. I pull back, all the way out of her, before slamming back into her, going deeper than usual.

Aria groans and shakes her head. "Too deep," she says, and I smile.

"You'll get used to it. I'll stretch your pussy out to fit me perfectly," I say, trying my best to control my movements a little better. She makes it so easy to lose control.

"I want you closer," Aria says, and I nod in agreement, slipping out of her.

"Ride me," I tell her, sitting back and pulling her on top of me. She looks startled, and I grin at her. She's beautiful, and I'm glad she's finally becoming more comfortable with her body. The sex was good back when she refused to take off her bra, but it's even better now that she doesn't feel the need to hide from me. Having her completely bare like this, the trust and this closeness... It's unreal.

Aria places her hands on my shoulders, her eyes on mine as she sinks down on me. She moves slowly, driving me crazy. The way she moves on top of me, the way she moans against my lips... Yeah, I'll never get enough of her.

Chapter Forty-Nine

ARIA

I stare at the bacon I'm frying, lost in thought. Noah is leaving today. Gray has repeatedly asked me to tell him, and I'm wondering if we should. The fears I have... I can't keep hiding behind them. I can't punish Gray for what Brad did to me. I'm going to have to learn to trust, to take risks. And Gray is worth it. Noah is right. If I keep being indecisive about our relationship, if I don't give him back as much as he gives me, he'll get tired of waiting. Rightfully so.

I look up when Gray walks into the kitchen. Last night comes to mind, and I smile as he walks up to me. "Morning, beautiful," he murmurs as he pulls me in for a kiss. I rise to my tiptoes, my arms wrapping around his neck, and I sigh when he pulls away, my eyes on his. The way he looks at me... he can't be faking that.

"Let's tell him," I say, my voice barely above a whisper. Gray's eyes widen, and I smile at him. "We can't keep this a secret. I can't lie to his face any longer. You're right. You were right all along."

Grayson smiles, and the happiness in his eyes makes the

butterflies in my stomach come alive. I never knew what love was until him. I just thought I did.

"Gray, you really want to tell him, right? You aren't worried you'll change your mind? That maybe you just needed to get this out of your system?" I ask, unable to eradicate my insecurities.

He frowns and tightens his grip on me. "What the fuck? No. This is it for me, babe. You're it. He's going to find out at some point. Wouldn't you rather we tell him now? The longer we keep it from him, the more we're betraying him."

I look into his eyes, searching for a trace of insincerity, but I find none. "Okay," I whisper. "Let's do it."

Grayson breathes a sigh of relief and drops his forehead to mine. He pulls away reluctantly when one of the doors in the house slams. Noah walks into the kitchen, looking exhausted. He glances at the two of us, and Gray grabs my hand, his grip tight.

"Noah," he says, looking my brother dead in the eye. "I'm in love with your sister."

I tense. When I said we should tell him, I didn't quite mean like *that*. I was planning on easing him into it a little more. Noah's eyes move from me to Gray, and my heart races so quickly that I feel sick. I'm scared. I'm scared I'm taking something away from Noah. That he'll feel like I'm betraying him. We both went behind his back, and I don't want to hurt him.

Noah nods slowly. "I know."

"I... you... what?" I stutter.

Noah crosses his arms and stares Grayson down. "I knew you were falling for her long before you did, buddy. *Nyx?* Aria has had an illustration of the goddess Nyx in her room for years. She uses that as her username on all her gaming platforms. I knew from the second you told me about her. I knew you were falling for her, and I knew you'd be done for if Aria started working with you."

He turns to look at me, his expression unreadable. "What I want to know is how *you* feel, Aria."

"I... I'm in love with him, Noah. I'm sorry. I didn't mean for it to happen, but it did."

Noah looks away, and I swallow hard. "Are you in love with him or are you on the rebound?"

Gray tenses next to me, and I glare at my brother. "I love him, Noah. This isn't a phase, it's not a fling."

He nods, his eyes moving between us. "Very well," he says. "It's about time."

I blink in disbelief, and Noah chuckles. "Ari," he says. "You've looked up to Grayson for years. I'm pretty sure you've had a crush on him your entire adult life. You might not have been able to see it, but I did. When Gray was around, you turned into the little sister of my memories, the girl I thought I'd lost. The way you smile at Grayson has always been different. The way he made you come alive... I *knew*."

He nods at Gray. "And you weren't much better. Aria is the only other person you really talk to, the only person you're patient with. She always has been. The way you look at her? It's like my little sister hung the damn moon. Don't think I don't know you went to beat Brad up after talking me out of it. The protectiveness you've always felt toward her... it wasn't brotherly. It never has been. I never minded it, though. Not if it's you. You're a great guy, Grayson, even if you can't always see it yourself. I couldn't have picked a better man for Aria."

I relax against Gray, and he wraps his arm around my shoulder. "I'm sorry we didn't tell you straight away."

Noah shakes his head. "It's okay, Ari. This is your relationship. All I want is for you to be happy. You don't owe me anything. Grayson might be my best friend, but I don't own him. You don't need my permission to date him. Besides, my two favorite people getting together? How could I be disappointed? Just don't break his damn heart, because that shit would get awkward fast. I'm really not up for taking him out and having to hear him reminisce about *you*. Ugh." He shudders, and I burst into laughter.

I walk out of Gray's embrace and straight into my brother's. He wraps his arms around me and presses a kiss on top of my head. "Just be happy, Ari. That's all I want for you. You deserve the world, little one. It's time you reach for everything you deserve, because it's right there, within your grasp."

I pull away, tears in my eyes. "Since when are you all philosophical?"

Noah looks away, a smile on his face, and I narrow my eyes at him. "You... you met someone! Didn't you?"

Noah tenses, but he can't keep the smile off his face. "It's complicated, Ari."

I gasp and grab his arms, a wide smile on my face. "Wow, there really is a girl, huh?"

He shakes his head. "She's a patient, Ari. It's really complicated. I can't... even if I want to, I can't be with her."

He takes a step away, his eyes filled with frustration. He's tense as he raises his hand to my face, brushing aside my hair. "Just be happy, okay? You be happy enough for the both of us."

Who is this girl that's got my brother looking so lost? He's never focused on anything but his career. Whoever she is, she's managed to capture his attention.

Gray looks at me and shakes his head, and I pout at him. How can I *not* question Noah? Gray throws one of his stern expressions at me, and I sigh, letting it go.

I look at Noah, unable to believe this is real, that I really could be this happy.

Maybe I was wrong all along. Maybe happiness does last.

Chapter Fifty

GRAYSON

Aria is sitting on the sofa when I walk in, and I smile to myself. She's grabbed the duvet from our bedroom and she's drowning in it, her head barely sticking out above the top. She looks up and grins when she sees me walk in, and I pause in front of her.

She stands on top of the sofa, the duvet falling away, revealing the black T-shirt she's wearing. It's petty, but I'm happy it's one of mine, and not one of Noah's. I love the guy like my own brother, but I'm happy he went back home. I'm happy I get to share this space with Aria again. It's different when it's just the two of us.

She spreads her arms, and I walk into her embrace, wrapping my arms around her. "Hey, baby," I tell her, squeezing her tightly. Standing on top of our sofa, she's almost as tall as I am, and I pull back to kiss her. Aria sighs against my lips, and my hands roam over her body. I can't get enough of this woman.

"How was your meeting?" she asks, in between kisses.

I lower my lips to her neck, kissing her just below her ear

where she's most sensitive. She moans, and I smile as I lower my lips further.

"It was good. Laura is doing a great job setting up the machine learning division."

My hands slip underneath her T-shirt, and she tugs my tie loose, letting it fall to the floor.

"That's good," she says, preoccupied with the buttons on my shirt. My eyes fall closed when she leans in and kisses my neck.

"We have a shit ton of work to catch up on," I remind her, and she nods as she presses a kiss to my throat. Aria and I both took a few days off to spend time with Noah, underestimating the amount of work we'd have to catch up on.

"It can wait," she tells me, and I grin as I bury my hand in her hair. I pull her face to mine roughly, my lips crashing down on hers. Aria moans and wraps her arms around my neck. I can't believe she's mine.

She pushes my suit coat off my shoulders, letting it fall to the floor. "Eager, aren't you?" I say, grinning.

She looks up at me as she sinks down to her knees on the sofa, her hands on my fly. Her movements are impatient, and I groan when she wraps her hands around my cock. She smirks at me before lowering her lips to my cock, taking me in deeply. Her mouth is hot and the way she sucks down on me is fucking unreal.

I groan and grab her hair as she takes me in deeper, moving my hips with her. "Look at you," I murmur, tightening my grip on her hair. "Didn't even let me undress fully before latching onto my cock, did you?"

She moans, and the vibrations her voice produces have me biting down on my lip. I watch her as she moves her head up and down, taking more and more of me. I tighten my grip on her hair and push into her mouth, and she takes it. I expected her to gag, but she doesn't, not until I hit the back of her throat.

"Tell me, baby. Are you wet for me? Are you getting off just sucking my dick? I haven't even touched you yet, but I'm betting I can slide right into you."

She glances up at me, and the look in her eyes tells me I'm right. I pull out of her mouth, and she whimpers, needy. "So fucking beautiful," I murmur, tilting her head up. "I fucking love you."

She smiles at me as I grab the edges of the T-shirt she's wearing, pulling it up. I chuckle when I see she's naked underneath. Of course she is.

"Tell me how you want it, Nyx."

Her cheeks redden, and for a couple of seconds, she looks shy. But then she smiles, a twinkle in her eyes. "I want it hard, Gray. I want to feel you deep inside me, and I want you to make me scream your name."

I laugh as I push against her shoulder, making her fall back on the sofa. "Of course you do, baby."

I grab her ankles with one hand and lift her legs up, my fingers finding their way to her pussy. "Soaking wet. I'm not surprised."

I grab my dick and align it with her, enjoying the way she squirms, wanting to feel me inside her. I've never been with a woman like her before. She's so honest about how much she wants me, about *what* she wants.

I push into her, and she tenses. "Too much?" I ask. Having her legs pressed together and up in the air like this makes her even tighter than usual. She shakes her head, and I push into her even further.

I love watching her lie there, her long dark hair spread over our sofa, her eyes glazed over with lust. I move slowly, driving her insane. I do it just to watch her squirm. "Grayson," she warns, and I grin, pulling out almost all the way before slamming into her deeply, the way she likes it. She moans, the sounds she's making filling up our living room.

I pull her hips up higher, fucking her at an angle I know she can't resist. Every time I slide back into her, she cries out in delight. Three minutes. That's all it takes for my girl to come on my cock. She fucking milks me, taking me right along with her.

I collapse on top of her, and she wraps her arms around me, her lips finding mine. We lie there together, lost in each other.

"I'm going to fuck you like that for the rest of our lives," I tell her, my hands threading through her hair.

Aria laughs. "Is that a promise?"

I grin and press a kiss to her neck. "It's a vow, baby."

We both have a fuck ton of work to do, but we'll get to that later. At some point, Aria will turn on the TV and put on my shirt. She'll reach for her laptop, and we'll work together, side by side, the way we do every night.

But not now.

For now, I just hold my girl in my arms, counting my blessings.

Chapter Fifty-One

ARIA

I yawn as I run the script *again*. My vision is starting to blur, I'm that exhausted. The hours we've been spending at the office in the last couple of weeks are unreal, and it isn't even enough. We're nearly at the finish line, though. The project is nearly done.

I rise from my seat and head toward the coffee machine, needing *something* to keep me awake. I place my cup in the machine and mindlessly press the buttons. At this point. I don't care what type of coffee it is, though I suspect muscle memory will result in yet another double espresso. I don't even like coffee that isn't mostly sugar, but I'm desperate. I worked through the night last night, and though I know the sun has since risen, I have no clue what time it is. Early morning, I guess.

I scroll through my phone as I wait for my coffee, tensing when I see the update on the Nemesis Platform. My eyes widen as I read through the additional information about the rape case we were struggling to find any evidence on. I didn't think we'd be able to crack it, considering how little we had to go on. Looks like the victim, Ida, came forward with information she's been keeping a secret for decades.

I read through the logs over and over again, but the report doesn't change. The rape didn't just result in lifelong trauma... it also resulted in a child. A child that she claims was left in a *church*.

My heart starts to race, and I scroll back up, reading through the report one more time. I don't believe in coincidences. I'm not sure I believe in fate, but I certainly don't believe in coincidences.

My hands are shaking so badly that typing takes me minutes rather than seconds. I'm operating almost entirely on auto-pilot, my mind scared to make the connection. I'm in such a weird detached state I barely realize what I typed, until I receive a reply, a confirmation.

I don't even recall asking to meet Ida in person, yet I'm staring at a meeting confirmation. She tells me she's grateful for my help, and that she's finally ready to tell someone her story. But am *I*? Am I ready?

I straighten my shoulders, forcing myself to get it together. Just because life has always let me down doesn't mean it's the case now too. Maybe, just maybe, I'm wrong.

I walk to my desk, a cold chill running down my spine, as though my subconscious is warning me as much as my brain is. I glance into Grayson's office. He's been working as hard as I have, but neither of us has minded it, because we've been going home together every night. We've been working late on the sofa, just the two of us. Every morning, we wake up together. The happiness we found together made everything bearable.

But is it strong enough to withstand this? If what I suspect is true, would Gray be okay? I drag my gaze away from him and grab my bag, making my way out of the office before he notices. I walk past Riley, but something in my expression must have warded him off because he frowns and looks away, though I notice the tinge of worry in his eyes.

My mind is carefully blank as I walk to the diner Ida told me she works at. Five blocks. She works five blocks from our office. I've been here before. With Gray.

My stomach is churning by the time I walk in. My hands are trembling, and I clench them together, forcing myself to stay calm. I might be wrong. I might be wrong about all of this. I need to know before I say anything to Gray.

I walk to one of the empty booths and sit down before my legs give in yet again. I see one of the waitresses eye me nervously, and I swallow hard. Those eyes. I know those eyes.

My heart sinks when she walks up to me, my eyes dropping to her name tag. "Ida," I say, smiling tightly.

She nods and sits down opposite me. "You must be Nyx," she murmurs, her voice soft. I nod tersely as I take her in. The familiarity guts me, and I pray I'm seeing things. Maybe I'm just tired, maybe my brain is playing tricks on me... because it sure looks like she has the same nose as Gray, the same eyes.

"Thank you for coming," she tells me. "Thank you for offering your help. You have no idea how many times I've been close to giving up... *on everything.* The thought that he walks freely, maybe even doing what he did to me to other women... Nyx, I can't sleep at night. It's coming up to thirty years. If I don't speak up now, I never will."

I nod and reach over the table to grab her hand. "Tell me as much as you can. Tell me the things you left out of your initial report. I'll do what I can to give you the justice you deserve."

She places her other hand on top of mine, gripping tightly. She nods, determined, but I see the pain in her eyes. Even her expressions are so much like his.

"George was a fellow church-goer. He seemed like a lovely fellow, and for a while, my parents considered him a potential suitor."

I nod, motioning for her to continue. Ida gulps and looks away, her eyes filling with tears.

"My parents had almost finalized our union... but then I fell in love. I fell for a childhood friend that had just returned from his studies, and when we met again, we knew that was it."

My ears are ringing as I listen to her story. I'm dreading what I know is coming, and I hate myself for it. I'm not the one that lived through this. If Ida can be brave, then so can I.

"My parents gave Jameson and me their blessing, and we were to be married within the year. I was the happiest I'd ever been, Nyx. Come to think of it, I believe it's the happiest I've ever been, because every moment after that became a living nightmare. George heard of my impending nuptials, and he asked to meet me. He said it was to get closure, to see me one last time. I was young and foolish. I felt guilty, knowing how much he'd wanted to marry me, so I agreed. I never should have."

Ida pulls her hands away and wraps her arms around herself, her gaze on the window beside us. "Jameson wasn't happy that I was meeting George, but he trusted me. Besides, George asked to meet me at a restaurant we'd been to before, so I didn't think much of it. I showed up, and I remember him standing there, a chilling smile on his face. Even then, I felt like something was wrong, but I was more concerned with politeness than I was with my own safety. I should've known better. The last thing I remember was finishing the cocktail he'd ordered me. Shortly after that, everything went black. When I woke up again, I was chained to his bed."

A tear runs down her face and she swallows hard in an attempt to keep her sobs at bay. "He kept me there all night, telling me he had rights to me, because I should've been his. He said he'd show me what I'd be missing, and that I'd be his whether I liked it or not. He told me Jameson would never look at me again once he was done with me, and I'd end up choosing to marry him instead."

She wipes away her tears, her eyes falling closed. "I ended up passing out eventually, my body hurting in so many ways. When I woke up again, I was alone. I got out of there as quickly as I could, wishing to leave it all behind me. I didn't dare tell my parents, and

I certainly didn't dare tell Jameson. I knew he'd never marry me if he found out, and I was desperate to pretend like nothing happened, like I wasn't damaged goods. So I stayed quiet. Until I couldn't. Until I started throwing up every morning, and my mother sat me down to ask me if I could be pregnant."

I try my hardest to keep my expression neutral, but my heart is breaking. Her case was bad enough as it is, but this? This is unfathomable.

"I told my mother everything, hoping she'd save me somehow. Instead, my parents sent me to my grandmother in the country-side, to hide out as my body started to change. You see, we were very religious, so abortion wasn't an option, especially not in those times. My parents didn't even allow me to give Jameson an explanation, and I was miserable. I had no way to reach him, no way to explain. All the while, the baby grew inside me, reminding me I could never go back to the life I once had."

A tear falls down her cheek and her eyes fall closed. She inhales shakily, and when she looks at me, her gaze is pleading.

"My father took my son from me days after birth, and he refused to tell me where my child went. It wasn't until he was on his deathbed that he told me. He said he took the baby to the same church George and I met at, the church that resulted in my downfall."

She looks at me with tears in her eyes. "I can't get back the life I envisioned for myself, Nyx. But I do want justice. Please, help me. Help me find my baby. Help me with this case."

I nod and take out my tablet, shutting my brain off as best as I can while she gives me every detail I might need to track down her child.

I didn't need to, though.

I knew the second she gave me the church's address.

Chapter Fifty-Two

ARIA

The sun has set by the time I walk up to the apartment building I've come to consider home. I've got over a dozen missed calls from Gray, and I can't imagine how worried he must be, yet I can't get myself to pick up the phone.

I walked around the area for hours after meeting Ida, trying my best to make sense of the story she told me, trying to think of a way to tell Gray. I can't...

He's been searching for his parents for years now. How do I tell him that none of the scenarios he imagined could be as bad as the truth is? How do I tell the man I love that his mother is the woman whose horrific case we've been trying to solve? Even worse, how do I tell him that the father he's been hoping to find... I can't even finish the sentence in my mind. If it hurts me this much, it'll destroy Grayson.

Yet I can't stay silent. Part of me wants to take this to the grave and hide it from him. But I can't. I can't do that to him. I can't make that decision for him.

I'm trembling when I walk into the building, and I'm second-guessing myself all the way up to the penthouse. Part of me wants to run. I don't want to be the person to tell him. I don't want to watch his heart break.

I'm shaking as I walk into the house and Gray rushes up to me, alarmed. "Aria," he says, relief coursing through his eyes. "Where the hell were you?"

His hands run over my body, as though he's checking for injuries. He's frantic, and I rise to my tiptoes, my arms wrapping around him.

"Aria, you're worrying me."

I lean in and kiss him, cutting him off. I don't want him to ask me where I was. I don't want to have to explain. Not yet.

Gray relaxes against me and kisses me back, his hands threading through my hair. He lifts me into his arms, and I wrap my legs around him as he pushes me against the wall. He kisses me with the same desperation I'm feeling, and I don't want this kiss to end. I whimper when he pulls away, and Gray drops his forehead to mine.

"Where were you?" he asks.

I hug him tightly, hiding my face against his neck.

"What the fuck is going on, baby?"

I squeeze my eyes closed and inhale shakily. "We need to talk, Gray. There's something I have to tell you."

Grayson tightens his grip on me and carries me to the sofa, sitting down with me in his lap. "Ari, talk to me. What happened? Where were you?"

I look into his eyes, wishing they weren't an exact replica of the tear-filled eyes I looked into earlier today. I raise my hand to his face, my finger tracing over his cheekbone.

"I... I went to meet someone, Gray. A woman."

He looks confused, and I don't blame him. I'm scared. I'm scared of not choosing the right words, of hurting him more than this story doubtlessly already will.

"She told me she had a child almost thirty years ago. Her son would be twenty-nine now, and just like you, he was left in front of a church."

I see the hope in his eyes, and it kills me. I force myself to keep my eyes on his, to be brave. I swallow hard, blinking back my tears. "The church she left her son at was the same one you were left at. It could be a coincidence, but maybe it's not."

Gray tenses, and the hint of happiness in his eyes kills me. "You found my mother?"

I'm messing this all up. I have to tell him what he needs to know.

"Gray, the woman... it was Ida, our rape victim."

He tenses, and I wish I could take my words back instantly. The incomprehension in his eyes quickly turns into horror, and I grab his shoulders.

"I could be wrong. I must be. I just... I don't know. I had to tell you. I couldn't not tell you."

Gray cups my cheek and leans in, pressing a kiss to my forehead. "I love you, Aria," he whispers, but his voice sounds pained. "Don't worry, okay? All of this might just be a crazy coincidence. Let's focus on the case, okay? Tell me everything."

I nod and wrap my arms around him, my grip tight as I repeat the story Ida told me. Or as much of it as I can.

Gray tenses, and though he tries his best to stay calm, I see the worry in his eyes as I tell him most of what Ida told me. I see the way he grimaces, the way he recoils in horror. I hope I'm wrong. I hope Gray is right, and this is all just a crazy coincidence. He listens to me as I finish telling the story, never once interrupting.

He runs a hand through his hair and looks away, his gaze on the window. "We found George, didn't we?"

I nod, knowing where he's going with this.

"We'll have to do a DNA test. I could be living proof of his crime. If there's DNA evidence, there's hope. We'll need to have the legal team look into that straight away."

"Gray," I whisper. "Forget about the case for a minute... what about you? Everything I just told you, it's a lot. What if you do that test, and you end up being Ida's son?"

Gray looks into my eyes and cups my cheek, his thumb brushing over my lips. "I don't know, baby. I've been looking for my parents all my life. Of course I don't want to be the son of a... a..."

I lean in and rest my head against his shoulder, and he hugs me tightly. "I bet it's just a coincidence," I whisper.

He presses a kiss to my hair. "Maybe it is, Nyx. Maybe it isn't. Either way, I need to know. The questions I've lived with all my life... even if the answers I'm seeking aren't the ones I'm after, I'd still rather have them than not. I can't spend the rest of my life wondering."

I nod, my lips brushing against his neck. I hope this is all a misunderstanding, a trick of fate. If it isn't, it might destroy the man I love.

Chapter Fifty-Three

GRAYSON

I stare up at the ceiling, unable to calm my thoughts. I've been looking for my parents for years, and never once did I consider this. I knew there would be a chance my mother gave me up knowingly, but I never could have even dreamt of something like this.

Could I really be the son of a monster? Does his blood run through my veins? I'll find out tomorrow, and I'm feeling conflicted. On the one hand, I want answers. On the other, I'm scared of what truth I might uncover.

It would explain the violence I struggle to suppress. The satisfaction I felt when I put my former foster father into a coma for touching one of the girls in our home. I've known something is wrong with me ever since then, when I realized I felt no remorse at all. I felt that same satisfaction when I wrecked Brad's face and his entire life, too. Do I get that from my father?

Aria turns in my arms, her lips brushing past my neck. "Can't sleep?" she whispers.

I pull her closer and tighten my grip on her. She might try to reassure me, but there's no way she could love me if the tests come back positive. There's no way a woman like Aria could ever be with the son of a rapist. She might try to convince herself it doesn't matter, but it does.

"Gray?"

I bury my hand in her hair, finding solace in her embrace. I don't even know what to say to her, how to explain my worries. I don't want to put her in a position where she'd have to lie to me to make me feel better.

"Just thinking about the test," I tell her. The way she was crying as she was telling me about Ida revealed the things she left unsaid. It betrayed her fears.

Aria pushes herself up on my chest and looks at me, the small amount of light from the window illuminating her silhouette. She's beautiful, and I barely deserve her as it is.

"It'll be okay, Gray," she says.

I nod and raise my hand to her face, stroking her cheek with the tip of my fingers. "I love you, Aria," I tell her, wishing the words were adequate to explain how I feel about her. "You are the missing part. You are what completes me. My life was empty, until you."

She leans in and lowers her lips to mine. She kisses me, and this kiss is different from all those that came before. I thread my hands through her hair, taking my time with her. I turn us over, so I'm lying on top of her. She spreads her legs for me instinctively, and I smile against her lips.

"I'll never get enough of you," I whisper.

"Grayson," she says, her tone pleading. I lean in and kiss her neck, taking my time, leaving marks all over her skin. Tonight feels different... It feels like it might be the last time I get to hold her, the last time I get to call her mine.

Tomorrow, the way she sees me might change forever. She might never smile at me the same, and while I know she'll try not to let it show, I know that I'll lose part of her.

I pull her T-shirt up and she lifts her arms for me. Just a few months ago, she wouldn't even let me see her naked. She and I have had to work so hard to get where we are. Will all that progress be undone tomorrow?

Her gaze is heated as I wrap my hands around the white lace panties she's wearing. She lifts her hips for me and I drag them down slowly, wanting to savor this moment.

I spread her legs and lean in to kiss the inside of her thighs, teasing her, slowly getting closer to where I know she wants me.

"Grayson," she moans. I love my name on her lips. I love that pleading tone of hers. Fuck. I love everything about this woman.

I press a kiss against her pussy before leaning in and getting a taste. Aria moans, and the sound of her drives me insane. I circle my tongue around her clit the way she likes it, getting her close within minutes. She pants my name over and over again, and I swear I could come just listening to her.

I make her come on my tongue, enjoying the way she loses control over her body. I pull away to watch her, the way her cheeks flush and her lips fall open... Beautiful.

She smiles at me and I'm lost. She owns me, every broken, battered piece of me. I grab her legs and push them over her shoulders. "You want my cock, don't you, Nyx?"

She nods and I push the tip in, keeping it there, torturing her. "How badly do you want it? I just made you come, but that isn't enough for you, is it?"

She shakes her head. "I will always want more of you."

I push in a little deeper and then pull back out almost all the way, making her whimper. "Look at you," I tell her. "This soaking wet pussy, your hair spread over my pillows... You're so nice and sweet at work and around everyone else, but you're a little slut for me, aren't you?" I push in a little deeper and smirk at her. "You want all of this big fat cock, don't you?"

Aria moves her hips up, trying to get me in deeper. I love how needy she is, how blatantly she wants me.

I push into her slowly, watching as her pussy takes all of me. She's so wet, so hot.

"Gray, please," she begs, and I pull out almost all the way before thrusting into her the way she wants it. I look into her eyes as I fuck her, slamming into her, making her tiny body take my cock.

"I love you," she moans. "I love this. I love this cock."

I grin and give it to her harder, loving the way her muscles contract around me when I push into her at the right angle. I bite down on my lip when she comes for me, and I follow soon after, making a mess of her pussy.

We collapse together, both of us a sweaty mess, and I wrap my arms around her, holding onto this happiness while I still can.

Chapter Fifty-Four

GRAYSON

I'm in a state of disbelief as I put my phone down on my desk. Positive. The DNA test came back positive.

I didn't think much of it when the prosecutor asked me to take the test. They had me go into a clinic, and I walked out of it minutes later, not expecting much at all. The entire process was efficient and painless, so much so that it was easy to forget what it was all for, what the results could mean.

I'm startled out of my thoughts by a knock on my office door, and I look up to find Aria walking in. She closes the door behind her. Her eyes meet mine, and the smile melts off her face, making way for a frown. "Gray?" She says, her voice soft. "Is everything okay?"

I shake my head and rise to my feet. She walks into my arms and my eyes fall closed as I place my chin on top of her head, hugging her tightly. "The results came back positive," I say, my voice barely above a whisper, a part of me unwilling to say it out loud.

Aria freezes in my arms, and my stomach twists. I've tried my best to keep my mind off the implications of a positive result, but I can't avoid the truth any longer. I'm the result of a horrible crime, and I don't know how that'll change how Aria sees me.

She pulls back, and I look away, unable to face her. "That means you finally found your mother, Gray," she says, her hands reaching for mine. "Ida told me her father took her child away from her shortly after birth. I wonder how she feels, knowing you've finally been found. She asked me to help her find you, you know?"

I raise my hand to her face and twirl a strand of her hair around my finger. "So far, all my communication has been with the prosecutor. I know next to nothing about Ida. I have no idea if she even wants to see me."

Aria purses her lips and nods. "She must want to see you, too. If she's trying to find you now to aid her case, she must be ready to meet you."

My heart races at the mere thought of meeting my mother. I've spent years searching for her, and she's been so close all along.

"I... I think I want to drop by the diner. Even if it's just to see her. I'm fine not even speaking to her, but I've got to see her."

Aria nods in understanding, a bittersweet smile on her face. The haunted look in her eyes tells me she's thinking of her own mother. She'll never see her mother again, but mine is only a few blocks away.

"Do you want me to come with you?" she asks, and I shake my head, cupping her cheek.

"I think this is something I need to do on my own, Nyx. She's so close... I'm just going to drop by. I've waited for years, and I don't think I can wait a second longer. I want to see my mother with my own eyes, even if it's just once."

She smiles and rises to her tiptoes, pressing a kiss to my cheek. "I'll be right here, my love. I'll be here when you get back, and you can tell me all about it."

I bury my hand in her hair and tilt her head up, kissing her with every ounce of gratitude and love I'm feeling. I'm so fucking lucky to have her. I was worried about what she'd think of me, but her only thought is how *I'm* feeling. The way she looks at me hasn't changed, and I should've known it wouldn't. This is my Nyx, after all.

"Go," she whispers against my lips, and I nod, pressing a lingering kiss to her forehead before grabbing my wallet and walking out of my office, a strange sense of wonder coursing through my veins. Years. I've been looking for my mother for years. How many Sundays have I sat outside the church I was left at?

By the time I reach the diner Aria told me about, my stomach is in knots. I'm rarely nervous, but I am right now. I walked here mostly on autopilot, trying to keep my raging thoughts at bay, but they overwhelm me now.

How many times have I walked straight past her? I took Aria here for coffee months ago. Was Ida there then?

I walk into the diner before I can talk myself out of it, before my thoughts turn negative, as I know they will. I feel sick as I walk up to the same table we sat at when I crashed Aria's and Riley's coffee date.

I glance around, seeing this place through different eyes. So this is where my mother has been working. All these years I kept wondering who she was and where she might be. Now that I have my answers, part of me wishes I'd left the past where it should've remained. Now that I'm sitting here, this morning's phone call is finally sinking in. I might be Ida's son, but I'm also the son of her rapist. I don't know how she'll respond to seeing me, and countless scenarios run through my mind.

A waitress walks up to me, and my heart starts to race. My eyes drop to her name tag, and a strange combination of relief and anxiety washes over me when I realize she isn't Ida.

I hesitate, and then I smile up at the waitress who, in hindsight, is far too young to be my mother. "Shabnam," I say, addressing her by the name on her tag. "Is Ida here?"

Shabnam pauses, and then she nods, turning to get her. I run my clammy hands over my suit trousers, unsure whether I should stand or stay seated, unsure what to say. Maybe I shouldn't even be here at all.

I freeze when an older woman walks up to me, and I see the exact moment she realizes who I am. Her face distorts into a disgusted expression, her eyes flashing with hatred.

"You," she spits out, sliding into the seat opposite me. "How dare you come here? You're his child, aren't you?"

His child? I nod, functioning entirely on autopilot.

"Wasn't it enough that you ruined my life? Did you come here to ruin this pitiful job as well?"

I frown, confused. "I don't even know why I'm here, Ida," I tell her. "I just wanted to see you."

"What for? To remind me of the sins of your father? You need to leave."

"I... I'm your *son*," I say helplessly.

Ida laughs, the sound hollow. "You're no son of mine. You're the Devil's son. You ruined my life, and even now, you're ruining it further. I thought your existence would at least get me justice, but it didn't. I'd never have tried to find you if I didn't think you'd help put him away, but you're useless to me."

Her eyes flash with what I recognize as frustration, and I can't help but hope that it's the *case* she's frustrated with, and that she's merely projecting that on me. Despite her words, a small part of me wants to believe she doesn't hate me.

"He was happy to give his DNA because of how long ago the offense occurred, I assume. He'd have been a lot more worried if he knew about your existence. Now he's lawyered up, swearing up and down that I *wanted* it. That he'd been courting me, and I'd been asking for it. Like I'd ever want to be defiled. Now it's his word against mine. Who do you think people will believe? The poor waitress or a successful businessman?"

She laughs, the sound filled with hatred. "You look like him," she tells me. "I bet you're just like him too, aren't you? Hurting women, using those weaker than you. I bet you've gone after someone vulnerable, just like your father did. You have, haven't you?"

I instinctively think of Aria. When she and I started dating, she *was* vulnerable. She was heartbroken, and I took advantage of it. She'd never have wanted to date me if she hadn't just come out of such an awful relationship.

Ida smiles at me, her expression chilling. "You're a monster," she tells me. "You shouldn't exist. If my parents would've let me, I'd have aborted you. The only reason you're alive is because my father took you away from me before I could kill you with my bare hands."

She rises from her seat and stares at me. "You should be dead," she says. "You know, for just a second I was happy you existed because I thought it meant I'd finally get justice. But it doesn't. You're useless, your existence is meaningless. You are born of sin, and darkness will follow everything you touch. Don't appear here again. Don't destroy what is left of my life."

She walks away, and I stare after her, her words reverberating in my mind.

Chapter Fifty-Five

ARIA

I glance around the office, my phone in my hand. I expected Gray to come back after meeting Ida, but he hasn't. His phone seems to be turned off too, and it worries me.

I'm anxious as I make my way home, overthinking everything. I should have gone with him. I knew this wouldn't be easy, and I should have been there for him. If nothing else, I should've waited for him outside. Why didn't I think of that at the time?

My heart starts to race when I walk into the house to find it dark and empty. Panic grips me, and I clutch my phone tightly. My first instinct is to try calling Gray again, but I already know his phone is turned off.

I lean back against the wall, my thoughts whirling. Where could he be? What could have happened? Maybe I should have dropped by the diner to check if he might still be there with Ida. Maybe they've been talking for hours, and his phone ran out of battery. That's what I want to believe, but I can feel deep down to my core that something is wrong.

I walk through the house, pausing by the door that leads up to the rooftop. My heart hammers in my chest as I walk up the stairs. I'm trembling as I walk out onto the rooftop, worried sick.

Intense relief washes over me when I see Gray standing by his punching bag through the glass walls separating the pool area from the gym. The force he's hitting the bag with tells me his meeting with Ida didn't go well.

He barely looks up when I walk into the gym, his expression haunted. What could have happened? She was actively looking for him, wasn't she?

I walk up to Gray and sit down on the floor a few steps away, watching him. He goes through sequence after sequence, hitting and kicking the bag, his muscles tensing with every move. I don't say a word as he keeps going, my eyes on his face. I watch his expression carefully, taking in the sorrow, the anger, the heartache. Whatever happened can't have been good. What could she have said to him?

Gray steadies the bag with both hands and drops his forehead to it, his breathing labored. I rise to my feet and walk up to him, placing my hand on his arm. He turns his head to look at me, and the pain I see in his eyes guts me.

He reaches out for me, the back of his hand brushing over my cheek. There's desperation in his eyes, and I wish I knew what it is he needs. I can't make it right if I don't know what's wrong.

"I love you," I whisper. "I don't know what happened, Grayson. I don't know how she responded or what she might have said, but *I* love you. I love you with all my heart. You're more than just my boyfriend, Gray. You're my family."

He swallows hard and pulls me closer. I wrap my arms around his neck and jump up the way I usually do. He instinctively lifts me into his arms, and I wrap my legs around his waist. He inhales shakily and buries his face in my neck as I tighten my grip on him, the tips of my fingers combing through his hair. We stand there together, my legs around his waist and his face buried in my neck. I hold him as closely as I can, doing my best to make him feel just how loved he is.

"You always know the right thing to say," he whispers, pressing a soft kiss to my neck. "I love you, Aria. I don't deserve you, but fuck... I love you. I love you so much."

I nod, my eyes filling with tears. I don't know what's going on, but my heart is breaking for him. Gray pulls away to look at me, and the vulnerability in his eyes has my stomach tightening. "What do you see when you look at me, Aria? Do you see the son of a rapist? Tell me honestly, baby. Do you think I'd ever hurt you? I need to know."

"What?" I cup his cheeks with both hands, keeping his eyes on mine. "Don't you ever even think that kind of bullshit, Grayson. Don't. I don't see you that way. I never have, and I never will. You're still the same man I fell in love with. You're still Noah's best friend. You're the person who helped make my dreams come true, the man that inspired me to keep going when life was too much to bear. You're the person who helped solve hundreds of cases, never even asking for recognition for all you do. That is who you are, Grayson. That is who you've always been."

He looks into my eyes, his gaze searching. I see the disbelief, the suspicion, and I don't know how to make it better. Gray inhales deeply and presses a lingering kiss to my cheek. "Come on," he says, sounding defeated. "I'm sweaty. I need a shower. Let's go down."

Chapter Fifty-Six

GRAYSON

I inhale deeply as I turn the shower on, feeling filthy right down to my soul. I'm not sure how long I've been in here when the door opens. I turn to find Aria walking up to me, her body bare, a tortured expression in her eyes. I did that. I put that worry in her eyes.

She takes my electric toothbrush from me, and I blink in confusion. I didn't even realize I was holding it. "I've heard you brush your teeth three times now, Gray. I think you're clean."

She puts it away and moves closer to me, her palms flat on my chest. She's so fucking tiny, and I've always loved that about her, but today it scares me. It'd be so easy to hurt her. Will I ever feel that same twisted satisfaction while hurting *her*? Is she safe with me?

Aria slides her hands up my chest and around my neck. "Grayson," she whispers, her head tilted up to face me. Even on her tiptoes, she can't kiss me unless I bend down to meet her lips. I look into her eyes, wondering what she sees. How long is it going to take for her to realize what kind of man she's with? How long until my touch becomes revolting to her?

"I'm done showering," I tell her, untangling myself from her. I see the disappointment in her eyes, and for a second, I want to stop and turn back to her. I want to take her into my arms, but then I'm reminded of Ida. Not even in my mind do I dare call her my mother, not since she told me I'm an abomination. After everything she went through because of me, I don't deserve to call her mother. She was right. Even before Aria was mine, I wanted her. When she wanted to move here with Brad, I stopped it from happening. I did it, knowing it'd hurt her. I did it because I was selfish. That was just the first step. In what other ways will I hurt her as time goes on? How long until it becomes physical?

What would have happened if we'd never started dating? Would I have been able to resist touching her the way I'd been dreaming of? Would my heritage make me incapable of respecting her wishes? Would I end up touching her against her will?

I'd like to think I wouldn't, but I don't know anymore. I don't know what I'm capable of.

I slip into bed, knowing it doesn't matter if I attempt to go to the guest room. Aria will follow me. I know she will. I tense when she gets into bed with me. I feel her inch closer until her arms wrap around mine. She spoons me, and it breaks my heart. I turn and take her into my arms, holding her tightly. "I'm sorry, Aria," I tell her, wishing words could accurately portray how sorry I am about everything. "I'm sorry for worrying you, for turning off my phone."

She settles in my embrace, her head on my chest. "It's okay, Gray," she murmurs. "It's okay to take some time to think things through and it's okay if you don't want to talk. I know what that's like. I'll sit with you in silence for as long as you want me to. I'm not going anywhere, Grayson."

I bury my hand in her hair, struggling to believe she's mine, at least for now.

"I love you," I whisper.

Aria looks up and presses a kiss to my neck. "I love you more."

She pushes herself up on my chest, shifting in my arms so she's lying fully on top of me, her forearms on my chest. I stare at her in disbelief. She's so beautiful. It isn't just her outer beauty. It's her heart.

She leans in, and I freeze when her lips brush over mine. She's so light on top of me, so fragile. The way I've touched her in the past... who knows how many times I've already hurt her unknowingly?

Aria sighs and lies back down, her hair tucked underneath my chin. I close my arms around her, my heart conflicted. I've always felt protective of Aria... but I can't protect her from myself.

Chapter Fifty-Seven

Aria

I'm anxious as I put the egg tarts in the oven. Portuguese egg tarts are Gray's all-time favorite treat, and I'm hoping this will cheer him up. He hasn't been himself all week. He's been distant and quiet. I haven't seen him smile once, and though he isn't actively pushing me away, he isn't reaching out for me the way he used to. He doesn't walk up to me when he gets home and he doesn't kiss me. When we go to bed, he'll hold me if I wrap myself in his embrace, but he won't reach for me.

Even at work, he isn't the same. He works insane hours, but he isn't checking in with us in person. He isn't speaking to any of us. Even Riley noticed he's been behaving differently. The atmosphere at work has changed, and it all points back to Gray. He doesn't even realize he's the heart of his company.

I don't know what's going on in his mind. He's constantly lost in thought, and I'm worried. I feel like I'm losing him, even though he's right here. I don't know what Ida said to him, but it's clear she's done some damage. I just hope it isn't irreversible.

I tense when the front door opens, my heart racing. I've never felt this type of desperation. I've never so badly wanted to make someone feel better. Even back when I wanted to put a smile on Noah's face by making him a birthday cake, it didn't feel this way. It didn't feel like my own heart would break if I failed to make him smile.

Grayson barely looks up as he walks into the house, seemingly lost in thought, as he always is these days. "Gray," I say, walking up to him. He pauses and turns to look at me. At least that hasn't changed. He still looks at me with blatant affection.

I place my palms flat on his chest and slide them up slowly, wrapping my arms around his neck as I push my body against his and rise to my tiptoes for a kiss. He leans in, bending down just enough for my lips to meet his, but the kiss is chaste at best. I don't remember the last time I managed to turn him on, and it makes me feel insecure. I keep trying to convince myself it isn't me, but I can't help but worry. I can't help but think that maybe everything just coincided. Maybe the big change in his life made him realize he doesn't have time or space for me, or he just doesn't want me enough. I'm fighting those thoughts as best as I can, but they're still there nonetheless.

"I made you egg tarts," I tell him, trying my best to smile as brightly as I can. If there's one thing I excel at, it's forcing a smile.

Grayson looks into my eyes and nods. "Thank you," he murmurs. "But I'm not hungry."

He pulls away and turns to walk to the bedroom, and it kills me. It kills me to watch him walk away. I hate feeling this helpless. I don't want to stand here and watch him suffer in silence, not when I'm right here, right by his side.

"Grayson," I whisper, my voice breaking. "Don't shut me out. Don't push me away."

He turns to face me, his expression as pained as mine must be. He walks up to me and I look up when he buries his hands in my hair, holding me tightly. He leans in and presses a kiss to my forehead, his lips lingering.

"I'm sorry," he whispers. "I'm sorry, Aria. I just have a lot of work to do. That's all."

He pulls away, and I miss him instantly. I take a step closer and rise to my tiptoes, pulling his head down to mine. I kiss him, silently begging him to kiss me back.

He tenses, and for a second, I'm certain he'll push away, but then he kisses me back, properly, for the first time in over a week. I moan against his lips, and he melts against me, his hands roaming over my body. I push myself up, and he smiles against my lips as he lifts me into his arms, turning us around so I'm pressed up against the wall, my legs wrapped around him.

His tongue brushes against my lips, and I open up for him, deepening our kiss. I've missed this. I've missed losing myself in him.

"Aria," he whispers, his lips moving to my throat. I groan when he sucks down on a sensitive part of my neck, needing more.

But instead, he pulls away, dropping his forehead to my shoulder, his breathing as labored as mine. "I can't do this," he murmurs.

He lowers me to the floor carefully, but I'm not letting him go. "Why? What's going on, Gray. You've barely spoken to me in days now. Talk to me."

He runs a hand through his hair and looks away. "It's not you, baby. It's never you. You're everything good in my life. You're my light when the world falls into darkness. It's me. I'm born of sin, Aria. I'm the son of a rapist. I've got his blood running through my veins. I carry that darkness inside me. I never should've been born. A man like me... it's only a matter of time before I hurt you, and I probably won't even realize it. Hell... I might like it. Then what?"

My stomach drops, and a chill runs down my spine as I try my best to stay calm. "Who told you this?" I ask, unable to hide the edge in my voice. "When you left the office to go see Ida, you weren't thinking any of this. You left with hope in your eyes and you returned clouded in despair. Did she do this to you? Did she tell you this?"

Anger unlike anything I've ever felt before rushes through me, and I'm tempted to remove her case from my platform entirely. How dare she make the love of my life question who he is. He's been looking for her for years, and this is what he found?

"I... it's okay, Ari. She's hurt, and she was lashing out, but she wasn't wrong. It's true. I *am* the result of a horrible crime, and nothing will ever change that. But maybe, just maybe, if we're able to give Ida the justice she deserves, some of those sins will be lifted."

I raise my hand to his face and cup his cheek, keeping my eyes on his. "Those are not your sins, Grayson. They are not your burdens to carry. It is not you who should be seeking redemption."

He nods, but I can tell he doesn't believe me, and for now, there's nothing I can do to make him see himself through my eyes. What I can do, is help him with his case. If that's what he needs right now, then that's what I'll do, no matter how badly I believe that Ida neither deserves Grayson nor the help we can offer.

Chapter Fifty-Eight

ARIA

I wake up alone and sit up, instantly panicked. My heart is racing as I slip out of bed and check room after room, knowing that I won't find Gray. I can feel it. It's crazy, but I can feel if he isn't home. I can feel when he's near, and when he isn't.

I glance at the clock in the living room, my stomach tightening in worry. It's seven in the morning, so he must have slipped out during the night. Lately I often find Gray staring up at the ceiling by the time I wake up, but he's always in bed with me.

This is a first, and it worries me. I walk back into our bedroom, looking for traces of him, any indication of when he might have left or where he might have gone.

I jump when my phone buzzes on my nightstand and reach for it frantically, hoping it's Gray, but it's not. Instead, a myriad of notifications from the Nemesis Platform pop up. I frown, confused by what could be causing this big of a commotion.

I scroll through, my heart stopping when I realize Ash uploaded a video and requested that the media team distribute it.

My hands are shaking as I press play, scared of what I'll find.

The video starts, and I instantly recognize George. Gray is sitting with his back to the camera, the two of them in an empty bar. George is clearly visible, but Grayson is mostly blurred. Not that it matters. I'd recognize him anywhere.

"There's this girl," Gray says, his voice slurred. "I think I love her, you know?"

I frown, a chill running down my spine. What's going on here? Why is he with George... and who is he talking about?

George takes another big swig of what appears to be whiskey and nods, indicating for Gray to go on. It looks like the two of them have been drinking together for hours.

"I thought she loved me too, but she doesn't. I'd have married her, man. Loved her with all my heart. Wanted to have fucking babies with her. But she? She was fucking around on me all along. She'd never let me spread those pretty legs of hers, but it turned out she spread them for everyone else."

George laughs. "Women are vicious creatures, boy. They play games and think they'll get away with it. It's up to you to take what you want."

Grayson tenses. It's subtle, and I doubt anyone but me would even notice it. I sink down to my knees on the floor, clutching my phone tightly. Part of me instantly feels betrayed, but a more rational part of me can see what's going on. He's getting a confession out of George. How did he even track him down? How did he get him drunk? Is a confession even legally admissible if he is? I'm not sure it is, but I can see how this would sway the jury nonetheless, if Gray can get them to see it. If our media team can get this to go viral, then there's no way George is getting away with what he did.

"I should have. If she was going to spread her legs for all my buddies, she should've let me fuck her. I'd have done her much better than any other man could."

"Take her," George says, slumping over. "She was yours first, wasn't she?"

Gray nods. "We were dating. She made me believe she wanted me, that she'd marry me."

George laughs and nods. "I knew a woman like that once," he says, gulping down more whiskey. Gray refills his glass the second he empties it, but George doesn't seem to realize what's happening.

"Matter of fact, she recently popped back into my life. I think she missed me because she clearly wants my attention. Maybe she regrets leaving me after all, especially now I'm rich."

Gray leans back and raises his arm. I can't see his face, but it looks like he's taking a sip of his drink. "What happened? She did to you what my girl did to me?"

George nods and laughs. "Yeah, but I aint no pussy. I wasn't going to let her away with it."

"I don't want to let my girl get away with this bullshit, either. If nothing else, I just want a taste of her pussy, you know? If everyone else gets to have it, why don't I?"

George claps Gray on the back, a wide smile on his face. "That's it, my boy. That's it."

Gray shakes his head. "It's not possible, though. She won't even speak to me."

George laughs and empties half his glass, quickly succumbing to the liquor. He's already slurring his words more than he did at the start of the video, and it's only been a few minutes.

"She doesn't need to speak. She just needs to spread her legs."

Gray runs a hand through his hair, frustrated, though likely not for the reasons George thinks. "How am I supposed to get her to do that when she won't even speak to me?" he says, agitated.

George smiles, and even through my screen, it makes chills run down my spine. That glint in his eye... it's pure evil. He glances around to check no one is listening, and then he leans in.

"In my time I used a liquid one of my buddies got me," he says. "Put it in her drink, and in just a few minutes, and she'll be putty in your arms."

"I don't know, man," Grayson says, an edge to his tone that

George misses entirely. "I'm not sure it'll be the same if she's just lying there."

George shakes his head and drops his hand on Gray's shoulder. "You'll still enjoy it. Just knowing you still get to have what you're owed will make it enjoyable. It'll be even better when she eventually wakes up and starts to fight you. Just make sure you tie her up."

I feel sick. This man... this man can't be Grayson's father. They can't be related. I can't believe he's sitting there without an ounce of remorse, telling Grayson to *rape* someone.

"You talk a good talk, but have you ever actually done it?"

George grins, and that smile of his makes my stomach turn. He empties his whiskey glass, and Grayson refills him yet again.

"There was a girl... much like yours. She told me she was mine, that she'd marry me. They're all the same, those whores."

He lifts his glass to his lips, his expression betraying the bitterness he must still be feeling.

"So you speak from experience then? I thought you were all talk."

George straightens. "I told you I aint no pussy. I met her at the place I took her on our first date, a vial in my pocket. She was done for within minutes. I took her home to the bed I expected to share with her and tied her to it. She looked beautiful, lying there."

Gray chuckles, but it's obviously forced. George doesn't notice, though. The liquor and the memories have him distracted.

"What was it like?"

George smiles, his expression gleeful. "Oh, it was glorious. I stained my sheets with her virgin blood the way I always knew I would. In hindsight, I wish I'd waited for her to wake up before I did it. She cursed me, but she enjoyed it. She was so wet, her body telling me how much she wanted me even though her lips lied."

Gray lifts his arm, taking another sip, I assume. "She cursed you, huh? Your girl got a name?"

George nods, grinning. "Ida. Oh, beautiful Ida. She cursed

the hell out of me, but she wanted me. She tells me we conceived a baby that night, but it can't be true. She wants my attention. I've kept an eye on her through the years. If we had a baby, I'd know. She'd have come for alimony years ago."

He takes another big swig of his drink, and my stomach churns. A confession. That was a confession. Grayson just sat there and listened to his father explain how he raped his mother. He sat there, and he played along.

He's ensured his mother justice by doing so, but at what cost?

Chapter Fifty-Nine

GRAYSON

I stare at the large cross at the center of the church. I've never sat in these pews. I've never even entered this church, but today I felt compelled to go.

I couldn't go back home to Aria after the filth I sat through, the things I heard. Not that this place will help. Aria told me that this is where Ida and George met. They attended church together, but that clearly couldn't save George from his twisted mind, nor Ida from her fate.

Despite all of that, I find myself here, where it all started. I find myself staring up at the cross, part of me hoping that there's some sort of purpose to all of this. Was everything that happened pre-destined? Was I meant to exist, or am I truly just the personification of my father's sins?

I can only assume I was left here because my grandfather blamed the church for what happened. Because he thought they should take care of the consequences of the crimes they failed to prevent. I chuckle to myself, the sound reverberating through the empty church. It's all absurd, really.

My eyes fall closed when I hear the clicking of heels resounding through the halls. I should have known. I should have known my girl would find me anywhere I go. I stare at the cross as she gets closer. I don't need to turn and look to know it's her. My heart knows.

If a God does exist, then he must have been the one to send her to me. She is all that is good in this world.

Aria slides in next to me, and I turn my head to look at her. She's beautiful. She always is, but today her beauty stirs my very soul. Seeing her calms the viscousness that claws at me. The thoughts I can't keep at bay are silenced when I look into her eyes.

"What are you doing here?" I ask, my voice soft.

She smiles, but I see the hurt in her eyes. I hate that I'm doing this to her. I might be hurting, but she is too, because of me. She wraps her arms around herself and leans back, her eyes turning to the cross I'd just been studying.

"My home is wherever you are, Grayson. Since you weren't at the apartment, I came here."

Pain, hope, and fear all melt together as I stare at her. I don't deserve her. She might be the best thing that's ever happened to me, but I can't be that to her. She's such an incredible woman, and she deserves better. She deserves better than a rapist's son.

"You should go," I whisper, willing myself to say the words.

Aria looks back at me and grins. "Funny how you think you can tell me what to do. I've never been very good at listening to instructions... you'd think you'd know that by now."

I fall silent and look at her. She's incredible, and I'll ruin her. I know I will. "Aria," I murmur. "Please leave. You... you can't be with a man like me. You can't. You have such a bright future ahead of you. You're beautiful, intelligent, funny — you're incredible. Don't waste that on me."

She sits in silence, as though she's thinking through my words, and it kills me. It hurts to have her walk away, but she must. I can't taint her. Not her.

"I think you're misunderstanding the whole church thing,"

she says, frowning. "Just because Jesus was a martyr doesn't mean you need to be."

I look down at my hands, feeling conflicted. "Aria, didn't you see the video? I'm the son of a rapist. That man... that vile creature... his blood flows through my veins. You and I don't have a future together."

She looks into my eyes, and the certainty I see in them startles and humbles me all at once.

"The man you were last week, and the man you are today... are they two different people?"

My eyes fall closed in an effort to hide the agony I'm feeling. She doesn't get it. Right now she might not think much of the situation, but reality will soon sink in. And when it does, she'll no longer look at me that way.

"I've been here. Maybe not quite in the same way, but I know what it's like to have your entire life fall apart around you. I did exactly what you did when I lost my parents. I shut everyone out. I lost my ability to speak, and I convinced myself no one could ever remotely like me with all my flaws, my traumas, my pain."

Her lips tip up into a bittersweet smile, and she grabs my hand, holding it in both of hers. "I love you, Grayson. Who your parents are doesn't affect me in the slightest. The only thing I care about is how it affects *you*."

I laugh mockingly, unable to hide my disbelief. "You say that now, but you'll change your mind, eventually." I turn to her, agony almost crippling me. "Tell me, Aria. Would you ever have children with me, knowing what type of DNA they'd inherit?"

She tilts her head in question and looks me square in the eye. "Tell me, Grayson. Would you ever have children with me knowing they'd have a mother that continuously has nightmares? That can't go to sleep without checking every single lock in the house? A mother that'll suffocate them because she'd always be worried about their safety?" She looks away and shakes her head. "I don't know if I want children, Gray. I'm not cut out to have them, and it wouldn't be fair to them. It wouldn't be fair to have them if I can't raise them in a healthy way. What I do know is that if I ever want children, I'd want them with you."

"Aria," I say, my tone terse. "Don't you ever say anything like that. Don't even think it. You'd make a great mother. Any children would be lucky to have you."

She raises her hand to my face, stroking my stubble with the back of her hand. "Why? Because my past doesn't define my future, the way yours doesn't either?"

She cups my cheek, and I place my hand over hers, staring into her eyes. "It's not the same, Aria."

She smiles at me, her eyes filled with the same sorrow I'm feeling. "It is, Gray. You just don't see it yet. But you will. I'll spend the rest of our lives convincing you if I must."

I want to believe her, but all I can think about is my father's words. The vileness I saw in his eyes last night left me wondering if that same evil has infected me, too. I worry that it's a slow-acting poison, something I have no control over, something I might not even realize is affecting me. Not until it's too late.

I can't take that risk with Aria. I can't risk hurting her.

Chapter Sixty

ARIA

I stare into Grayson's office, watching him work himself to the bone. He doesn't rest, nor does he sleep these days. He's losing weight, and there are permanent dark circles underneath his eyes. I'm worried. Thanks to him working on our software personally, we're due to finish ahead of schedule, but at what cost?

I tear my gaze away when I notice Elliot approaching me from my peripheral vision. He looks crestfallen, and I look down at my hands.

"The blurring was well done, but I recognized him nonetheless. I don't think anyone else will, though. But wow... I never would have thought... and for him to do that, get a confession like that, that was insane. It all makes a bit more sense now, the way he's been acting lately."

I nod and wrap my arms around myself, as though that'll keep me from falling apart. I look up at Elliot and decide to follow Grayson's wishes. Ida doesn't remotely deserve our help, not after what she's made Grayson believe, but if this is what he wants, if this is what he needs, then I'll be here to support him.

Besides, getting that video destroyed him. I'm not sure he'll ever be the same again. He was distant after speaking to Ida, but that was nothing compared to what he's like now. All he does is work. He barely even eats or sleeps, and it's been days since we last had anything that even remotely resembled a conversation.

"He asked the social media team to circulate the footage, but it still hasn't been picked up by the mainstream media. Can you get it into the inboxes of whoever can either make the video go viral, or whoever can get it onto the news?"

Elliot purses his lips and nods. "I can, but that might not be enough."

I nod, grimacing. "We need the video to pick up enough media attention, and we need to make sure the arraignment judge sees it, so the case is pushed through to a trial. Once it is, I need you to find out who the jury consists of. We'll have to work together to make sure each of them sees the video, whether that be on social media, a media panel by the bus stop, or through an ad on their phone. I don't care how, but before the trial, I need every member of the jury to have seen the video."

Elliot's eyes twinkle, and I can tell he's enjoying the challenge. If anyone can make this happen, it's him. He's a much better hacker than I am.

"Do this for me, and I'll owe you a favor to be called in whenever you need, provided it doesn't go against my morals."

His eyes widen. "Are you serious?"

I nod, my gaze turning back to Grayson. "I need this case resolved in as little time as possible."

Gray won't be able to leave this behind until the case is over. He's set on fighting for justice for Ida, and he won't rest until he's got it. The longer it takes, the more of himself he'll destroy.

"You and Grayson..."

I turn back to Elliot and smile. "We're dating. We have been for months now, and he's *it* for me. I'm not sitting back and watching him lose his spirit. I'll be damned if I let him do this to himself."

Elliot smiles. "I get it. I feel the same way about my boyfriend. There was once someone that almost broke Lucian's spirit, and at the time, it was Grayson that I turned to for help. Working here was never a true repayment of the favor I asked for — it was yet another favor he granted me. But this... this might help even the scales. Anything you need, Aria, I've got you."

I nod and stare after Elliot as he walks back to his desk. Grayson has no idea how many lives he's touched, how many people admire and appreciate him.

Elliot is about to break half a dozen laws for him, and he'll do it with a smile on his face. That's how much of an impact Gray has had. So many of us are willing to go further than he'd ever imagine, if he asks us to.

I rise from my seat and walk toward his office. It hurts that he doesn't even notice me anymore. He's so caught up in his work, using it to distract him from everything that's going on. He doesn't even realize how much he's pushing me away, how much he's hurting me.

"Grayson."

He looks up and smiles tightly. When was the last time I saw him smile at me? Truly. Not one of these fake forced smiles. When is the last time he looked at me with that twinkle in his eye that I've come to love?

I walk toward his desk and lean against the edge, my legs brushing against his chair. Usually he'd have rolled his chair closer, so I'd be stuck between his legs. He'd steal a kiss and try to convince me to have an office quickie, and I'd be all too eager to agree.

Today, he doesn't so much as touch me. He hasn't touched me in days now, or has it been weeks? It's been so long I can't remember.

"I asked Elliot to help with the case. He recognized you in the video, but he assures me no one else will."

He leans back in his seat, looking conflicted. "I figured we'd need his help... I just didn't know how to ask."

I nod. "You don't need to, Gray. We're all here for you."

He sighs and runs a hand through his hair. "I need him locked up, Aria. It won't change the past... but maybe it'll change Ida's future. Maybe it'll quieten the words I keep hearing him say in my mind."

I want to reach out for him and sit down in his lap so I can throw my arms around him. I want to hug him tightly, and promise him I'll do everything in my power to make things better.

But I don't. I stay where I am, my eyes on his. If it's distance he needs right now, then I'll respect that. I won't put my needs above his.

"I feel like I'm suffocating in the darkness he spewed," Gray murmurs, looking away. "I'm trying to trudge through, but I can't get ahead. I can't get past this. I keep thinking about the conversation I had with him, and I struggle to hold back the violence I feel. Violence, Aria. I wanted to hurt him, and I almost did. If not for the confession we needed, I'd have hurt him beyond repair. And that's the problem. The evilness he portrayed, it doesn't just surround me, it's within me."

I inhale shakily, wishing there was a way to tell him that isn't true. "We'll put him behind bars, Grayson. *You* will. You'll do that, instead of physically hurting him, because it's the right thing to do."

He nods, but I'm not sure if he's really hearing me.

Chapter Sixty-One

GRAYSON

I walk into our bedroom and freeze when I see Aria sitting on top of our bed; her legs crossed, wearing the sexiest nightgown I've ever seen. She's got her laptop in front of her, her gaze focused.

She looks up and smiles at me, and my breath catches. I pull on my tie and swallow hard, unable to drag my eyes away. She's so fucking hot, and the way she's sitting gives me a glimpse of the red lace she's wearing underneath. Fuck.

"Hey, Gray," she says.

I nod, trying my best to form a reply, but I can't take my eyes off her tits. What the fuck is she wearing? It's got all kinds of straps, and the way it sticks to her body... it was definitely designed to torture me.

She looks back at her laptop, seemingly not noticing my reaction, and I run a hand through my hair, frustrated.

"Look," she says, turning her laptop toward me. "Elliot just sent me a list of the jury members. I'm working on making sure they've all seen the video you took. I'm targeting the people around them, to ensure they're forwarded the video by those they trust. Elliot and I are working on monitoring all devices and communication, to ensure they see it."

I stare at her in astonishment. What have I ever done to deserve her? I've never once asked her for her help with Ida's case, but she's gone all out. She's made everything more bearable, and the solutions she's thought of are nothing short of brilliant. Aria isn't just stunning, she's a fucking genius with a heart of gold.

I sit down on our bed, my thigh grazing hers, and she turns to look at me. "Thank you," I whisper. She rises to her knees and presses a lingering kiss to my cheek. I turn, my lips brushing past hers, and my eyes fall closed at her sharp intake of breath. When is the last time I kissed her? I only ever dare hold her at night when she's fast asleep. I keep fearing that I'll hurt her, that I won't be able to hold back, that the evil inside me will infect her. I can't take that risk with Aria. I'd never forgive myself if I hurt her.

She raises a trembling hand to my cheek and leans in, pressing a soft kiss to my lips. I freeze, trying my best to control the need to push her flat onto her back. I want my hands wrapped in her hair and my cock deep inside her. I want that look in her eyes, the one that tells me I'm slightly too big for her, but she's taking me eagerly nonetheless. The things I want to do to her... they border on violent. These feelings aren't romantic. This is pure lust. Aria deserves better than that, but there's no way to make her see it.

She pushes against me, pushing me down on the bed the same way I imagined doing to her. There's a hint of anger in her eyes, and she grits her teeth as she climbs on top of me, her eyes widening when she feels how hard I am.

"Oh, so you do want me? Or is this just a physical response to having a woman on top of you?"

She rolls her hips, and I wrap my hands around her waist, struggling to stay calm. I want to push her against the wall, my cock buried balls deep inside her. I want her screaming my name, every push inside her hitting so deep that it borders on pain.

I gulp and look away. But tonight, Aria won't be ignored. She leans in and yanks on my tie, pulling it loose, before moving her hands to the buttons on my shirt. "Baby," I whisper. "Stop."

Aria freezes and looks away, hiding her expression from me. "What is it, Grayson? You're hard, but you're still turning me down. It's been weeks since you last touched me. You barely even kiss me back. Tell me, what is it? What did I do? I know you're hurting Gray, but this..."

I tighten my grip on her waist and shake my head. "You didn't do anything, my love. It isn't you. It's me."

She laughs, the sound hollow. "That's what you're going with? You're really telling me that *it isn't me, it's you*? Just say you don't want me."

I look into her eyes and grab her hand, pulling it toward my erection. "Tell me, Aria... does this feel like I don't want you?"

Her eyes widen, and I flip us over so my body is on top of hers. She moans when I grind my hips up against her and I lean in, kissing her the way I've been wanting to. She melts against me and I bury my hands in her hair, pulling her closer the way I've been imagining. The way she moves her body against mine, *fuck*.

I lower my lips to her neck, kissing and sucking down on her skin, wanting to mark her as mine. It's been so fucking long, and I want to fucking brand her. She pushes her breasts up and I smirk, pushing the fabric away with my teeth. "You look like a fucking slut with this shit on, Aria. You're wearing this for me, huh?"

"Of course," she moans, her eyes falling closed as my tongue swirls around her rapidly hardening nipple. The way her body responds to mine... amazing.

She pulls on my clothes, sending some of the buttons on my shirt flying, and I pull away briefly to undress. She rises to her knees on our bed when my suit trousers hit the floor, and she places her hands on the waistband of my boxer shorts.

Her eyes are on mine when she pulls it down, and the way she licks her lips has my dick jerking. Fucking hell. Why does she have to be so fucking sexy?

Aria leans in, grabbing my cock by the base, her lips lowering onto me slowly. I groan when her tongue swirls around the tip and bury my hand in her hair, pulling her further down.

"You want to know whether I want you, Aria? Tell me, how does all that desire taste? Look at you, on your knees for me... you're such a fucking good girl, aren't you? Sucking me off like that."

I push my hips further forwards, my cock slipping deeper into her mouth. I fuck her mouth like that, going deeper until I hit the back of her throat. Aria chokes on my dick, tears springing to her eyes, and she pushes away, her hands wrapping around her throat.

I freeze, realization dawning. I hurt her. I was so fucking lost in how good those lips of hers feel, I didn't think of her. I take a step away and shake my head.

Aria grabs my hand, clearing her throat. "I'm fine," she tells me, but her red eyes tell me she's not.

"Fucking hell," I say, looking up at the ceiling. What did I just do? I keep trying to convince myself I won't hurt her, yet the second I touch her, I take it too far. I should've known better.

That same icky feeling rolls down my spine, and I grit my teeth. "I need a shower," I tell her, walking away. I'm desperate to get rid of this feeling... this feeling that evil oozes from my very pores.

Besides, I need distance. I can't stay near Aria. I can't be trusted not to hurt her again. What the fuck do I do? I can't let her go, no matter how much safer it would be for her. I can't lose her, but at this rate, I'll destroy us both.

Chapter Sixty-Two

GRAYSON

I lean back against the wall in the corner of the bar, my eyes on Aria. We're supposed to be celebrating the completion of the project her team has been working on, but she doesn't look happy. This is her moment. Having her name on software like the one her team created is all she's dreamt of for years — yet she looks like she'd rather be anywhere else right now.

I watch her as Laura hands her a glass of wine, taking in the fake, forced smile on her lips. When is the last time I saw her smile?

A real smile. One of those that makes her eyes light up and her cheeks flush. When is the last time I saw true joy in her eyes?

I miss her. I miss the woman she used to be, the one I'm slowly but surely destroying. I'm to blame. I'm the one that took the joy from her and I continue to hurt her day by day. My mind replays the look in her eyes when I last touched her. I used her. I lost control when she wrapped her lips around my cock, and I used her for my own pleasure. I keep telling myself that I love her and that I'll never hurt her, but when it came down to it, I was only concerned with my own pleasure.

Every part of me wants to reach out to her and tell her that I need her with every fiber of my being. I want her in my arms so my heart can be at ease, so my father's words can't reach me.

But I can't use her that way. I can't put her in harm's way out of pure selfishness. The way she clutched at her throat just a few days ago, the tears in her eyes... I can't put her through that again, no matter how badly I need her.

Aria nods at Laura, the two of them engrossed in conversation, and I sigh. She's so fucking beautiful. I wish she'd look at me, I wish she'd smile at me. I want her to walk up to me with that look in her eyes that I've always loved, the one that tells me she and I are the only ones in on secret. I need her... yet I don't dare let it show.

A selfish part of me wishes she'd realize how much I crave her attention. I want her to treat me the way she did when she found me sitting in church. Back then she told me that my past doesn't define my future, but I guess it does.

I knew she'd pull away from me eventually. I knew reality would catch up on us. Hell, I knew I lost her the day I hurt her. She hasn't looked at me the same since. The faith and hope she clung to lost its hold on her the second I touched her in a way I shouldn't have. I lost her trust, and rightfully so. I can't keep her safe. Despite all of the promises I made myself, I can't protect her from myself. I can't run from the monster within.

Aria looks up when Riley approaches her... and she smiles. She smiles at him in that way that was always reserved for me. I swallow hard and try my hardest to pull my gaze away, but I can't. I'm transfixed. I'll take whatever I can get from her. I'll take every one of her smiles, even if they aren't aimed at me.

She looks into his eyes, and I tighten my grip on my glass, raising it to my lips. The liquor burns down my throat and I revel in it. She's been pulling away from me recently, and I can't even blame her. All I can do is stand back and watch her slip away, knowing she deserves far better than me.

The son of a rapist... Aria deserves better than that. I have no right to even touch her. Hell, I shouldn't even get to call her mine. And soon I won't. I know it. I see it in her eyes. All I see reflected back at me these days is the sorrow I surround her with. I'm infecting her with my vileness, and it's robbing her of all that makes her *her*.

Riley offers Aria his hand and she tenses as she raises her head to look at me, our eyes meeting across the room. I force myself to look away. I see the pleading look, the hope in her eyes, but I can't intervene now. I can't stop her from taking Riley's hand, not when I can't offer her my own. She deserves to smile the way she did seconds ago. She deserves to dance like I know she loves to, the way Riley is asking her to. If I can't give her what she needs, I have to step back and let her reach for the happiness I'm taking from her.

My heart twists fucking painfully and I swallow hard as Riley twirls around the woman of my dreams. A man like him... yeah. I don't think anyone would ever be good enough for Aria, but Riley would be better for her than I could ever be. She laughs as he spins her around, and the sound makes my heart race. That happiness... she doesn't experience that around me. Not anymore.

Why does she stay? Is it out of guilt? Is it because I offered her the job she wanted above all else? Or is it simply because of Noah?

I shake my head and run a hand through my hair. Nah... I bet it's just her heart. Aria probably can't walk away right now, not even when she knows that she should. I bet she's waiting for the right time. I bet she's starting to feel trapped. She's probably regrets all the promises she made me but just doesn't know how to get out of them now. A woman like Aria... her conscience won't allow her to walk away.

I tense when Aria pauses on the dance floor, her eyes on Riley's and her hands on his chest. That's how she always used to touch me. He leans in to speak to her, and my heart fucking breaks. She's moving on right in front of my eyes, and there's nothing I can do or say to make her stay. I don't even deserve to speak up, to fight for her. I don't deserve her.

The glass I'm holding shatters from the force I'm gripping it with and the shards cut into me deeply. I glance at my hand, blood rapidly staining my skin, and I welcome the pain with a type of detachment that's hard to put into words. The sting of the cuts can't keep me distracted for long, though. Not when Aria is a mere few steps away.

I look up at her, silently begging her to notice my pain, to notice me. She doesn't. Her eyes never leave Riley's and I turn to walk away, leaving her in the arms of another man.

Chapter Sixty-Three

ARIA

I stare at my phone, a bittersweet smile on my face. Ida won the case, and it ended up being a landslide victory. I'm not surprised, considering the amount of work we put into it behind the scenes.

I wonder if Grayson has heard about it yet. He must have. I wish I knew what he was thinking, whether he's happy and relieved, whether this makes him feel better.

He's only a couple of steps away, but his office door is closed. It often is, lately. Part of me wants to walk in and find out how he's taking the news, but a larger part of me has nothing left to give.

My phone buzzes in my hand, and my eyes widen when I read the message. I smile humorlessly and grab my handbag as I reply to the request to meet.

My thoughts are whirling as I walk over to the diner Ida works at. I've been working on this case for months, and it's cost me everything. But maybe it always would have happened. Maybe Gray would always have lost interest in me. Maybe Ida's case just accelerated that process.

She smiles at me when I walk in, and the similarity hits me right in the chest. It's the eyes. Gray has her eyes. "Nyx," she says, grabbing my hand. I stiffen as she leads me to a table, sitting down opposite me. "I can't thank you enough. I've never felt freedom like this before. For years, I thought he got away with what he did, that no one would ever listen to me. Until you."

I lean back in my seat and cross my arms, my eyes roaming over her. She looks happy, and I can't help but feel like she stole that happiness from Grayson and me.

"It's not me you should be thanking, Ida. It's Grayson."

She falls silent and looks away, a tinge of guilt in her eyes.

"Do you have any idea what it took to win your case? Things aren't as simple as they seem. They never are. That video that moved the odds in your favor? Who do you think orchestrated that? Who do you think got that confession?"

I laugh, the sound shrill. My heart is bleeding, and staring at her makes me feel like whatever is left of it is being stabbed with a blunt knife.

"It killed him. Grayson was devastated after he met you, and when I found out what you told him, I was ready to drop your case. You do not deserve him. You do not deserve everything he's done for you, the hell he put himself through. If it were up to me, I'd have let you burn. I'd have let you live with your sorrow for what you put the man I love through. But not Grayson."

I swallow hard and grit my teeth, trying my best to remain in control of my emotions. "Since you had the guts to sit here and tell him he was born of sin, you'll sit here and listen to what it took for him to win you that case. Because it was him that did this for you, not your lawyer."

I lean in, looking into the eyes that are identical to the ones I love more than life itself, and all I feel is hatred. "You destroyed him, Ida. He'd been searching for you for years, going to the church he was left at every single Sunday, hoping for a glimpse of you. Do you have any idea how hard he's worked? How he grew up? Do you even know who Grayson Callahan is?"

I glance down at her phone and shake my head. "That phone of yours? It wouldn't work without the software Grayson's company developed. The man you say never should have been born, is the same man that runs one of the most influential software companies in the world. He's the same man that personally worked on hundreds of cases just like yours — *pro bono* and completely anonymous. That is the kind of man Grayson is. He's brilliant, he's kind, he's compassionate... and without him, you'd still be living with unresolved crimes haunting you. You think it was your lawyer that won you the case?" I laugh humorlessly and clench my hands.

Ida looks at me, disbelief flickering through her wide eyes.

"That video Grayson made? It killed him to take it. It killed him to sit there and hear how he was conceived. He hasn't been the same since. Despite everything you said to him, he went and did that for you, forsaking himself. But that's not all he did, Ida. Grayson ensured the right people saw that video. At first, it was the judge that pushed your case forward to a trial instead of dismissing it. Then it was the jury, earning you that landslide victory. He broke countless laws to give you the justice he thought you deserved, but that's not all he broke. He broke his own heart — and mine too."

I look away, disgusted by her. "The next time you feel even an ounce of relief, the smallest sense of justice... remember who you owe it to. Remember what it cost. Grayson paid for your happiness by sacrificing his own. Every smile on your face for the rest of your life, is one you took from him. He might have been born as a result of a crime, but it doesn't compare to the sins you committed against the one person who stood by you even when you turned your back on him. He didn't choose to be born the way he did, but *you chose* to give him up. You chose to turn your back on him when he came to find you, his heart filled with hope. You looked him in the eye and destroyed him. You might be enjoying a sense of freedom now, but you'd better remember what it cost."

I rise to my feet and turn to walk away, a tear rolling down my cheek as I walk out the door. My heart aches for everything Grayson went through, everything *we* went through. I hope it was worth it.

Chapter Sixty-Four

ARIA

I glance around the apartment Grayson and I turned into a home. It's in the little touches, the throw blanket on the sofa, the candles, the cushions. Then there are the little kitchen tools I bought myself, the photos of the two of us.

I was never supposed to get this comfortable here, and I'm wondering if I invaded Grayson's space without even realizing it. He only offered me a place to live as a favor to Noah, after all. He thinks I don't know, but the two of them aren't as sneaky as they think they are.

"Aria?"

I turn to look at him, surprised to find him home at all. Lately he spends all of his time at the office, and when he gets home, he goes to the rooftop gym, using up whatever energy he's got left. By the time he comes to bed, he's ready to pass out from pure exhaustion.

We don't eat together. We don't talk. We don't discuss our days, nor do we work together the way we used to. I don't remember the last time we had a full-length conversation, something beyond casual pleasantries.

Grayson's eyes drop to the suitcase beside me, and he tenses. "Where are you going?"

I look at him, searching for a trace of panic, a hint of pain. I find nothing. His expression is completely unreadable. I thought things might change once Ida's case got resolved. I thought that helping Ida get justice would ease his pain, and I think it has. There's less tension in his shoulder, and the look in his eyes is less haunted. But his attitude toward me hasn't changed. It's been a few weeks, and other than thanking me for my help, he hasn't spoken to me. He hasn't sat down to have dinner with me, and he certainly hasn't so much as touched me. He hasn't even held my hand, let alone hugged me. He comes to bed after I fall asleep, and he's gone before I wake up. Some nights I'm not even sure he sleeps next to me. I know he's home, but I suspect he's been spending some nights on the sofa or in the guestroom, and I hate feeling like I invaded his space, like I took his bedroom from him.

"Home," I tell him, and it kills me to say it, because I thought home was wherever Grayson was. I thought *home* was the apartment I'm standing in right now. But then, I thought the same when it came to Brad. I'm so desperate for a normal life that I turn blind to reality. I fail to see that I'm inserting myself where I'm not wanted.

Grayson walks up to me, and my heart starts to race. I hate myself for the hope I feel, for the way I can't keep from silently begging him to ask me to stay, to take me in his arms and kiss me the way he used to.

"You're leaving, huh?"

I stare at him, my heart shattering into a thousand pieces. That's all he's got to say? I smile mockingly and look away. He's been showing me he doesn't care about me for weeks now, so why is a part of me still surprised?

I glance around the house, my eyes lingering on one of the photos of my parents that Gray put there for me, my stomach tightening. "Tell me to stay, Grayson," I whisper. "Tell me you don't want me to go. Tell me we can get past this, that you'll talk to me. Tell me we can work this out."

I look at him, desperation clawing at me. "It's been weeks since we last really talked. You're killing me, Gray. You've got me wondering whether it's just me, whether you just fell out of love with me, whether you just don't want me anymore. And you know what, if that's the case, just tell me. Tell me... don't push me away like you have. Don't make me feel unwelcome, like I'm intruding in your home."

Gray runs a hand through his hair and looks away, his jaw locked.

"Tell me what you're thinking, Grayson. Even if it's just to tell me you want me to leave. *Please*, just speak to me. I'm begging you," I whisper, my voice breaking.

He looks into my eyes, and it kills me to find nothing there. There's no love, no affection, no intimacy. "Are you coming back? You signed a contract."

I blink in disbelief and laugh humorlessly as a tear rolls down my face. I swipe it away angrily.

"Yeah, unless you don't want me to. I love my job, Gray... but if you don't want me to come back, I won't."

He nods and looks down at his feet. "No, you should keep your job. You're good at what you do, Aria. It'd be a loss for the company if you left."

My heart twists painfully, and I look away. A loss for the company, but not for him. How could this have happened? How did we grow this far apart?

"While I'm at home, I'll start searching for a place to stay on some of the housing forums and online groups."

Gray raises his hand to my face, but he pulls it away before touching me, letting it drop to his side. "My house is big enough, Aria. You can stay here if you want to."

I swallow hard. Stay here? And do what? Watch him move on with his life? Watch him pick up the pieces of his broken heart and hand them to someone else? Am I supposed to watch him eventually fall for someone else? Listen as he brings other women home? Grayson won't stay single for long. He's too big of a catch. Even if he doesn't want to date right now, he'll get lonely, eventually. He's far too passionate to go without a woman for too long, and I don't want to be around to watch him find the girl that manages to keep his attention in ways I failed to. Maybe that's all I was to him. I was accessible and easy.

"I don't think that's a good idea, Grayson."

He nods and takes a step away. "Would you like me to drive you to the airport? What time is your flight?"

It hurts. It hurts that he isn't in any way asking me to stay. My last few hopes disappear, leaving me feeling empty. I didn't even realize I wanted him to fight for me, not until just now.

"No," I tell him, my voice barely above a whisper. "My flight isn't until tonight, but I just wanted to check in already. And I... I just want to go. I need to leave."

I can't explain how I feel. I want to run from the pain, the emptiness that surrounds me in this house, the memories of us.

Grayson nods, and I force a smile onto my face as I walk past him, the sound of my suitcase's wheels filling the silence. I turn back to look at him as I reach the door, knowing this is the last time I get to look at him and consider him mine.

We might not have said the words, but we both know this is the end for us. We were over before we ever really began. Grayson and I... we're two damaged souls that sought salvation in each other, our quest ending in mutual destruction instead.

I brought devastation to him through my platform and his mother's case, while he... he destroyed me by making me believe in love when I should have known better.

"Goodbye, Grayson," I whisper, before turning and leaving behind the best thing that ever happened to me.

But here's the thing about that... just because he's the love of my life doesn't mean I'm his.

Chapter Sixty-Five

GRAYSON

I stare out my office window, my mind replaying this morning's scene. Aria standing in the living room with her suitcase in hand, telling me she's leaving. I knew it was coming, but it didn't make it hurt any less.

I knew I was losing her, and all along, I knew I only had myself to blame. I pushed her away, and I did it knowingly. Every time she looked at me, silently begging me to kiss her, to hold her. Every time she wore something sexy, just to get a reaction out of me. Every one of those times, my non-response was speaking louder than any words I could say.

It fucking killed me to watch her walk out the door, but what right do I have to ask her to stay? She might be hurting now, but she won't for long. A girl like her... she isn't for me. I don't deserve her. I never did, but even less so now.

I can't even touch her without hurting her. If it's this bad now, how much worse will it get through the years? Over time, I might truly become like my father, and I need Aria out of harm's way. I'd never forgive myself if I hurt her again. Watching her clutching her throat, tears in her eyes, all because I couldn't hold back? That can never happen again.

It's not just physically that I'm hurting her. I can't even fulfill her emotional needs. I can't put her fears to rest, I can't take away her insecurities. Aria needs someone that can love her fearlessly, someone that can touch her without holding back, make her feel as beautiful as she is, and that can never be me.

"Grayson?"

I look up to find Elliot standing in my doorway, his expression torn. He steps aside, and I freeze.

"Ida?"

She nods and hesitates before walking into my office. Elliot steps back and closes the door behind him. I sit up, surprised to find her here.

"Grayson," she says, and I stare at her wide-eyed. I've never once heard her say my name. "I named you that, you know?"

I look away, unsure of how to reply. I see her fidget in my peripheral vision, and I force a polite smile onto my face. "What brings you here?" I ask, gesturing toward the seat opposite me.

She inhales deeply, almost as though she's bracing herself. "Nyx," she says, and I tense. "She messaged me this morning to let me know my case is officially considered resolved on her platform." The mere mention of her makes my heart squeeze together in a way it never has before. My heart has only ever beat for her.

"I asked to meet her a few weeks ago, to thank her for helping with my case, and she told me it isn't her I should be thanking. She told me what you've done for me, and I had no idea, Grayson. I didn't know. I'm sorry it took me so long to finally gather the courage to come see you. Words will never be able to express how grateful I am, and how incredibly sorry I am for everything I said to you."

I stare at her in surprise, and she smiles shakily. "It's okay," I tell her. "I never intended for you to find out. You don't need to thank me. It's the least I could do."

She shakes her head and places her hands on my desk. "You're wrong, Grayson. You didn't owe me a thing. You didn't know me, and I *abandoned* you. You were an innocent child, brought into the world against your will, and I took my pain and helplessness out on you. I never even considered how my actions then, or my words now, would affect you. I've been selfish through and through, and if not for Nyx, I'd never have realized it. Grayson, you saved me. I don't even dare ask for your forgiveness, because Nyx was right. I don't deserve a son like you. I'm so sorry, Grayson. I'm sorry, and I'm grateful that you have her in your life. The love she so clearly has for you... I'm grateful that you have that, that you have *her*."

I grimace and clench my jaw, the pain almost overwhelming me. "*Had*," I murmur. "Nyx... she left."

Ida freezes and looks at me with raised brows. "Impossible. Why?"

I smile humorlessly and look into her eyes. "Because you were right. I'm a monster, and darkness does follow everything I touch. The woman you know as Nyx... she's all that's good in life, and I can't taint her, I can't dim her shine. I can't risk hurting her."

Ida leans back in her seat, her gaze piercing. "She left... and you let her go?"

I nod, my eyes falling closed as I try my best to stay in control of my feelings. Fuck. I never expected it to hurt this badly.

When I open my eyes again, I find Ida staring at me. I'm startled when she smiles at me.

"If you were the monster you think you are, you'd have chained her to you. You'd have kept her trapped, whether she liked it or not. But you didn't, did you?"

I shake my head. "I wanted to... but I can't. I can't do that to her. Never her."

"So you put her happiness above your own?"

I nod, and Ida stares at me. "Are you sure?" she asks, and I frown. "When you let her go, were you putting her happiness first, or were you caving in to your fears? The woman I spoke to would have burned down the world for you, Grayson. There's no way leaving would have made her happier than being with you."

I stare at her and blink in confusion. Ida rises from her seat and smiles at me. "You're no monster, Grayson. You're nothing like the man that conceived you. I was wrong. I've never been more wrong about anything in my life. Everything you did for me, never expecting me to find out... It means you're a far better person than I will ever be. I don't know if I'll ever have the honor of getting to know you, but even if I don't, I can tell you this much: I'm proud of you. I'm proud of the man you became despite the way I abandoned you."

Ida picks up her bag and stares down at her feet before looking back at me, a conflicted expression on her face. She takes a sticky note out of her bag and sticks it onto my desk. "This is my phone number," she murmurs. "After everything I did, everything I said... I'd understand if you want nothing to do with me. But if you ever change your mind, I'll be here, waiting. I've made countless mistakes in my life, but nothing will ever be as bad as abandoning you twice. Once when you were a baby, and then again when you found me at work."

I stare at the sticky note in surprise as she walks to the door, turning back to me. "Put her happiness first, Grayson. Just now you told me you can't risk hurting her, but isn't that exactly what you're doing right now? It's listening to my words that brought you harm, so I shouldn't ask you to listen to me again, but please do. Please don't let her go because you believed what I said in spite. Please don't let my moment of despair rob you of the love of your life. I've already taken too much from you — don't let me take more. You know who you are."

She smiles and walks out the door, leaving me staring after her. Her words keep repeating over and over in my mind, a small seed of hope sprouting deep within me.

Chapter Sixty-Six

ARIA

My heart feels heavy as I sit down in one of the seats by the gate, my mind automatically replaying the last time I was on a plane. It was with Gray, and I was heartbroken then, too.

It didn't feel the way it does now, though. Back then, it was the betrayal that pained me. This time... this time it's *Gray* that's killing me. It's the memory of him, the love I still carry deep within. Boarding this plane doesn't feel like a fresh start like it did then. No. Now it feels like I'm leaving my heart behind.

A tear runs down my cheek, and I can't help but wonder if I'm making the right choice. I stayed for weeks even as he pulled away, giving me no indication that he wanted me with him. Should I have stayed nonetheless? I want to be there for him, but my presence only seemed to be an additional burden to him.

All of my doubts and insecurities melt together, making me second-guess everything. I truly thought Grayson and I could get through anything together. That our love was strong enough to carry us through the darkest days. I was wrong.

I'm snapped out of my thoughts when all the lights at the

airport suddenly flicker. Every screen in the vicinity goes dark, only to be lit up with an image that has me freezing in shock. I stare up at the video of Grayson with wide eyes.

"Aria?" The sound echoes through every speaker, and my jaw drops. All around me people stare up at the screen, most of them as shocked as I am. What's going on? Grayson pulls on his tie and stabilizes the camera. The video seems to be streaming from a mobile device.

"Don't get on that plane. I'm begging you, Aria. I'm begging you to stay. I'm on my way to the airport right now," he says, glancing at his watch. "I know you'll start boarding within the next ten minutes, but I beg of you, don't get on that plane."

He runs a hand through his hair, his expression pained. "Aria, you are the best thing that has ever happened to me, and letting you go was the worst thing I ever could have done. It's only been a few hours, and I can truthfully tell you that these are the single worst hours of my life. I thought I was doing what's best for both of us, but I was wrong. I was so wrong, baby. My fear of hurting you blinded me to the pain I put you through, Ari."

Grayson sits up, seemingly urging whoever is driving to go faster. "I love you," he says. "I love your smile, your wicked intellect, your heart. I know I don't deserve you, Aria... but I'll spend every waking moment for the rest of my life working on being a better man. That still might not be enough, but Aria, I swear, if you give me a chance, I'll never stop trying. I'll never stop doing whatever I can to make you happy, to make you smile."

The camera shakes, and Gray appears to be on the move. "I know I've hurt you. I know you think I don't care, and that I didn't notice you in the last couple of weeks. Baby, have a look at the contents of my phone."

The screen flashes with what must be hundreds of photos of me, one after the other. Some are of me at work, some at home. They're all photos of me doing the most mundane things, all of them taken without me even realizing it. There are photos of me doing simple stuff like working on my laptop at home, some of me standing by the coffee machine at work, then there are selfies of the two of us, with me asleep on Gray's chest.

"I'm desperate, clearly, because at this point, I don't even care about the world knowing how obsessed I am with you. I'm so fucking in love with you. Even when my fears were at their height, and I was convinced you'd leave me, I wanted to capture these moments to cherish for the rest of my life. But you know what, Aria? The memories aren't enough. I need you. I love you so much that life has no meaning without you, and I know you love me, too. I know it, Aria. I know you do, and that's enough. So long as you love me, we'll make this work. I'll do anything to have one more chance. I know I've hurt you, but I'll spend the rest of our lives earning your forgiveness."

There's a commotion around the corner, countless people murmuring and stepping aside, revealing Grayson walking up to me. His eyes meet mine, and he puts his phone away, the video cutting off.

"Aria," he murmurs, pausing in front of me. He grabs my hands and holds them tightly. He sinks down to his knees and looks up at me. "I'm begging you. Please stay. I'm not asking you for your forgiveness. All I'm asking for is a chance to earn it."

I look into his eyes, completely thrown. "Grayson, why are you here? Why now? The screens... what were you thinking?"

Everyone's eyes are on us, and countless phones are pointed at us too. I glance around, flustered.

"You turned your phone off, and I was scared you'd get on that plane. I had no choice. I couldn't let you go. I couldn't care less about the repercussions I'll face for hacking into the airport's systems."

My heart twists painfully, and I swallow hard. "You've been letting me go for months now," I whisper, and he shakes his head.

"Never, baby. I know it seemed like that to you, but I never stopped loving you. Will you give me a chance to prove it? I'll do anything."

I stare at him, trying to assess his sincerity. The desperation in his eyes; that can't be fake. "Can you promise me you'll communicate with me? Promise me you'll actively work on overcoming the challenges we're facing. I don't think this'll get better without therapy, Gray. Promise me you'll do whatever it takes, that you won't shut me out again when things get hard. Promise me, Gray."

I expected him to hesitate, but he doesn't. He nods and tightens his grip on my hands. "I promise. Anything you want me to do, I'll do. All I want is to be a better man for you, Aria. There's nothing I won't try. Please, just tell me you'll stay."

The pleading look in his eyes has my heart racing. I've doubted him for weeks until I was certain we were at a point of no return. I thought he gave up on us. But maybe it's not only his vision that was clouded by insecurity and fear. Maybe it was mine too.

I smile at him, my eyes filling with tears. "Then yes, Grayson. I'll stay."

Chapter Sixty-Seven

GRAYSON

Aria is quiet as we walk into the apartment, her expression telling me she didn't expect to return here. I leave her suitcase in the corner as she walks to the window, just like she did the very first time she walked in here.

I follow and stand behind her, my hand covering hers. Aria tenses and turns around, finding herself trapped between the glass and my body. She looks up at me, and I hate seeing the insecurity in her eyes. I hate knowing I put it there.

I place my index finger underneath her chin and tilt her face up as I lean in, slowly, carefully. Her eyes fall closed before my lips brush against hers, and she inhales shakily as I bridge the distance between us, my lips meeting hers.

Aria rises to her tiptoes, and I deepen the kiss, taking my time with her. I push against her, and she moans, her hands finding their way into my hair. By the time I pull away, we're both panting. It's been so long since I last kissed her. "I missed you," I whisper against her lips, leaning in for another kiss. She tightens her grip on me and kisses me back, her movements slow and passionate.

I'm rock solid by the time she pulls away, her forehead against mine. "I missed you too, Grayson. You have no idea how much."

Her hands run over my body and I lean in, pressing a kiss right below her ear before moving on to her neck. A soft moan escapes her lips, and I smile. Her hands tremble and she presses them flat against my chest in an effort to hide it.

"Tell me what you're thinking," I whisper.

She looks so vulnerable, so hurt. "I'm wondering if you want me, Gray. You chased me down at the airport and asked me to stay, but I'm having a hard time believing what you said. I don't want to be led on again. If there's something you want from me, please just tell me. There's nothing I won't do for you, so please don't use me. Don't think you need to be in a relationship with me to avoid letting Noah down."

What the fuck? I've been so busy focusing on my own pain I never thought about how my behavior might have reopened old wounds of hers. Every time I pulled away from her physically, she must have been reminded of Brad. Fuck. I can't believe I made my girl question herself like that. Even worse, I was too blind to see what I was doing. I still remember the way she cried as she told Noah and me what he said about her, and all this time I was reminding her of that, making her think I feel the same way Brad did.

I cup her cheeks and look into her eyes. "All I can think about is wanting you naked, my dick buried deep inside you. I'm scared I want you *too much*, the way I did when you wrapped those beautiful lips around my cock. I want to fuck away every crazy thought going around in your head, but I'm scared I'll be too rough with you. That's all it is. My biggest fear is hurting you. You make me lose control, Aria, and I don't ever want to see you in pain. But at the same time, I'm a selfish bastard, and though I tried, I just can't let you walk away — not even when I know there's every chance I'll end up hurting you."

She nods and moves her hands to the buttons of my shirt, taking her time undoing them. "But baby," she whispers. "I like it rough."

She looks into my eyes as she undoes the buttons, as though she's assessing my response, and I bite down on my lip when her hands move to my suit trousers. "Can you feel that, Nyx?" I ask her. "Does that feel like I'm messing around with you? Like I don't truly want you?"

She shakes her head, her eyes lit up with hope. I lean in to kiss her, my hands tugging at her clothes. She deepens the kiss and raises her arms for me as I pull her dress over her head. She stands in front of me wearing nothing but black lace, and I swallow hard. "Fuck."

Whatever she's seeing in my eyes seems to put her at ease, because she smiles at me, a hint of satisfaction in her gaze. I raise my hand to her face and brush her hair out of the way. "You're so fucking beautiful," I whisper.

Aria grins and rises to her tiptoes, her lips finding mine. When she kisses me like that, I fucking lose it. I lift her into my arms and push her up against the window, eliciting a moan from her. The way her hands move over my body, the way her nails graze over my scalp as she buries her hands in my hair, deepening our kiss. Yeah... fuck.

She pushes her hips against mine, grinding up on me as I kiss her, and I know I need to be inside her. "I need you," I whisper, and she nods.

The type of desperation I feel doesn't allow me to carry her to our bedroom. Hell, I don't even manage to get us fully undressed. Instead, I shove my underwear down and hers aside, loving the way she squirms when the tip of my cock presses up against her.

She moves on top of me, trying to get me in deeper, and I grin as I pin her against the window. "You want this cock, huh?"

"Please," she says, her eyes glazed over with lust.

I chuckle as I push the tip in, loving the way she wants me. My girl... yeah, she's the one. She's perfect in every fucking way.

She *wants* me. I don't need to worry about forcing my desires on her. She wants me as much as I want her. "You want more, baby?"

Aria pushes against me, and I grab her wrists, pinning them above her head. She stares me down, her eyes filled with passion, her lips half open.

I look into her eyes as I slam into her, watching her eyes fall closed in delight. Fucking hell. "Always so wet and tight, Nyx," I whisper, holding her by her hips as I fuck her slowly, deeply, never taking my eyes off her.

"I love you, Grayson," she says, and I grin as I increase the pace, thrusting into her the way I know she likes. I watch her every expression, every sigh, every moan. Yeah, she wants this as much as I do.

I listen as her pants get quicker, her moans higher, and I shift her in my arms, fucking her at an angle I know she can't resist. I watch my girl come all over my cock, taking me right along with her.

Aria and I collapse against each other, and I carry her to the sofa, lying down with her on my chest. She pulls the blanket she bought for the sofa over us, and I wrap my arms around her, trying to calm my raging heart.

Aria pushes up against my chest to look at me, and I bury my hand in her hair. "I really thought you didn't want me, Gray," she whispers. "I thought you didn't know how to tell me that you were done with me, that maybe you feared harming your friendship with Noah."

I shake my head and cup her cheek, my thumb brushing over her lip. "Baby, I'll always want you. I won't lie to you and say I'm no longer scared because I am. I'm terrified I'll hurt you, but I'll work on that. I... I'll go see a psychologist, Ari. I know my issues are all in my head, I know it. I'll get better. I'll do anything to make sure I don't break your heart again. Anything."

She nods and presses a kiss to my cheek before lying back down in my arms. For her, I'll go to the ends of the world if need be. The issues I'm facing... they can't affect her. I need to make sure of it.

Chapter Sixty-Eight

GRAYSON

I stare at the tombstones in front of me, feeling surprisingly nervous.

"Are you sure you want me here for this?" Noah asks. I glance at him and nod. There's no one I'd rather have with me right now.

Since Aria had a few weeks off between projects, we decided to spend a couple of days with Noah. Coming back here as her boyfriend has been different, to say the least. Thankfully, it hasn't been overly awkward, but joining her in her bedroom at night has been a little awkward. I can tell it makes Noah uncomfortable, but he's been supportive. Much to my surprise, learning about my past hasn't changed his mind about letting me be with Aria. In fact, it changed nothing for him.

I clear my throat and wipe my clammy hands on the jeans I'm wearing. "Hi, Mr. and Mrs. Grant," I say, my heart racing. "I've never had the honor to meet you, but it feels like I have, because that's how well your children keep your memory alive."

I shift my weight from one foot to the other, unable to calm my nerves. "I'm here today to thank you for bringing into this world the two people I love most. Noah has been my best friend for well over a decade, and Aria... well, your daughter... she's the love of my life. She's beautiful, astonishingly intelligent, humble, and she has a heart of gold. I can't tell you what she sees in me, because I ask myself that question every single day. I'm well aware that I don't deserve her, but for whatever crazy reason, she's chosen to be with me. When times got tough and I wasn't sure I'd make it through, she stuck with me. She is, quite honestly, the best thing that ever happened to me. And I know... I know I'm not good enough, but I'm working on being better."

It took me a few weeks to get into it, but I actually look forward to sessions with my psychologist now. I'm not sure how long it'll take me to be completely sure I'm not as harmful as I think I am, but I'm getting there, slowly but surely. I've gotten far enough to know I won't ever hurt Aria, and she'll always be safe in my arms. I haven't been able to change the way I see myself, nor have I managed to quieten my father's voice completely, but I'll get there.

I straighten my shoulders and inhale deeply. "I guess what I'm saying is that I'm here to ask for your blessing. I love your daughter beyond reason, beyond measure. I always will. I didn't know feelings this pure existed until her. All I want to do for the rest of my life is show her how amazing she is. Every day, for as long as I live, I'll do everything within my power to make her happy. I'll cherish her and never stop appreciating all the little things she does. I'll support her dreams and I'll always be there to catch her when she falls. I'll be everything she needs me to be, for as long as she'll have me. Hopefully, that'll be for the rest of our lives. So here I am... asking you for your daughter's hand in marriage. I want nothing more than to make her my wife."

Noah drops his hand to my shoulder, his eyes suspiciously watery. "Mom, Dad," he says. "Grayson is the best person I know. I can't think of a better man for Aria, and I know you'd have loved him if you were still around. Hell, you'd probably have loved him more than you love me. He's just that type of guy. I truly wouldn't want anyone else as my brother-in-law. I know you'd approve of him, so I'm giving him your blessing on your behalf."

I look at him in gratitude, and he smiles, clapping me on the back. "I see the way you treat my sister, Grayson. I see how you look at her. You think you don't deserve her, but you do. You two are perfectly suited for each other, and I'm happy you found each other. The two of you were always meant to be. I could see it long before you did."

I look down, humbled by his words. "Come on," he says. Noah presses a kiss to his palm and places his hand on the tombstones before turning toward the exit. "We'd better hurry if we want to make it home before Aria does."

I nod and follow him out, nearly walking into an old lady with a dozen flowers in her hands. I steady her, my hands on her shoulders. "I'm sorry, ma'am. Are you okay?"

"All good, sweetheart," she says, pushing the flowers in her hands against my chest. "Here, you take these. I was just about to throw them out," she explains, tipping her head toward the small flower shop behind her. "You look like you have a lady that'd love them, so you have them."

I stare at the flowers, wide-eyed. Aria *would* love these. "Thank you," I murmur, nodding gratefully. She grins and walks back to her shop before I can even offer to pay her for the flowers, and I turn to Noah, finding him staring at me in shock.

"White tulips," he whispers, his voice barely above a whisper. His eyes meet mine, and his expression has me tensing. "They're my mother's favorite. My father always used to buy them for her."

My eyes drop back to the flowers, a rush of emotion overcoming me. I'm not a superstitious man, but this feels a lot like a sign. Noah smiles at me and then looks up at the sky, the emotion in his eyes matching what I'm feeling.

"Let's go," I say. "I can't wait another second to ask your sister to be my wife."

Chapter Sixty-Nine

Aria

I'm surprised when I see a text message from Ash. Grayson and I haven't really been communicating on the Nemesis Platform anymore, but it still brings a smile to my face to see a message pop up.

Ash: *I hear there are plenty of fish in the sea and all that, but you're my sole-mate.*

I burst out laughing, pausing in front of Noah's front door.

Ash: *Nyx, Aria, baby... I whale always love you.*

I love this. I'm not sure why, but these messages have the butterflies in my stomach going wild. It took a little while, but things have never been better between us. Gray is actively working on overcoming the doubts instilled in him by his parents, and I've been working as hard as I can on overcoming my recurring nightmares and my compulsions related to locked doors and safety. We've both been encouraging each other to stay on track, to keep healing our pains. It hasn't been easy, but knowing we're together and actively working toward our happiness makes all the dark days worth it.

Ash: *When do you think I fell for you? Was it before I ever realized who you were?*

Nyx: *I'm not sure, but I was falling for you both online and offline. I think you stole my heart long before I knew you were the hottie I've been crushing on half my life.*

Ash: *Did you? Crush on me?*

Nyx: *Of course. You were my brother's hot friend, the guy I looked up to growing up. You may or may not have played a role in all my teenage fantasies.*

I walk into the house, expecting to find the boys in the living room, watching the game like they told me they would. Instead, I'm met with silence.

I frown and walk around in search of Noah and Gray, pausing when I notice the lights in the garden. My heart starts to race when I spot Grayson standing in the middle of the garden, wearing the same T-shirt and jeans he wore on what I've come to think of as our first date. I'm trembling as I step out, the breeze making my hair flutter. Grayson's eyes meet mine, and my heart skips a beat.

"Did I fulfill those fantasies?"

I smile as I walk up to him, my thoughts going wild. This feels... *different*, and my heart can't help but hope that this is what I think it is.

"You did. You do, every single day."

He raises his hand to my face and cups my cheek gently. "I think I fell a little bit more for you every time I saw you. The first time we met was right here, in this garden. Noah invited me over for a study session, and you walked in. You were beautiful, but it was your eyes that stayed with me. You were just like me. You had demons chasing you, but you put a brave face on nonetheless. I found myself wanting to learn more about you. I wanted to learn what made you smile. And oh, when you smile. Fuck, baby. When you smile, it lights up my whole world. You did that to me then, and you still do that to me now."

Grayson bends down on one knee, and tears spring to my

eyes. "Aria, I didn't know what love was, until you. I didn't know life could be this good. I didn't know I could be this happy, this fulfilled. You make me want to be a better man every single day."

He pulls a ring box out of his pocket and takes my hand. "For the rest of my life, I want to find new ways to make you happy. I want to tell you totally unoriginal puns and hear you laugh at them. I want to lift you into my arms when you can't reach things that are too high for you, and I want to be by your side as the world discovers your mad coding skills. Will you let me? Will you let me be the one that you lean on, the one you turn to when your nightmares wake you? I want it all with you, Aria. Good and bad. I want every part of you... Aria, will you marry me?"

I nod. "Yes. Yes, Grayson. Yes."

He smiles and slides the ring onto my finger. I don't even have chance to look at it, because the second it's on, he rises to his feet and pulls me closer, his lips finding mine. I rise to my tiptoes to kiss him back, my hands roaming over his chest. By the time Grayson pulls away, we're both panting. He drops his forehead to mine and smiles. "I love you, Aria."

"I love you more," I whisper. "I can't wait to become Mrs. Callahan. I can't wait for the rest of our lives together, Gray."

He pulls away, a twinkle in his eye. "I desperately want to carry you to your room and keep you there for the next few hours... but Noah wants in on the celebration," he says, tipping his head toward the house.

Gray grabs my hand and pulls me along, pausing in front of the dining room. I walk in, curious, my eyes widening when I see Noah standing by the table, a large ring-shaped cake by his side, two photos of Mom and Dad beside it.

"Congratulations, little one," he says, his gaze filled with pride.

I walk up to Noah and wrap my arms around him, bursting into tears all over again. "You made this for me?"

He nods and pats my head. "I had a little bit of help," he says, and the look in his eyes tells me it's Amara that helped him — my brother's mystery girl. The girl he claims is nothing but one of his patients, yet he can't even say her name without smiling.

"What would you have done if I said no?"

Noah shrugs and glances at Grayson unapologetically. "More cake for me," he says.

I burst out laughing, and Grayson shakes his head as he walks up to me, his hand wrapping around my waist.

I've never felt more loved. I thought happiness wasn't meant for me, but Grayson proves me wrong every single day, and I know he always will.

I look into his eyes, my heart overflowing with love. I can't wait to find out what life has in store for us. I know that whatever it is, we'll face it together, and we'll always come out on top.

Always.

Epilogue

ARIA

Gray's lips find mine as I wrap my arms around his neck. He lifts me up and pushes me against the wall, my legs wrapping around him. I whimper when he pulls away, missing him instantly.

Gray sighs, his forehead resting against mine. "Noah will be here soon. Don't interrogate him, okay?" he pleads. I pout at him, and he presses an indulgent kiss to my forehead. "Don't do it, baby. He's bringing Amara, so don't freak her out."

I nod reluctantly just as the doorbell rings. Gray lowers me to the floor and I bite back a smile as I walk into the hallway, excited to finally meet Noah's mystery girl.

I stare at the beautiful redhead standing in front of my door, her blue eyes filled with trepidation. She's hiding behind Noah, and I grin at her.

So this is Amara. She's drop-dead gorgeous. Her beauty is unreal. No wonder Noah is so smitten.

"Come in," I tell them, stepping back as I open the door wider. Noah throws a grateful glance my way and leads her into the penthouse. I expected Noah, but Amara... I didn't see that coming. Gray only informed me she'd be coming with Noah a few days ago, and Noah has been hesitant to mention her to me, probably because he knows I'd ask him countless questions.

Noah was meant to come over for the weekend so we could go visit venues for the wedding and ensure that he doesn't feel left out. I was looking forward to spending some time with my brother, but I'm far more excited to find out more about Amara. He's been so incredibly tightlipped about her, and the curiosity is killing me.

"Hey, buddy," Gray says, walking into the hallway. His eyes find mine, and my heart skips a beat. I wonder if he'll ever stop having that effect on me. I doubt it. Every day I fall a bit deeper.

"Aria, Gray," Noah says, "meet Amara Astor."

Her eyes move between Gray and me, and she hesitantly offers me her hand. I can see her trying to gather her courage, and it pulls at my heartstrings. How often have I felt the way she must be feeling right now, out of place.

"I'm Aria," I tell her. "I'm Noah's sister."

She nods and wraps her hand around mine, her palm clammy. She's nervous, huh? "It's lovely to meet you," she says, smiling tightly before turning to Gray, repeating the process.

Gray throws me a warning look and I pout at him. How does he know I was about to question the two of them? Surely I'm not that transparent...

"Remember when I told you about the company I thought you should invest in?" Noah tells Gray. "She's the founder."

"Hmm," Gray says, glancing at his watch. "I need to get to the office. Something came up. Walk with me and fill me in," he tells Noah, who nods before turning to Amara.

I watch as he places his hand on her lower back and leans in to speak to her. I've never seen him so attentive before. He's crazy about her.

"I was about to go cake tasting," I tell Amara. "How about you come with me while the boys catch up? I think I'd have much more fun with you than I would with Noah."

She looks up at me, startled, and then turns to look at Noah, who nods at her. That look between them... yeah, I can see it. This girl is going to become my sister-in-law.

I struggle to hide my giddiness and Gray shakes his head at me as he walks up to me. He wraps his hand around the back of my neck and tilts my head up as he leans in for a kiss, his lips lingering. "Be good, Nyx," he tells me, grinning as he walks away, Noah in tow.

"Nyx?" Amara repeats, her eyes wide.

I glance at her as I grab my handbag. "It's a nickname," I tell her. "No one but Gray calls me that, though."

Amara follows me down to the garage, her gaze intent. "You're Nyx, aren't you? *The* Nyx. It makes sense... Noah told me you're an engineer too."

I look at her with raised brows as I get behind the wheel of one of Gray's precious babies. "You've heard of the Nemesis Platform?"

Amara smiles as she buckles herself in. "Yes. Who hasn't?"

I grin, trying my best to hide my excitement. "So you're an engineer too?"

Amara nods and tells me that she's a mechanical engineer doing a post graduate degree at the same college that Noah's clinic is at. Now that it's just the two of us, she seems far more relaxed, and much more talkative.

I listen to her as we walk into the bakery, a sense of pure joy washing over me. I'm engaged to the love of my life and Noah seems to have met an amazing girl. This... this is what I always wanted for the two of us.

I take a bite of a coconut flavored cake slice and offer Amara a bite. "So, tell me, how did you meet Noah?"

Amara blushes and looks down. "Well, um... the company Noah asked Grayson Callahan to invest in... it's mine. I, um, well... I founded a company that creates sex toys. I basically use my engineering skills to create unobtrusive yet revolutionary toys."

I smirk, unable to help myself. Sex toys? Noah is done for. He's as straight-laced as they come, and Amara is perfect for him.

"So, I... well... I was testing a new invention," she says, her cheeks bright red. "It, um... it got stuck in me, so I had to go to the doctor's office to get it removed."

I burst out laughing, loving every second of this story. "Doctor Grant... *Noah*, he was startled, to say the least."

Her flushed cheeks and the look in her eyes tell me more than her words could. Just as I'm about to question her further, my phone buzzes, a notification from the Nemesis Platform popping up.

Ash: *I'm grabbing a coffee with Noah, and I was just thinking about how you looked this morning, your hair spread over our pillows and that look in your eyes that tells me I fucked you good. You're Brew-tiful.*

I giggle to myself, my heart skipping a beat. I'll never get enough of this man.

Nyx: *Love you a latte.*

I glance at Amara, my heart overflowing with happiness. Noah and I have been through so much, yet here we are... I'm loved beyond measure by the man of my dreams, and Noah? Noah is falling for Amara far harder than he realizes. I'm going to enjoy seeing him lose his mind and heart to the redhead sitting opposite me.

Ash: *I love you more, baby. Words can't espresso how much.*

This... I never thought I could ever be this happy. For so long I thought Gray, Noah and I would never escape the sorrows of our past, but I know better now. Our future is what we make of it, and I can't wait for Noah to discover that too.

"That story better than anything I could've imagined," I tell Amara, a smile on my face. "So tell me, what do you think of my brother?"

She blushes, and I lean back in my seat, a wide grin on my face. Yeah... I'm without a doubt counting my blessings. The life

I'm living right now is a dream come true, and I'll never take it for granted.

I can't wait to see what the next couple of years might bring. I have a feeling life will only get better...and I'm ready. I'm ready for all life has to offer.

———

Don't want Grayson and Aria's story to end? Download an exclusive scene from their wedding day from my website

You'll also catch some glimpses of them in *Dr. Grant*, Noah and Amara's story.

Also by Catharina Maura

Dr. Grant

Dr. Noah Grant's dream job at a prestigious private college came with three rules:

1. Don't sleep with the students

2. Don't sleep with a patient

3. Stay away from Harold Astor's granddaughter

Seems easy, right?

It was. Right until Amara Astor walks into his office with one of her own inventions - *an adult toy* - stuck inside her.

She's a patient, a PhD student, *and* she's Harold Astor's granddaughter. She's entirely off-limits.

Getting involved with her puts his promising future at risk, yet he can't turn her away. Not when doing so means she'll find someone else to test her crazy inventions with.

*Author's Note: This is a **standalone** romance with a guaranteed HEA.*

Dr. Grant, Amara and Noah's story, is available now

Made in the USA
Las Vegas, NV
21 September 2024